DEVIL IN THE WIRE

MT Clark

Shaved Dog Book Press

CHAPTER 1

L ike waves breaking to shore and receding, everyone in line at the Running-a-Ground coffee shop made space for the courier balancing four hot drinks in a flimsy cardboard tray. Dangling from one wrist was a bike helmet and the other a plastic bag filled with oversized pastries.

The shop was proud of its eclectic, independent streak by fighting New York coffee shop chain conventions. Bike parts hung from the ceiling and the kaleidoscopic collection of tables and chairs seemed to be sourced from the parents of college kids headed to campus.

The courier's face was a mixture of grit and grimace as his messenger bag strap shifted down his shoulder. With no free hand to save himself, he counterbalanced, leaning sideways as if he were ducking a Manhattan sidewalk tree branch. Despite his desperation, no one looked up from their phones while they patiently shuffled along the queue for a post-lunch coffee.

Jay, however, was not under the spell of his phone. He had tried to call Jenni several times over lunch with no answer. *Don't look desperate. Two or three calls a day. That's it.* For now, all he could do was wait for an unlikely return call. It made him feel even more lonely than he already did. Three months apart after more than a decade together was a new kind of hell.

Jay was acutely aware of the courier's rapidly failing luck. His light blue eyes, following the courier's awkward dance, stood out among the sea of brown eyes and dark hair. Jay's thirty-year-old beer belly was always at odds with his shirt length. At least he had a full head of sandy blonde hair, neatly trimmed with a tuft raised with mousse. Jenni loved to call it his "tin-tin." Thankfully, she didn't have a nickname for his waistline.

Despite New York social conventions, Jay put out a hand and said, "Ah, let me help." His deep south roots forced politeness out of habit, but his offer of assistance was too late.

The strap of the bag dropped to the crook of the courier's elbow like a guillotine and sent four hot drinks into rising waves of brown and black. To Jay, it was like watching a commercial for a refreshing drink; joyful splashes in slow motion with hip background music. In anticipation, he jerked sideways to spare his suit and white shirt from calamity.

No one with their nose buried in their phone was spared. The cups used the table, floor and window to backsplash hot drinks at the patrons from every direction.

A loud murmur drowned out the slow jazz playing over the coffee shop speakers. Up at the front of the line, someone grabbed a handful of napkins and started passing them back. One of the workers behind the counter called out, "Don't worry, sir. We'll get started on replacing your drinks and I'll be over there with the mop."

The line let out a collective groan. It was going to take forever to get their drinks now. Jay glanced out of the window of the coffee shop and mentally calculated his chances of bolting for another shop and catching his train. He decided on the path of least resistance and settled on waiting.

One of the spilled drinks was hot chai. The pungent spices mixed with burned milk reminded him of his Louisiana childhood. Losing interest in the monotony of the clean up, Jay returned to his daydream of Jenni.

Steam rose from the oversized serving of gumbo cooling on top of a cinder block. The dense, white mist collected into droplets swinging heavy from the tarp just inches over Jay's head. He was sixteen and hungry.

Jenni's eyes, bright in the reflecting flashlight, danced with the droplets for a second then returned to Jay with a concerned gaze. "I didn't mean to microwave that so hot. I was in a rush."

The knot in Jay's stomach pulled even tighter. His hunger was a dull ache; a side show to the main feature of pangs of guilt. Once again, he was at the mercy of someone else's grace. It didn't hurt that Jenni was beautiful, smart and a part of the prominent Delacroix Louisiana creole family.

Jay's family history consisted of one incomplete sentence scribbled inside a bible he had long lost. *Not from Louisiana.* As if his blonde hair and blue eyes weren't evidence of that.

"None of the folks that I lived with had homemade shrimp gumbo for leftovers. This smells incredible." The tiny tarpaulin tent, hidden behind neatly stacked logs in Jenni's backyard, was enveloped in the pungent aroma of seafood and spice.

Jay leaned over and put his hand on Jenni's arm. "So, thank you." The gesture was intentional and he hoped she was blushing. Her midnight-dark skin hid all the clues of potential desire as he searched her face. This was the first time they were together alone. Up until then, Jenni delivered Jay's food at a local park filled with shrieking kids and the shouts of overprotective parents. Underage, he could not walk into a food pantry without being dragged back into state guardianship.

She smiled faint and gazed back at the bowl. "I didn't intend to come so late. I needed to make sure my mother hadn't forgotten something and turned back home. I can't take chances. She'd bring the gris gris down on me."

Her legs, crossed under her loose white dress,

4

unwound as she brought a knee up to her chin. There, she rested her head and neatly folded her skirt, all proper and practiced. Countless braids of black hair danced; falling strand by strand, from her shoulders to dangle across the front of her dress. Her voodoo, made to look unintentional, was of a skilled temptress.

Jay's gaze never wavered as his heart pounded like a timpani in his chest. It was certain they were to be more than friends, but he collected bad luck and bad decisions like baseball cards. He wanted to blurt out that he stopped his runaway trek across the south because of her. He opened his mouth but could only let out a croak. His desire to nudge his advances further fell second-fiddle to his stomach. It had been nearly two days of only scraps, and for a sixteen-year-old it was all he could bear.

Eyes heavy-lidded with concern, Jenni offered an oversized silver spoon with an elegant vine pattern running along the edges. He paused for a half-second before devouring the soup. Her long, matte-black nails were perfectly manicured and captured his attention against the delicate lace trim of her dress.

The explosion of spices on his tongue was even more majestic than the haunting aromas that arose from the bowl. For a homeless teen, hell became heaven only in these fleeting moments.

Back at Running-a-Ground, Jay's middle-aged reverie was broken by a plump kid's oversized face only inches from his nose and puckered with disgust. The football jersey that hung over the kid's ballooning stomach hid the brown shorts that extended only a few inches beyond the shirt's hemline.

The face enunciated every word. "You are a turd."

Jay shook his head. "Huh?" The memories of his time in Louisiana was so real. The monstrosity next to him at the counter crushed any remnants of the daydream. On autopilot and shuffling as the line moved, Jay had ordered his usual drink and was waiting for his hot nectar when he was jolted awake.

He hurriedly fished out his credit card to escape the mounting confrontation.

"I'm standing right here." The kid leaned closer to Jay's face. The stench of days' old sweat and bad breath wafted into Jay's nostrils. Red hair, matted and hanging in clumps, framed his rotund, pale face.

Jay squinted one eye and tilted his head with his nose raised to escape the odor. He pushed his credit card across the counter and murmured, "Just let me get my latte and I'll be out of your way."

He returned his eyes to the counter to avoid escalation. He nervously pulled at his cuffs and tucked his shirt deeper into his suit slacks. In the back of his head, he could hear Jenni's calm voice. *Don't make things worse, Jay.*

The kid rolled his eyes at the barista behind the counter and jerked his thumb at Jay's chest. "Can you believe this snob? Thumbing his nose at me like I'm some crazy homeless guy?"

Streaks of red crept up Jay's neck to his cheeks. The nerve of this kid. His voice shook as he poked his finger at the kid's oversized breasts. "You reek, buddy. It's so bad that my eyes are watering." Anger welled up from a place rarely tapped. He never had the nerve to talk back, but the kid's accusation pressed his emotional triggers. Worse, his nerves were raw from days of dialing Jenni's number with no reciprocation.

The kid clenched his jaw and replied, "You ordered your *latte* while I was in the middle of talking to Mary. Do you uppity snobs even see people outside your income level?"

"Listen kid, I'm in a hurry." Jay held up his hands. His self-control was a sand castle in the rising tide. He was a bystander watching his own emotions overtake logic. He spoke with the condescending tone of kindergarten teacher. "*I'm sorry. Does that make you feel better? Do you want a band-aid?*" His voice wavered, but he held his place.

The kid let out an exasperated huff. "You don't know who you're messing with. I can make your life miserable."

Ignoring him, Jay turned to Mary behind the register. "May I have my drink?"

Poor Mary's eyes were wide, darting left and right, following the verbal melee. She pushed the cup across the counter and swiped Jay's credit card. In a meek voice she asked, "Do you want a receipt?"

The kid slammed his palms down on the counter. "He doesn't need a receipt unless it helps with tax avoidance. A credit card for a latte? Is cash too dirty for your hands?"

Jay shook his head in disbelief. He dealt with angry customers every day over the phone. He was trained to empathize in order to de-escalate. The hell he was going to try to relate to this emotional wreck. No one was paying him to deal with this.

More importantly, he needed to get away. He was going to escape this one before he did something really stupid. This was rapidly turning into a similar mess that precipitated his summer break up with Jenni. He repeated his mantra. *Don't make things worse.*

He blew out a breath to calm his nerves, gave a dismissive wave with his free hand and walked away.

His conscience urged him not to speak, but his anger won one last battle.

"I hope," said Jay at full stride, "that you get the right mix of meds figured out someday."

Jay returned to normal breathing when he stepped onto the crowded New York sidewalk. His hands shook as he tucked his credit card back into his wallet. He descended the stairs to the subway and fought every urge to look behind him.

It took a few sips of the scorching latte to settle his nerves, making a mental note to avoid the Running-a-Ground coffee shop in the future as he waited for his co-worker on the subway platform. It was their daily habit to get out of their office over lunch to recharge for the last half of their workday. The B train train pulled in with a rush of cold air and teeth-rattling screech. Jay scanned the platform for his co-worker one last time before boarding.

As the doors closed, a well-manicured hand appeared and forced it back open. Mike slipped inside and straightened his suit with a short tug at each cuff. He scanned the subway car with a confident smirk and spotted Jay. He sauntered over to an open overhead harness, bouncing his steps like Fred Astaire under a streetlight. A couple of ladies watched him with fascination.

Mike shook his head and said, "Another family of tourists caught in the turnstile. I think they were trying to use an ATM card to get through."

Despite the clamor to board, Mike looked on top of his game. He always did. Today, his slightly-too-small, mod suit was single-buttoned at the waist with a purple handkerchief rising out of his breast pocket in a neat double triangle. His dark suede shoes bore no scuffs. Not one of his short, wavy blonde locks that hung over his blue eyes were out of place.

Jay cracked a weak smile in return. His face was pale.

"Bad sushi, bud?"

"I wish," said Jay. "Ran into someone who was having a bad day. If he had possessed a weapon, I'd be dead and front page news."

Mike chuckled. He waved his hands to the windows and said, "More like back page police blotter. Yet we still appreciate the beguiling societal beauty that is Manhattan. Maybe you need to drop your habit of lattes after lunch."

Jay's eyes widened in mock horror. "That would be worse than death."

CHAPTER 2

"**D**ude, he actually held his nose up to me like he was a king holding court. I wouldn't be surprised if he powdered regularly," said Scott. He was fuming from his run-in at the Running-a-Ground coffee shop earlier.

He was home in his apartment; nestled in the center of a couch that moaned with his every movement. Yellow foam peeked through the ripped and well-worn pattern of the brown fluer-de-lis. The center of the backrest was broken, lending the illusion of fabric-covered wings rising from behind Scott's three-hundred-pound frame. The stench of days old pizza wafted in each lazy rotation of the fan that was clipped on the end of the coffee table.

His roommate, Karl, nodded absentmindedly and did not look up from his own computer by the window. Brown cropped hair, cut monthly by a vintage Flowbee purchased on eBay, neatly lined his equally brown eyes and eyebrows. He showered every day, unlike Scott. Karl also had a job, unlike

Scott.

"Are you even listening?" Scott's voice was a borderline whine.

"Yes, I'm listening. I just gotta get this app done. I promised a working version last week."

Ignoring Karl's hint of annoyance, Scott continued, "I want to punch this guy. He walked out and got the last word on me. Right in front of Mary, too."

"Aw, man, let it go." Karl didn't miss a beat tapping on his keyboard. While Scott didn't contribute to paying rent, he more than made up for it by being entertaining. Scott had amused Karl since they were friends in junior high. TV was boring compared to Scott's daily, psycho-paranoid rages.

"Thanks for the sympathy. You know, he had a CityTrust badge clipped to his shirt. I bet he works there."

Karl nodded in acquiescence and continued typing.

"I bet he's some big shot VP. Some elitist Wall Street trader who skims the little guy and blows it on prostitutes."

Karl nodded again.

"He was ordering a *latte*."

Karl smirked and said in a semi-serious tone, "Then he's definitely part of the proletariat. Present Exhibit A to the judge. The latte." It was fun to wind Scott up. All it took was a nudge in the right direction. Of course, a nudge in the wrong direction resulted in expulsion from high school and the loss of a few jobs. Both dodged enough trouble to graduate and Karl eventually got his college degree. Scott never finished his first semester.

The guilt of being the instigator of the mess in high school in part paid Scott's rent. *At some point, thought Karl, maturity will teach Scott how to channel his energy into a more productive endeavor.*

Scott's nostrils flared as he continued in a fevered, high pitch. "I was making small talk with Mary. But he was in a *hurry*. I think she was starting to warm up to me and that jerk blocked my mojo."

Karl laughed out loud. "Sorry, bud, but Mary is way out of your league. She *has* to be nice to you. You're a customer."

Scott grunted, leaned back and tugged at his shirt. "Speak for yourself."

The couch creaked and moaned as Scott lifted his thick legs onto the coffee table and perched his laptop onto his belly. Colored wires rained out the side to a jumble of metal boxes under the glass tabletop. With a tap at the keyboard, the equipment came to life with a series of clicks and whirs, flashing blinking lights of green, yellow and blue.

"I'm going to make that jerk regret he ever lived. Time for some devil in the wire." His fingers jumped across the keyboard in a blur. Sweat ran down the sides of his face and met the ends of his wide grin. After a few minutes, Scott cried out in a high-pitched squeal, "Well, helloooo, Mr. Jay Wilson of CityTrust. This is definitely my man. Ugh, that's one crappy corporate mugshot."

Karl stopped typing and looked up with a

mischievous smile. "Okay, I gotta see this lucky guy before you get started."

◆ ◆ ◆

"CityTrust, can I help you?" Jay's boss had been listening in on his calls so his voice was extra cheerful today. In a weak moment, more hungover than tired, he strayed from his assigned script last week and fumbled a potential account upgrade into an irate customer. That explained the latte. Full focus was required.

The cubicle did nothing to help with focus. It was bland, undecorated and brightly lit by buzzing fluorescent bulbs. As far as his eyes could see, the cubicle pattern repeated in all directions filled with agents wearing headsets like foot soldiers in corporate warfare.

The high-pitched voice on the line creaked. "Yes, I need to close my checking account."

"I'm sorry to hear that." Jay's voice was soothing. "CityTrust strives for all customers to be completely satisfied. I'm sorry to hear you want to close your account. Before I do that, may I ask if there anything I can do to keep you as a happy customer?"

Jay heard a faint click in the headset. Yep. Earl was listening.

"Well, my friend tells me his bank will deposit his paycheck a day earlier than mine. Why can't you?"

"Is the paycheck a direct deposit?"

"No."

"We will deposit your check a day early just like your friend's bank. With your permission, I can set up a direct deposit for you."

"Yeah, really? That would be great."

"I just need your member number and I'll verify some information to confirm you are the owner of this account."

Jay entered the number into his computer. No response. He hit the spacebar a few times. The computer did nothing. Jay glanced at the clock in the menu bar. It was blinking. At least the computer hadn't crashed.

"Um, I'm sorry. I'm having computer trouble."

The lady laughed. "Yeah, IT sucks at my company, too."

Jay smiled. He remembered his training. They said customers can hear your smile through the phone. "Thanks for your patience."

After a few more seconds of no response, Jay closed the program and reopened it. Nothing. He stood up in his cube to look around the office. Everyone was merrily tapping away on their keyboards. Whatever was wrong, it was with his computer alone.

"I'm really sorry. I'm going to have to reboot my computer. Would you be willing to wait a few minutes or would you like me to call you back?"

The customer sighed loudly and said in a frustrated tone, "Never mind." She ended the conversation with a loud click.

With a crackle, Earl's voice rang in his ear. "Jay. Come to my office."

"In a minute," said Jay, "I need to call the help desk."

Jay blew out a breath, rubbed his face and leaned back in his chair. "What luck."

Earl's office was immaculate and that was because he had nothing to do during his working hours but torment his call center staff. Rumor was that he slept with pet snakes and spiders at home. His bookshelf was filled with business books, sorted from large to small; each end propped up by a book-stop. One was a decorative bowling ball. The other a bowling pin.

Earl straightened his fingers into a peak over the clean blotter on his desk. "Jay, a broken computer is not a good excuse."

"It was the truth."

"Is that so?"

"Yeah, I called the help desk. They said I can't access anything because something happened to my account."

Earl rolled his eyes and leaned back in his leather chair.

"It's worse. Apparently, there is no record of me being an employee. They told me I need to go to HR and sort it out."

"Maybe I should fire you and make it easy for everyone."

"Please, sir, I'm sure it was someone's honest mistake."

Earl leaned forward and made no effort to mask his smirk. "I tell you what. Clock out. Go visit HR and then go home. We'll talk about this first thing tomorrow."

Jay left the office without responding. There was no use in letting things escalate like it did at the coffee shop earlier in the day. He took this low-rung job at CityTrust with hopes of a career built on the slow grind of good work earning the steady return of job promotions. Failing at the start line would mean he'd have to start over somewhere else.

Down the hall, dapper Mike leaned out of his cube into view, his suit jacket still buttoned neatly, talking to a customer in his headset. His eyebrows were curled up with concern. He mouthed, "Are you okay?"

Jay shrugged, waved half-heartedly and walked to the elevators to HR.

"The help desk said I'm not showing up as an employee," said Jay. "I need to get it fixed right away. I can't handle customer calls if I don't have access to the ROGN system."

HR was down a few floors in the CityTrust office building. It housed the same farm of blue cubes filling every open space. Just outside the elevators was the employee service center. If you didn't want sit on hold for forty-five minutes on a phone, you had the option of waiting in the lobby without hearing an automated message every sixty seconds. Here, it was the soft sounds of muzak.

The HR staffer looked up with tired eyes. She pulled her keyboard closer to the edge of her desk.

"Name?"

"Jay Wilson"

"Date of birth?"

"July 11th."

"Age?"

"Thirty."

The HR staffer looked up from her monitor and pulled her reading glasses down to her nose to get a better look at him. "You look older than thirty."

"Gee, thanks."

She blushed. "Oh, uh, I'm sorry."

"It's okay. I'm having a bad day. I feel twice my age."

After a few more punches at the keyboard, she asked, "When did you start here?"

"Three months ago."

"Well, there is no record of a Jay Wilson as an employee."

"I got paid last week. I'm certainly an employee unless you've taken up a policy of paying random people walking into your offices."

She stared humorlessly at Jay. Apparently HR

was having an even worse day than someone getting erroneously removed as an employee. She flipped off the monitor, pushed her keyboard under the desk and rose. "Let me talk to my manager."

The DMV would have shown better customer service. The line behind Jay murmured impatiently. After a few minutes, the lady waved Jay to join her inside a glass-walled office behind her desk.

The HR manager looked at Jay with disgust. He seemed to be twenty years past retirement. His thinning grey hair rose in light wisps across his balding head. Similar to his own boss, Earl, retirement would be considered boring compared to the daily joys of employee torment.

"May I see your ID?" he asked. Jay unclipped it. The manager turned the card over several times in his hands as if it were contaminated with a virus. He tapped on his keyboard and raised an eyebrow.

"I'm sorry, Mr. Wilson, but you aren't listed as an employee. We have no record of your application or employment status."

Jay blew out a breath. "Just talk to my boss, Earl Tanner. As much as he hates me, he will admit that I work for him."

"I'm sorry. If you'd like, just fill out this reinstatement form and turn it in to that gal down there." After handing over a sheet that rivaled a tax form, he pointed at an old lady pounding piles of paper violently with a stamp the size of a postcard. "She knows the ROGN system like the back of her hand. She will sort this out."

As if it were done every day, the HR staffer wordlessly guided Jay out of the office.

Jay stood in the hallway, stunned. His brain flipped from confusion to frustration. His bad day was spiraling in the wrong direction. Fighting it would only make things worse.

The queue of employees, waiting for HR to tell them what they can't do, watched him with disinterest. He pulled out his cellphone and texted Mike.

MEET ME @ PUB TONIGHT - DONE FOR THE DAY

A few seconds later Mike texted back.

DON'T DO ANYTHING RASH

Jay gritted his teeth. He had heard the phrase a million times. Jenni and Mike drilled the mantra into his head over the years like an Indian guru.

Mike texted again.

U OK?

I WILL BE

Jay decided to skip the subway and hummed *With A Little Help From My Friends* while he walked the seven blocks to Gordy's Pub. He could always find a new job if this one didn't work out, but it was too soon to give up. Jenni was the one that convinced Jay to start on the floor and, with some elbow grease, turn it into a career in banking. After all, New York was the financial capital of the world and what better place to start?

Scott woke up in the middle of the night with a pounding headache. He stretched out his hands in the dark and searched the side table; knocking over a half dozen bottles of meds. The clatter was punctuated by a lid rolling and settling across the room with a loud wobble. A muffled grunt arose from Karl's bedroom, but fell back to the deep breaths of sleep.

Scott's hands were trembling. Even in the pitch black, his eyes burned from staring at the screen all day. He wiped the eternal sweat that fell from his brow and smiled.

It was a sweet victory deleting Jay's employee records.

He flicked his finger across the laptop's trackpad to wake up the screen. After entering his password, the laptop flashed, casting a blue glow on Scott's pallid face. His smile widened as he followed the numbers and letters flashing by the screen in a blaze and blur. Earlier in the day, he cracked the administrator password on CityTrust's ROGN system. Now, he was cracking Jay's password in the event he used the same one in other systems. There were only two million possibilities left. That would only take a few more minutes and he had been waiting all night.

"Oh my dear Jay," said Scott, "you will soon live like the rest of us. I'm going to wipe that elitist smirk off your face."

This was more fun than passing time trolling conspiracy forums on the Internet. He loved stoking conspiracy theories and arguing point and counterpoint. Whenever someone demanded facts, Scott would hack a reputable source, edit some material and post a link. Over time, his anonymous identity swayed opinions and grew influential. The elitist deep state driving the engines of commerce and swamp of government must be destroyed and the human masses were easy to manipulate.

His anonymous personality was infamously known as Deetwuh. It was derived from his signature at the bottom of every post.

DITW.

Devil in the wire.

The whirligig of characters on his screen stopped. A window popped up and flashed, PASSWORD DECRYPTION SUCCESSFUL.

"Let's see what kind of password this clown uses. A football team? Dog's name? Oh my."

"J3NN1"

"Hmpf. Probably his high school crush."

Scott glanced at the clock, which read eleven thirteen p.m. He adjusted the laptop on his belly, unwrapped a Snickers bar, popped it in his mouth like a cigar and got to work.

CHAPTER 3

Gordy's bar was average in every way. The narrow room was half filled by the bar, complete with an overworked bartender who only smiled at the regulars. The opposite wall was lined with ice-cream tables that wobbled from uneven legs unsuccessfully leveled by coasters. The bathrooms were in a perpetual state of needing to not only be cleaned but repaired.

Mike sat in his usual spot; the corner of the bar that was closest to the entrance and best lit by the streetlights. His confident posture and impeccable fashion brought an air to Gordy's that encouraged the New York fashionista walking by to at least consider satiating their thirst inside. Gordy's owner and bartender knew this. "Nobody takes their car to a mechanic that has no cars in their parking lot."

That's why Mike got the benefit of half-off drinks at Gordy's. He was the lion at the gate of a bungalow. He appreciated saving money on the drinks because he spent more on clothes than anything else, including his rent. Nice clothing was rarely referred to as a vice. But for Mike, shopping for a new outfit was his drug of choice.

Mike was already enjoying his scotch when Jay sat next to him and blew out a breath. The bartender read the cue and poured a glass of whiskey.

"We had a lot of calls today and there were some no shows. Earl was looking for a reason to vent his frustration. Today was the wrong day to get on his dark side," said Mike.

"I didn't know Satan had anything but a dark side," replied Jay. He took a sip and continued, "The mountain in front of me got taller. CityTrust has no record of me being an employee. How is that even possible?"

"I'm sure it was a simple mistake."

"I'll sort it out tomorrow. You'd be proud of me. I left before losing my patience and digging a hole I can't get out of."

"Wow. The tiger is finally changing its stripes. Good on you to step away and not press your luck."

"I'm beginning to think that I don't have bad luck in life. I have a guardian demon."

Mike raised his glass. "I hear you, bud. Next time you roll the dice, I suggest you let 'em fall off the table."

Jay grunted. "Good one. I don't think things can get worse."

"I don't know. That day you, me and Jenni almost got caught shopping for clothes was pretty bad."

"I'm not sure I'd call it shopping when we were in a store after it was closed."

"When fashion calls, you answer."

"Especially when you were broke like us. Did you know that was the first night I kissed Jenni?"

"Now that you've told me that a dozen times, I think I'll be able to remember."

"Har har."

"You two are meant to be together."

"I wish, but she deserves better than me. I can't stand the silence anymore. If we could just talk. Be friends again. I'd be okay with going back to that."

"Give it time. We have a long history together. Despite the fact that I was eventually introduced to the concept of juvenile detention, I think of those times in Louisiana as good times."

"Indeed. No money, no food or place to stay, but I had the promise of a new day and we had a whole life ahead of us."

"To be young again. How the three of us ever became friends is crazy. A lawyer's daughter, a demon-possessed magnet for bad luck and the rumored love-child of Armani and Versace."

Mike chuckled and motioned to the bartender. "You need another drink."

Sunglasses sometimes aren't dark enough. Jay pressed his palms against his temples, walking in the bright New York morning sun. Rays bounced and glistened off the Manhattan high-rises, driving the piercing light deeper into his head. Though he had drunk too much last night, he had managed to get Mike to unbutton his suit and let a collar hang open. He smiled. A chink in Mike's silver armor of fashion apparently required only four drinks.

Jay shuffled along the line at CityTrust's employee entrance, moving slower than a line at a DMV. It was the same daily routine; two security officers flanked the metal detector watching with complete disinterest. Jay stepped up, swiped his badge and walked through the square gate.

One of the security officers stopped him with an outstretched arm. "Sorry, sir."

"Yes?"

He nodded at the light at the scanner. It flashed red.

"Oh, sorry. Let me run it through again."

He swiped, and after a short pause the red light flashed again.

Jay tilted his head back and closed his eyes. "There was a problem with the HR system yesterday. I thought they would have fixed it by now."

The guard did not care. He wanted the morning rush to end, so that he could sit back behind his desk and enjoy a weak coffee. "Step aside, sir. We need to let the others through."

Jay nodded, turned around and pointed at the phone at the desk. "Can I make a call?"

"Yup."

Jay punched zero. "Earl Tanner, please."

After three rings, Earl's voice snapped, "Hello?"

"Uh, it's Jay."

"Jay? Umm." Earl stumbled over his words. "Can you hang on for a sec?"

"Yes, but I only need you to let me in. I'm at the side employee entrance."

The phone let out a loud crack from hitting the wood desktop. Muffled voices talked over each other in the background. Jay plugged his other ear but could not make out what they were saying.

Jay nodded and shrugged his shoulders at the stream of co-workers crossing into the building. Despite all his efforts to drink away yesterday's mess, it looked as if today was going to be more of the same.

"Jay?"

"Yeah."

Earl fumbled over his words. "Uh, I need you to, uh, just stay there for a bit. Is that okay?"

"Sure."

"I'll send someone to...uh, let you in."

"Thanks. Sorry for the trouble, Earl. I owe you one."

Earl hung up without a response. Jay stared at the phone for a moment and returned it to the cradle. Earl was holding something back. He hoped it wasn't more bad news.

The security officers were distracted, talking into the radio strapped to their chest pocket. In unison, they turned and stared at Jay. One of them leaned over to press a button behind the desk. The exit doors locked with a loud metal clank. The employees already in the lobby murmured in frustration. More delays.

The security officers unsnapped their holsters. Their eyes never wavered from Jay.

Jay's brain worked overtime, trying to comprehend what was happening. Authority figures always made him nervous, even feel guilty. Every time he passed a police car, he slowed down to well below the speed limit.

Jay's mouth opened and closed like a fish. "Uh, wha? What's going on?"

"Sir, you need to come with us." The officer grabbed Jay's wrist gently. "Everything is going to be okay."

Jay jerked his hand back. "I can walk just fine by myself. Where are we going?"

"We're going to talk somewhere safe."

"*Somewhere safe?* Tell me what's going on."

One of the officer's radios cracked and buzzed. "Seventy four, are you code four?"

"Seventy four, negative," replied the security officer.

"What's a code four? Guys, you're making me nervous."

Without a word, the two officers glanced through the glass doors out to the Manhattan street filled with CityTrust employees, holding their morning coffee and waiting for the doors to reopen.

Flashing lights, red and blue, reflected faintly in the glass. Police.

Jay's cell phone vibrated in his pocket. He pulled it out and read a text from Mike.

WTF? U GOT A BOMB?

The security officer reached for the cell phone. "I'll take that."

Jay jerked it out of reach and replied rudely, "I don't think so." His heart was pounding in his chest.

"Sir, please stay calm." The two officers stepped back and held out their hands defensively.

"I don't know where you're getting your information but I don't have a bomb. Besides, it's hard to stay calm when you're treating me like this."

A panicked voice shouted from behind him in the line. "HE'S GOT A BOMB! RUN!"

Jay spun on his feet. "No no no!"

It was too late. A scene from a medieval battle unfolded. Instead of shields, it was briefcases. Cups of coffee were tossed in the air as employees struggled to rush back through the glass front doors. Ear-piercing alarms, trigged by emergency push bars, kicked in and added to the chaos.

What was once a polite queue of co-workers had turned into a storm of elbows to the face, kicks to legs and shoves to the back. The police outside, wielding batons, swam through the panicked throngs, shouting orders to make way and failing to make progress.

Jay felt a wave of humanity from behind, pushing his feet out from underneath him. He crashed to the marble floor, using his hands to protect his face from the unending rush of corporate hooves.

After a whirl of shoves and grunts, Jay fought to his feet. He worked his way further into the lobby and away from the chaos. One of the security officers grabbed Jay by the arm and pulled him to the wall.

Jay croaked, "I don't have a bomb. This is a mistake. Why don't you believe me?"

"Sir, no one needs to get hurt. Put the phone down and we can sort this out. Tell us where the bomb is." A second officer came to assist.

His pleas were not changing the minds of the officers. Just like an accusation from a foster parent, he was powerless to defend himself from authority. He was terrified and his childhood survival instincts kicked in. *Escape. Run. Hide. New family. Clean slate. Start over.*

One of the officers spoke slowly. "This doesn't have to get worse. Help us help you."

Jay paused, flicked his eyes at the collection of bags near the metal detector and returned his gaze at the security officers. Realization washed over their faces. They read the misdirection perfectly. The officers jumped at the pile of bags, scooped several of them up and bolted to the fire exit leading to the alley.

Wheezing from panic, Jay climbed over the

security desk, sending papers into the air and onto the floor. He slipped and knocked over a garbage can. The clatter echoed metallic and harsh on the marble lobby floor, adding to the rancor of the emergency alarms. The white walls were filled with flashing red lights and the white flickers of strobes. He could hear his childhood voice shouting through the rancor of panic in his head. *Escape. Run. Hide.*

Cornered in the lobby, Jay scanned for an exit and locked his eyes on a door adorned with a bright yellow sign. Stairs. He bolted through the doors. Skipping steps, he ran up the half flights using the railing to whip his body around each turn. Above him, doors flew open on every level and confused murmurs preceded the streams of employees that quickly filled the stairways. Jay fought against the crowds trying to push him back down to the lobby. They shouted in panicked voices.

"I don't think you want to go up, bud."

"Terry said it was a bomb."

"Oh my God. I need to call Tom."

"I can't get a cell signal."

The voices grew more frantic as the minutes marched by. Jay tried to calm the crowds. He repeatedly shouted, "It's a prank. There is no bomb. Calm down." No one listened. Like Jay, panic tripped the circuit breakers of logic in their brains. Only in safe confines would rational thought return.

Thankfully, the crowds thinned after a few flights for Jay to quicken his pace. After stopping to catch his breath, he glanced at the sign on the wall.

FLOOR 11. A childhood of running from authorities that claimed to have your best interests at heart was inextricably burned into his psyche. Despite the empty stairwell, he felt the walls closing in on him. He was not safe yet.

Jay wiped sweat from his face. "Three more floors." He forged on, using his arms to assist his tired, sore legs up the endless steps. Sweat soaked though his shirt and it was difficult to retain a grip on the railing. At the top of the stairs, in a dead end, was a short ladder to the rooftop door. He climbed to the small indoor platform and used his shoulder to push open the "emergency exit only" bar and stepped onto the roof of CityTrust.

He closed the door, grabbed an old, rusted lounge chair and wedged it in place with a hard kick. The rooftop was a junkyard of rusted exhaust tubes, air conditioning units and metal structures ready to collapse.

Jay put his hands on his knees and sucked in the refreshing, cold morning air. He was a child again, hiding from an abusive foster parent. With no one to help, he did what he did best. Survive. He resisted the urge to find a dark corner by an air conditioning unit and curl into a ball.

Sirens for multiple emergency vehicles clashed into a relentless jumble of alarms. Jay thought to himself. *Jenni better not hear about this.*

◆ ◆ ◆

Karl spun around in the chair at his desk to face Scott who was still sitting on the couch, unmoved from the same place yesterday. He was livid. "Scott, did you call from our phone?"

Scott cackled, his oversized belly jiggling like a waterbed under his hockey jersey. "I bet this is going to be on the news tonight. I can't wait to see the headlines tomorrow: CityTrust employee's bomb threat stops morning traffic."

"Scott, I'm serious. Did you call that threat in from our phone?" Spittle filled the corners of his mouth.

"Relax, bud. Yes, I called from our phone, but ran it through an anonimizer."

Karl shot upright and ran his fingers through his hair. "You know they can eventually trace that call, even with an anonymous server. I can't believe you did that!"

Scott rolled his eyes and continued to chuckle. "You've forgotten that I have access to Globecom's servers. I'm deleting the call records right now, dude. For all intents and purposes, the call was never made. I even crashed their reporting environment so they can't run any queries while I finish up."

Karl squinted his eyes at Scott. It was days like this that he felt less a friend and more the parent, ever watchful of Scott's enthusiasm crossing the line to irreparable consequences.

Scott felt the stare, like a cold breeze from a casino entrance when walking by on a hot day in Vegas. He connected eyes and spoke slowly, "Karl, have I ever let you down?"

Karl's shoulders fell, resigned to lose the debate. "No, you haven't. But this isn't like playing a prank on the prom king and queen back in school."

Scott's fingers never stopped their dance across the laptop perched on his stomach. Click clack click click click thunk.

Karl asked, "What are you doing now?"

Scott paused and looked up with a sneer. "As of yesterday, Jay no longer has a job. The poor guy doesn't know that it was just an appetizer."

Karl blew out a breath. Scott never let anything go. He didn't have anything to deter him from his mission. No job. No girlfriend. No commitments. Karl begged, "I think you've done enough."

Scott smiled. "Hardly. When I'm done, Jay simply won't exist."

◆ ◆ ◆

"I thought you'd be here. Good lord, what have you done?" asked Mike.

Jay fell into his usual stool at Gordy's. Black stripes of grease cut across the sides of his khaki pants. Red skin poked through the tears in his shirt on both elbows. His hair was tipped with sweat.

Mike waved to the bartender.

"The usual, Bert...and a glass of cold water, please." Jay continued, still out of breath, "I was barely inside the front entrance and security was all over me."

"Security was looking for you when I clocked in. They were searching your cube. They asked me if I knew where you were. I was lucky enough to hear them talking in the men's room with Earl. The moment I heard 'bomb', I was out of there."

"I can't comprehend how a bomb threat got linked to me."

"You need to call the police," said Mike. "You can't run away from this. This isn't Louisiana. It's New York and they have a severe allergy to bombs. They will find you before nightfall. Worse, you'll appear more guilty the longer you hide away."

Jay downed the scotch with a toss of his head, splashed the water into his face and waved for another. "I made it clear that I had nothing. They didn't believe me. It'll all be on their security footage. But it didn't matter, I was guilty in their eyes."

"They never found a bomb. Chalk it up as a misunderstanding. Just explain it."

Jay let out a breath and looked up at the ceiling. "You're right. What do I have to hide if I'm not guilty? Perhaps they'll give me an apology and my job back. But the question is: Who would call in a bomb threat with my name on it? Outside you, I have no friends."

"Maybe Jenni would know. Whenever we're out on the town, she always seems to run into a lot of interesting characters that know her. That one guy last weekend looked like a dead ringer to Robin Williams' Fisher King and seemed to be in love with her. Maybe you were a threat?"

"Well, she volunteers every weekend at the homeless shelter. There are so many people that come in and out, she's bound to run into them somewhere. They all certainly have their quirks and are mostly harmless. Besides, Jenni isn't returning my calls. Worse, I'm not sure a chat on how my life is unraveling is the best way to break our silence."

"I'll call her."

"No, don't."

"If there is any crazy chance she knows, we can make this stop."

Jay put his face in his hands and willed the world to go away. He was hoping a promotion at CityTrust would be the perfect opportunity to break his silence with Jenni. His last boss was relentless with criticism and incredibly demeaning. It only took a couple weeks before he lost his temper. Quitting on the spot was the emotional band-aid that felt better than being fired. It later formed a deep wound that Jenni and Jay never recovered from.

After a few beeps, Mike said, "Jenni. It's Mike. You got a sec?"

Mike held a thumb up to Jay, who peeked out between his fingers.

"What's going on? Any friends run any pranks lately?" Mike paused and then smiled. "Yes, Jay is here. How did you guess?"

After a pause, Mike handed the phone to Jay.

Jay let out a breath. "Hey, Jenni."

Jenni's voice was syrup. Her words enunciated like a southern belle awaiting someone to court her in the parlor, "We need to talk."

Jay stiffened. He did not want to relive their last conversation. He answered through his teeth, "Now is not a good time."

Mike's eyebrows curled into a frown. He mouthed, "Calm down."

The sweet drawl continued, "Jay, I'm sorry for not calling back. I needed to think."

"No bomb threat? Is there a new boyfriend that wants me destroyed?"

Jenni let out a breath of frustration. "What are you talking about? I don't understand what you're saying."

"Sorry," said Jay as he rubbed his face. "I'm having a really tough day. Week. Whatever you call it."

"Why don't you call me when you get things right?"

"Jenni?"

"Yes, Jay?"

"I miss you."

"Well, darling, don't get the wagon ahead of the mule. Call me back. But not until you're ready. I'm not...I can't do this again unless you're... sorted."

"Well, this situation that I'm dealing with is really bad."

"Isn't it always? Look, I need to go." Her tone cut like a knife.

Mike stared as Jay handed the phone back.

"So?"

"Jenni doesn't know."

Mike looked at his feet. "You know, she called me last week about you."

"She did? Why didn't you tell me?"

"She swore me to secrecy."

A faint smile broke across Jay's face. "I really do miss her."

Mike patted his shoulder. "I know you do, bud. You need to find a way to look beyond your nose."

"What's that supposed to mean?"

"Give up a little now to gain a lot in the long run. Jenni's worth it."

Jay sighed. "Of course she's worth it but I don't deserve to be with her. She needs a Wall Street investor type who can give her a beautiful house in the country. Not someone who is a magnet to fake bomb threats on a slow day."

Mike rocked his head back and chortled. "Why don't you let Jenni decide that, instead of deciding for her?"

"It's pretty obvious I don't deserve Jenni. Remember that guy I told you about that got on my back yesterday at the coffee shop? He was a three-hundred-pound whale trying to make the moves on a poor girl that couldn't have been ninety pounds soaking wet. Batting way out of his league. She didn't deserve him. This is the same thing."

"That's really not fair, Jay. You, of all people on this planet, should know not to draw a conclusion based on first impressions. Would someone look at you and see the incredible story of your upbringing?"

"Sure, I overcame poor odds. Sadly, no employer wants to place a bet on someone who grew up bouncing between foster families developing skills such as avoiding inappropriate gropes from adults and making lemonade from lemons sourced from a dumpster."

"I bet on you. Jenni bet on you. The payoff is coming. Just be patient. You have another hurdle to jump right now with this bomb threat. If anything, we'll have another great story to tell and we are full of them." Mike laughed as he poked Jay in the ribs.

His jocular expression melted into concern. "What's wrong?"

"I just realized," said Jay, "all this mess started when that kid got ticked at me at the coffee place. Is that coincidence? A prank call is classic teenage angst."

"That sounds likely. Even so, what are the chances of finding him? Getting him to fess up?"

"He knew the barista's name. Remember? Gotta be a regular. If we can find him, maybe the police can get me out of this mess."

"There is only one way to find out. But police first, coffee shop kid second."

The bar grew quiet. The hair on Jay's neck crawled, like Peter Parker's spider-sense. Two men at the end of the table stared at the duo. The bartender stopped cleaning his glasses, towel still stuck up inside a clean pint glass. Behind the bartender, the TV flashed a picture of Jay's employee badge from CityTrust. He couldn't make out what the news anchor was saying, but the intent was clear. The manhunt for Jay had already begun.

Jay looked down at his glass and whispered. "Mike, grab me like you're going to turn me in. You can't be an accomplice."

Mike whispered back, "I don't think so." He flashed a concerned look at one of the men at the end of the bar who reached into his jacket. Jay's eyes followed Mike's. They saw the grip of a pistol poke out from a holster. Nestled among a half a dozen empty PBR bottles on the bar top in front of the men was a camouflage baseball cap that read, "NRA."

Another New York vigilante. We'll be dead before proven innocent.

Mike held out one hand. "I don't think you want to do that, bud."

The man froze. His eyes were bloodshot from an afternoon of anti-government rants surely fueled by healthy doses of PBR.

Mike pointed at Jay. "When he he gets pissed, bad things happen."

All eyes jerked to Jay. His survival instinct kicked in. They've weaseled out of scarier situations as teens and had a little practice as a duo. Mike said it best. *All it takes is a little crazy to put people on their heels.*

Jay slowly raised his hand from his side and pointed an index finger to his own head. Everyone stopped breathing, more confused than terrified.

Jay puckered up his lips dramatically. "Bang."

One cue, Mike shot out his arm and cleared the bar-top in a wide sweep. Glasses, ashtrays and bowls of popcorn rained to the floor in a clatter. The men protectively held up their arms to their face and stumbled away from the bar.

Standing on his stool, Mike leaned over to grab several bottles of liquor from the shelf. Holding the neck, he swung a bottle to the floor in front of the men. It shattered, exploding liquor and glass in every direction.

With the distraction, Jay spun on his stool and bolted for the rear exit. He could hear Mike's fashionable boots clomping loudly behind him. After kicking the door open, Jay found himself in an empty alley the length of a full block. He jerked his head left and right. Running either way would leave them within shooting range. The trigger-happy vigilantes would shoot first and ask questions later.

I've got to get to the police before the crazies get to me. Jay cursed his guardian demon. Things were escalating out of his control.

Mike burst into the alley behind him, still cradling several bottles in his arms. Jay rolled a half-empty barrel over to bar the door.

Mike looked down at his bounty, half confused and half amused, and gave a shrug. "Guess I forgot to drop them."

He nodded above Jay's head at a rusted fire escape ladder.

"The guys with the guns are behind us. They're stumbling drunks, but weaponized. To the roof."

Jay shook his head. "Not again."

◆ ◆ ◆

"Right there." Jay leaned to peek around the alley corner and pointed at the corner coffee shop. The sign over the door hung at a lazy angle, as if it were embarrassed by the pithy name lined in gold letters: Running-A-Ground.

Mike squinted. "Do you see him in there?"

Jay shook his head. "Too far to see anything. Let's cross the street and peek in from the side."

"Not until we call the police first."

"Really?" Jay's eyebrows almost shot off his forehead. He let out a short, dismissive chuckle. "Let's tell the police that the real guy that they're looking for is a hockey fan lounging in a coffee shop, not the guy who lost his CityTrust job the day before and just ransacked Gordy's bar? I'm sure they'll immediately start a manhunt based on my good word."

Mike pursed his lips.

Jay crouched, still fighting the instinct to hide. He could feel the panic edging in from the edges of his vision. "Sorry, Mike. You shouldn't even be here with me, you know. I appreciate it."

"How can accosting this kid now be the more rational option? Are you planning civilian arrest? A confession?"

"We can talk it out. He was pretty upset with me. He totally mistook my intentions. He seems the kind that quickly blows things out of proportion."

"Like running from the cops when they're there to help you?"

"Very funny." Jay returned his gaze to the coffee shop. "It'll only take a few minutes to even see if he's in there. If he's not, then let's make a phone call to the police."

Mike acquiesced with a shrug. "Fine. If he's not there, let's call the police right away. I suppose it can't hurt to check."

The coffee shop smelled more of baked goods than of coffee. Tables and chairs filled the tiny dining area. The furniture appeared to be pulled from trash containers as they were a mishmash of the last century's upholstery styles and were decorated with scratches, tears and missing rivets. Jay smiled. It was endearing.

The place was horrifying to Mike. He held up his hands as he negotiated the furniture. It was as if the chairs would infect him. The edges of his lips were curled up in disgust.

"Ack. My eyes can't handle this excrescence. Someone needs to light a match!"

Jay stopped and motioned with his chin. "He's here. In line."

Mike peered over Jay's shoulder. "Wow. I don't even need three guesses to figure out which person. Why someone of that body shape would choose to wear something that oversized is beyond me. A little fashion sense would go a long way. Yikes, that shirt is probably bigger than my shower curtain!"

"Shhhh. He doesn't take criticism well."

Karl regretted leaving his jacket behind. The New York air had a crisp bite that turned his fingers into frozen fish sticks, but Running-a-Ground was only a few blocks away. It would take a few seconds to warm up after circling his hands around a piping hot cup of joe.

Scott always left for the coffee shop well before dinner time for baked goods. He wanted a little chat time with Mary before the evening rush lined up at the counter. Scott was never one to know what league he was in, but Karl appreciated his persistence. He was too shy to even connect eyes with most women.

This was Karl's favorite time of the day. His work was behind him and the evening would be filled with caffeine-fueled debate. Running-a-Ground was transformed into a geek-infused version of a barbershop once the rush hour traffic blew by. Sure they were immature, young adults, likely living with their parents. Karl had a regular job and sometimes looked at them with contempt, but their sophisticated humor and smarts garnered his respect.

Through the large windows, Karl saw that a

line was already forming at the counter. Dark over-
coats hung from the shoulders of those who slaved
at their desks all day, ties choking them and fluorescent lights sapping their vitality. They shuffled,
wordlessly, to purchase an overpriced cup of dirty
water that would keep them awake during their last
leg of the subway trip home.

A potbellied, blonde man stood out in the
line wearing a bright, sweat-soaked white shirt
striped with brown and black smudges. He shifted
his weight back and forth nervously. Behind him,
a well-dressed man with unbelievably perfect hair
reached into his mod-style blazer, pulled out a cellphone and snapped a picture of someone further up
in the line.

That someone was Scott.

Like a short fuse on a bottle-rocket, Karl connected the dots. Scott had shoved Jay's headshot in
Karl's face incessantly over the last day to celebrate
every little virtual strike he made online. In the
dull moments of running brute force cracker software that took hours to process, Scott did the virtual version of drawing mustaches and black eyes
on Jay's headshot. There was no doubt in Karl's mind
that it was Jay standing in line.

Karl shoved his hands into his jeans pocket
and stared. He was unsure of what to do. Calling the
police was out of the question. He had to extricate
his friend before they got a clear shot of Scott's face.
While he wanted to keep his friend out of trouble,
he'd be implicated just as harshly as Scott if anyone

discovered what he had done to Jay.

Jay and his friend began to circle Scott.

Karl scanned the sidewalk. The broken and uneven concrete was dotted with cigarette stubs and a wild pattern of black and grey paint stains. A garbage can was chained to a light post. He pulled off the metal lid to look inside. The can was empty.

He looked back in the cafe. There was no time.

Karl closed his eyes, blew out a breath and muttered, "Here goes nothing." With a grunt, he threw the lid into the Running-a-Ground sign that hung over the entrance. After a metallic clang, sparks rained down onto the sidewalk. One of the rusty bolts secured into the wall shot out into the street with a tungg! It was all that kept the sign in place.

The sign dropped and jerked into a short arc when the short power line connecting from above broke its fall. It swung into the glass facade of the shop. Glass shattered into tiny pieces, raining across the sidewalk, wood tables and tiled floor inside.

A short buzz and snap preceded the electrical short that blacked out the interior of the shop.

Everyone inside froze in confusion and horror. The whites of their eyes were stars in the darkness.

Like watching a YouTube video of a horrible accident, Karl's feet were stuck in concrete and he could not move. Everyone stared back at him.

Scott shouted out from the darkness, "Dude?"

Like a slap, Scott's voice brought him back to reality. People were pulling out their phones, turning on tiny flashlights and recording the aftermath.

Karl pulled his t-shirt collar up over his nose to cover his face. "Get out, bud. *Run!*"

Scott burst out of the darkness of the cafe, tossing chairs left and right. If he had a ring in his nose, he'd be a bull running the streets of Pamplona, tossing people asunder. He let out a high-pitched squeal when he tripped over the window sill onto the concrete sidewalk. Karl rushed over and tugged at his arm to help him back to his feet. All Scott responded with were dry whooping sounds, sucking for air in deep heaves.

Karl glanced back into the coffee shop. Some folks clamored through the disarray of furniture. Others walked slowly to the exit, talking in low voices. Like fireflies, cell phones lit up the dark interior. Karl and Scott's digital anonymity was disappearing as the seconds marched by. Worse, they only had minutes before the police arrived.

"No time, bud." Karl kneeled, reached under Scott's arms and pushed up with his legs. He let out a huff and finished with a guttural yell as all of Scott's weight bore down on his legs and back. He blinked with surprise when Scott spun around once on his feet. "Thanks, dude. Needed to catch my breath. What just happened?"

"Later. We need to get out of here."

If things weren't already live-streamed, something incriminating surely was going to be posted online. Karl pointed to the alley that separated Running-a-Ground from the street's liquor store. "Over there."

Karl led the way, running in the long awkward strides of a teenager who doesn't know what to do with his oversized feet. Scott followed, bouncing from one leg to another with steps that seemed to defy balance and gravity. Every part of his body protested, but fear and panic provided all the motivation and energy he needed.

Halfway down the alley, police sirens grew so loud that Scott could not hear Karl's footfalls. Both ends of the alley flashed in the colors of police lights, sirens echoing and ringing from every concrete and metal surface. They huddled, out of sight, in a dark alley door cutaway. The light above the door thankfully was not on, or more likely, was broken.

Scott whispered over the din, "Dude, what was that all about?"

"Your Jay. He was inside."

Scott's eyes jerked wide. "Why?"

"I dunno. They were right behind you. He had people with him."

"Police?"

"Nah...unless they were undercover. One of them snapped a picture of you from behind."

"Whoa."

"How did they find you? How did Jay know it was you?"

"There is no way anyone knows it's me.

Everything I did online was completely untraceable."

Karl let out a huff. "Ah, so this is all just a coincidence?"

The sirens snapped off. Footfalls echoed down the narrow walls of the alley. A police radio chirped and buzzed with static.

Scott bit his lip. He turned and tried the doorknob on the metal door behind them. It opened.

Karl's mouth broke into a smile. They darted inside the pitch-black room. In a smooth motion, Scott eased the door latch into place with a soft click. They allowed themselves to breathe again.

"We sit here until the commotion clears," said Karl, "then we take the long way back home."

"I'm in no hurry."

"When we get back, I want you to pack up and leave."

"What?"

"I'm not going to be implicated in this. You crossed the line."

"I'm telling you, they don't know it's me. It's impossible that they could trace my setup." Scott paused and said, "Uh oh."

"What?"

"Nothing...It's impossible."

Karl's voice was stern. "Scott. What is it?"

"You think he would remember the argument we had?"

Karl let out a chuckle. "Why wouldn't he? Look at you. You're not even mad at me, and you frighten me."

"Not nice. But you're right. But why wouldn't he just go to the police? Why would they chase us down? You said it was two guys."

Karl shrugged. "Yup. Jay and some well-dressed guy. He definitely got a picture of you."

Scott put his hand over his mouth, eyes wide with shock. He asked, "What kind of people don't go to the police and settle the score on their own?"

"Get to the point, Scott.

"We're in New York, dude. There are plenty of guys named Vinnie that are happy to help you snuff out somebody with nothing but ten grand, a name and a picture."

Karl gulped and replied, "You think they're going to order a hit? Come on. That makes no sense."

"Dude. He has no job. I deleted his employment record. A bomb threat is a felony. He's probably being chased by the police like Navy Seals on Bin Laden. In all that chaos, he's going to take the time to have someone take a picture of me? I highly doubt it's for social media. He's got to be absolutely livid. Plus, maybe Jay already knows all the other things I've done."

"Other things you've done? Oh my god, Scott. What else did you do? Never mind. Maybe he's going to give your picture to the police?"

"The police aren't going to trust someone who has Jay's police record."

"No way. You hacked the NYPD? That's crazy! Just as crazy as thinking you've got the mob on your tail."

"Doesn't matter what you think. I can find out if it's true. Just need some time on my laptop back in our apartment."

Jay and Mike stood in stunned silence. Glass shards crunched under the feet of those who were milling about carefully, hands outstretched for balance. Red and blue lights flashed across the darkened cafe, reflecting through mirrors and tabletops.

"What was all that?" Jay wasn't really speaking to anyone in particular.

Mike was busy brushing his hands through his hair, swatting out the dust and debris from his golden curls. One of the shop workers stood in the empty facade of the store and pointed down the sidewalk, shouting to the police. "They went that way. The skinny guy did it. In the alley. I'm sure folks here got a picture."

Two uniformed police officers bolted out of view. One stayed behind and calmly pulled out a tablet, wrapped rugged like a tire, and asked, "What happened here?" As the worker talked, the officer pecked on the screen that glowed in his face. Customers milled around the tables and chairs, confused and unsure of what to do.

"Hold on," said the officer in a clipped tone. "This thing is frozen up. I need to reboot."

Mike grabbed Jay's shoulder. He put his finger

up to his lips and pointed to the back of the store. Jay nodded in silent agreement.

The blue-red flash slowly dissipated the deeper they walked into the back room. Confident they were out of view, Mike pulled out his phone and brightened the screen to light their way. They exited through a delivery door, far from the chaos only a block way.

"The hockey kid. Where did he go?" asked Jay.

"He was the first one out of the shop. He ran like a little girl who stepped on a snake." Mike stifled a chuckle. "It's too bad you missed the sight."

"We're never going to find him now. That shop will be closed for weeks."

"True," said Mike, "but we got a good look at him. Can't forget that face. But there's something else."

"What?"

"Right after the ruckus, someone called out to the hockey kid from outside the shop. He helped the kid up after tripping over the sill. They were quite eager to leave the scene."

"Then why are we out here? Let's go in and get the police after them!"

"They're surely in pursuit. I wouldn't worry about that part."

"What part do I need to worry about?"

"The part about a person of interest for a bomb threat being in a coffee shop that looks like ground zero. Worse, we didn't leave Gordy's on the best of terms. I hate to say it, but your luck is getting worse than your decision making."

Jay closed his eyes. He'd be guilty before proven innocent. Mike was right. The disasters following Jay's footsteps would be evidence blocking even the most open-minded officers from believing his story.

Bile collected in Jay's throat. He had impossible choices again. It was hard not to flash back to his childhood; torn between suffering abuse as barter for warm meals and a warm bed, or to run blindly into the unforgiving life of homelessness. Neither were good choices and it came down to which was more bearable.

Mike asked, "Did you see what the kid was wearing? He had a Rod Gilbert Penguins jersey. I swear it was an original, highlighted nicely with a yellowing patina from months of never being washed."

"So?"

"More clues on who this kid is. No one else is going to have that jersey, much less be wearing it." Mike held up his phone. "I also got a nice shot before all hell broke loose."

Jay squinted at the picture. "It's the back of his head. But we've got height, weight and build. He's lucky if he sees the sun twice a month. That's something to work from. Maybe this can match security footage, if they have any. This is definitely the kid."

"We've got a general sense of age, too. A teenager? Maybe twenty?"

With a smile, Jay said, "We've got enough for the police. This is a teenager playing a prank. Simple."

"I say we go home first. Let's type up a timeline of what happened and explain all the details in a document that you can hand over. You'll be calm, professional and completely believable." Mike nodded at Jay's sweat-stained, street-mucked outfit. "But you need to clean up before you show up at the detectives' office."

"You're right," replied Jay looking at his sweaty, grime-scuffed clothes. "I need something that screams less crazy."

CHAPTER 4

"You think it's safe to go to your apartment?" asked Mike. As if answering his question, a sea of taxis broke free of the red light at their intersection, jerking out and braking in the most inefficient way one could travel Manhattan. It gave them a few more minutes to think before crossing. Black exhaust burped and broke the bright headlights cutting through the darkness.

Jay pulled his hood further down over his face. He grabbed a sweatshirt, tossed by a dumpster on the way back and replaced the clothes he wore at CityTrust. Despite the darkness, Jay was wearing Mike's sunglasses. "The police know my name. My address. The cops are probably reading a magazine in my bathroom right now. A bomb threat probably means the whole place has been ransacked."

"A *prank* bomb threat that you repeatedly denied," clarified Mike. "They don't ransack apartments over a prank. They never found a bomb."

"My face was breaking news! It's a manhunt. They don't post your face on the TV unless you're a threat."

"You know, I thought about that."

"Wow. Color me impressed."

Mike cocked an eyebrow. "I'm serious. I assumed there was a manhunt when I saw your mug on the TV. It could have been the evening news explaining what stopped up traffic. You did stir things up."

Jay blew out a breath. "I didn't hear what they said. I saw the picture and my brain froze. You mean we overreacted at Gordy's bar?"

"Um, you saw the gun right? The camouflage hat? There was no way we were going to survive capture by those two vigilantes. They'd beat us to a pulp before handing us over to the police. I'm sure they'd have more fun shooting us in the alley. They'd love the drama of saying how difficult a catch we were."

"I get it. But is there a manhunt for me or not?"

"At this point, it doesn't really matter. We're going to the detectives. Why don't I run up to your place and confirm it isn't crawling with eyes and ears. I'll text you when the coast is clear. Then you can clean up and put your story together before anyone wises up."

"Good idea." Jay pulled up his phone to check its battery. Along the top of the phone's display, NO SERVICE blinked rapidly. He shook the phone and looked again.

Jay held up the phone to Mike. "I can't get a signal. How is your phone?"

Mike fished his phone out of his blazer jacket and glanced at his display. "No problems for me."

"Maybe this is not a good idea. The police could have shut down my service."

"Relax. It won't take me but a few minutes to check on your place. I'll come back down and wave you over. Stay here and look inconspicuous."

Jay indicated his clothes. "I'll pretend to be homeless."

"You've got the experience to pull it off." With a wink, Mike dashed, actually skipped, across the intersection.

Jay sunk a few steps deeper into the dark corner of concrete steps of a row house to wait for Mike. He thanked his luck that the house's lights were off and moved to a crouch, hugging his knees to stay warm.

The exhaustion of the day pulled at Jay's eyelids and transported him back to Louisiana. He was crouched, out of view, in the darkened, recessed entry of a closed storefront. Across from him, was a food pantry in downtown New Orleans. Jay was waiting for it to close.

Underage runaways were always welcome at the pantry. The difficult part was leaving. The volunteers had good intentions but they didn't realize calling social services didn't help. State guardianship meant more foster families. At sixteen, he was finished with the cycle of generosity mixed with abuse.

He was most successful befriending another adult in need of the pantry's services. It was ironic that the most giving people he knew were the ones who had the least. However, his time sitting outside the pantry waiting for a handout revealed an opportunity with better results.

After closing, volunteers gathered spoiled vegetables and fruit and tossed it into a compost pile behind the pantry. Expired canned food, deemed no longer safe, was tossed in the dumpster. If he was lucky, he'd get a week's worth of food in one night.

The lights to the interior of the pantry switched off. On cue, the front door opened and a large black man, dressed impeccably in Adidas training pants and jacket, carried two large trash bags. The grunt of effort to toss the bags into the dumpster gave Jay hope. The heavier the bag, the more likely it was filled with cans. He salivated over the thought of apple sauce or green beans.

The man walked, confident and precise, from the rear of the building to his car parked across the alley. With a chirp, the lights came on inside, exposing the elegant leather interior of a four door Jaguar.

Jay bolted for the dumpster. Finders keepers, losers weepers wasn't just a mantra for children. It was a mantra for survival. No one hungry needed to raid the dumpster, as they got what they needed during the day. Jay was more worried about the potential of other teens beating him to his reward.

Inside the dumpster, Jay tore at the thick plastic bags. He was discouraged that one bag was filled with carpet remnants. The other bag revealed no jackpot, but a small reward of two plastic bottles of vegetable juice. Jay climbed out of the dumpster and almost dropped the bottles from fright.

A black girl stood in front of him holding a small plastic bag. Her eyes were wide, but not frightened. Her head was full of beautifully thin-braided strands held up in a ponytail. A few strands hung in front of her face.

"Oh. Sorry," gurgled Jay. He tried to clear his throat. His body was preparing for a feast and was not ready for the burst of adrenaline. It was fear. He felt exposed. *Escape. Run. Hide.*

The girl did not move. "I guess my dad didn't see you. My name is Jenni."

Jay's eyes darted left to right. He couldn't run back through the alley. The man with the nice car might still be there. His only option was behind the girl and she blocked his way.

Jenni continued in her southern drawl. "What's your name?"

Escape. Run. Hide. He shuffled in a wide arc around Jenni, keeping his distance and eyes on her.

"Do you want food?" She held up her plastic bag. "I have some."

He hesitated. Without a word, Jay held out his hand but kept his head on a swivel. It didn't matter if it was a priest or a policeman, he had a strict rule to follow. No adults. The girl was certain not to be alone and he needed to escape. All he had to do was run a couple blocks to one of his favorite spots to hide and he'd be safe again.

Jenni handed over the bag. "Old bagels. There is no mold, but I'd eat them right away. They are kind of hard."

She didn't flinch when he snatched the bag and hurried away.

"I'm here Tuesday nights," Jenni said in a soft voice as Jay slinked into the night. "If you wait for me, I'll have something better next time."

A man's voice called out from the alley. "Jenni, darling, it's time to go home."

A loud honk of a taxi woke Jay in time for him to see Mike frantically waving Jay over to his apartment lobby.

Mike shrugged his shoulders when Jay entered and said, "Nothing happened at your place. I even talked to your neighbor, Miss Bianchi, and she said it was just another day of kids hollering in the hallways."

Inside his apartment, Jay found an envelope with flamboyant cursive writing waiting for him on the floor. Jay scooped it up and grimaced at the letter.

"Love letter?" asked Mike as Jay opened it.

"My landlord says I'm six months behind on rent. I never, ever miss a payment. I can't even sleep if I think I might possibly be late on a payment. They have me mixed up with another tenant, I'm sure." His voice turned into sarcastic glee. "I'm so excited that I get to waste time sorting this out. Can't anyone do their jobs correctly for once?"

Jay flipped the letter over. "Here it says I'll be evicted if I don't pay in the next three days. Such lovely customer service."

Mike put his hand on Jay's shoulder. "I can cover you for this month, Jay."

Jay cringed inside. He wasn't looking for handouts. His whole life had been about receiving handouts. He knew Mike was just trying to help and fought his irritable demeanor. "I've got plenty of money to cover it. I'll do a quick transfer online and I'll clear this up with the landlord downstairs on the way out."

Mike opened the fridge. "Empty."

"Yeah, sorry." Jay nodded to the cabinets. "But I do have scotch."

"Even better." Mike collected a couple glasses, clinking happily as Jay scooted his chair up to his computer. A familiar chime rang from the computer as the screen brightened the living room.

After a few clicks, Jay slapped his forehead. He muttered, "Can't connect to the internet. Seriously?"

Mike dropped a glass of scotch on the desk next to Jay and sipped his own. "Reboot your computer. Where is the internet router? I'll reboot that for good measure."

"The hallway table, next to the phone."

A couple sips later, Mike sauntered back. "We have blinking lights. Try it again."

They both silently watched the laptop work its way back to life from its reboot. Blue, orange and red lights flickered, announcing all the hard work being done inside the case to ready the computer. The clicks and chittering were a protest, as if it was waking from a nice nap.

After a click and a roll of the mouse, Jay sat back in his chair. "Still no internet. I can't make payment if I can't get online."

Mike rolled his eyes. "Who's your provider?"

"StateComm. There's a customer service number on the bottom of the router."

Shaking his head, Mike returned to the hallway table. He held up the router to Jay. Lights were blinking. Mike picked up the phone and started to dial.

"Hey, Jay."

"Yeah?"

"Did you forget to pay your phone bill, too?"

"Now what?"

"Phone's dead."

Jay slammed his laptop closed. "Unbelievable!"

"I don't think so."

"Don't make fun of me, Mike."

"I'm not. This is all too much a coincidence."

Jay stared at the ceiling. "It's a sign from God that he can't do anything about the demons. I will start a warm bath and find my razors."

"Knock it off. It's not funny."

"Am I laughing?"

"This person who called in the fake bomb threat. He's messing with your billing. It sounds like a prank call to the bank wasn't the only thing he did."

Jay scratched at the stubble on his chin. "A prank call is far less difficult than shutting down my phone, internet and cancelling a rent payment. There are security measures preventing this kind of stuff. Plus, we work for CityTrust. There is extra security and monitoring on our accounts. No teenage loser could do anything this sophisticated."

Mike fell into the couch, holding his scotch out to avoid a spill. He took a sip and declared with swirl of his drink, "I have a theory."

"Let's hear it."

"Someone at the bank doesn't like you."

Jay took in a breath and rolled his eyes. "Find me someone at the bank who *likes* me."

Mike ignored the sarcasm. "Are all your accounts at CityTrust?"

"Yup. I was once a loyal employee. I moved everything I could to CityTrust accounts. Even got a CityTrust credit card."

Mike waved his drink like an exclamation point.

Jay pondered out loud, "I see your point. Call

in a bomb threat. Get in cahoots with someone in HR and delete my employee records. Bounce my checking account to the moon with errant transactions."

"So the question is: Who and why?"

Jay walked into the kitchen and grabbed the bottle of scotch. He freshened their drinks and joined Mike on the couch.

Jay continued, "I really don't care who and I don't care why. This has to end. I'm about to lose my job, my credit and my apartment. I'm not going down without a fight."

"Hear, hear, brother!"

"The police. We go to the police."

"Now you're talking sense! Let's go."

Jay took a sip. "I'm not going to the police drunk. It's late. I need to shower and shave. Plus we need to get all of this documented. In the morning."

"You're not drunk, Jay."

"Not yet."

"Then let's enjoy the evening. Maybe the police will come to us," said Mike.

He saluted with a clink of his glass. "To a mystery solved!"

Scott held his hands up in defense from his couch. "If you really think a hitman is onto us, you better let me do this." The computer equipment under the glass-top coffee table clicked and whirred in agreement. It was late, and that meant the blue LED lighting was on, pulsing in wild patterns over the motley collection of black and aluminum boxes. Karl hated it because it wasn't enough light to get around the apartment but when he switched on the lights Scott complained that it killed the vibe. He wasn't sure what vibe he was going for. Space cantina?

Karl opened the bag holding their dinner. The sharp smell of spice meant it was Wednesday's India Palace special. He unloaded styrofoam bowls of curry, dal and soups onto the side table. Scott reached for the small mountain of donut-shaped fritters, medu vada, dipped and popped one in his mouth with a single bite.

Karl leaned back in his easy chair and slurped his hot tea. "But why the government servers? It's not like the police aren't already after the mob."

Scott raised his eyebrow and a sinister smile broke across his face. "I have a plan."

"A Lex Luthor kind of plan or a Dr. Evil kind of plan?" asked Karl with a grin.

"Something you'd expect from a practical villain," replied Karl. "I'm thinking cockroaches with lasers."

"Very funny. But seriously."

"What one place can the mob not walk and communicate freely?"

Karl scrunched his eyebrows. "Where there is another mob family?"

"Wow. Didn't think of that one but not along

the lines of where I was going. I'm thinking jail."

"Captain Obvious to the rescue."

"No, I'm serious. If I can get the police after Jay, then it makes things really complicated for him." Scott popped another medu vada into his mouth, smacking his lips loudly. He wiped his hand on his chest and continued, "I figure hitmen don't get paid until the deed is done, right?"

"They make a deposit up front for a kill?"

"Yeah, how else? If you paid in full, what would keep the hitman from just walking away with the cash?"

"I guess," said Karl. He paused and continued, "You talk like you've done this before."

"You watch enough movies, you get the idea. So, I figure if I can lock Jay up in the brig, the hitman will walk away with his deposit. I need to make Jay's criminal record worse. Way worse. Why would a hitman finish his hit if his benefactor was in jail and unable to pay?"

Karl rolled his eyes and stared.

"You have a better idea?"

"Yeah, I'd go back in time and unplug your computer. I told you to drop it and you didn't listen."

"And I'm sorry. I've said it a hundred times. What else can I do?"

"Fix it. Then find another place to stay. Keep me out of this."

Scott pushed his food aside. "Come on, man. My parents aren't going to take me back in. You know that."

"I don't blame them for pushing you out. Get a job."

"Yeah, right. Go work somewhere for two weeks and then get kicked to the curb. Let me work for you again."

Karl pointed an accusing finger at Scott. "We've been through this before. You can't follow through. Why would I sign a deal only to have you bail on me?"

"I can't code under pressure!"

"Welcome to the real world, Scott," chided Karl. "They call it work because that's what it is. Do you think your dad bought all those hotels and turned them around with no effort?"

"He was lucky. Excellent timing."

"No one is that lucky. How many hotels was it? Fourteen? You're the one who is lucky; being born into your family. You've got the inside track to a decent job at your dad's company and you choose not to follow in his footsteps."

"I can't help it that I can't focus! It's not like I didn't try. Why are you riding on me like my own parents? Jeez!"

"Because you've got me pulled into your silly antics! I swear, this is the last time." Karl got up, grabbed his food and stormed into the kitchen.

Scott snorted, shook his head and returned his focus to his laptop. He pounded on the keyboard in frustration. Everyone was ganging up on him. His parents ragged on him all the time and now Karl had joined in.

There was no escape. Why didn't anyone understand? Of course, he wanted a job. He wanted to be able to work under his father's direction. It was so simple and easy for everyone to sit at a desk and write code or a report. The more he tried to focus, the louder the buzzing was in his head. Voices called out, layers upon layers of whispers, harkening him to all the other things he could be doing. Scott imagined chopping up his brain and letting all the little pieces chase down each tendril of thought independently, just so he could relax.

He gritted his teeth. If everyone was going to abandon him and not bother to understand what it was like, he was going to make them pay. His pulse quickened. Scott was going to make Jay pay dearly for getting him kicked out of his friend's apartment.

Ironically, the anger and helplessness helped him do the one thing he normally could not — focus.

Jay pressed his hands against his temples. The jarring din of the morning rush was exacerbated by the jackhammers excavating a sidewalk. It could have been the scotch from last night. Either way, the combination rattled his brain. It only felt better if he pressed the ball of his hands against his temple. Hard.

Messengers on bikes whizzed in front of him,

oblivious to the hazards to their safety. Food vendors hawked their breakfast foods, all conveniently packaged to be eaten on the run. Everyone had a place to go and quickly at that. Jay's mission was to deliver a statement the police he spent all morning typing up. The sooner he handed over his statement, the sooner this nightmare would end.

He wore a knit hat pulled tight over his ears. His sunglasses felt small for his face, but he wanted to pass for someone much younger. His pants were wound tightly around his ankles and he carried a messenger bag. The goal was to look no different than any of the other couriers in New York and it was working. No one gave him a second look.

The light signaled the crowd on the street corner and the herd broke free. Suits and dresses were followed by computers in bags, rattling along on wheels. Jay wove through the crowd, keeping his urgent pace. Nearly everyone had a coffee in hand. They were expensive hand warmers, but most New Yorkers gladly paid the ransom.

The police station broke the monotony of glass office buildings. Stately in its Greek marble architecture, it exuded history, significance and permanence. Even the doors were thick wood, probably a hundred years old.

The interior was dank and smelled of dried sweat and old paper. A marble counter extended from one wall in the lobby to the other. If each person behind the counter was behind glass, it could pass for a bank. The countertop was chest height, but the officers who worked behind the counters seemed to be walking on stilts. When Jay made his way to the front, the officer stood two feet over his head.

"Can I help you?" asked the young officer. He didn't even look at Jay. He was likely only a few years out of school and massively bored. His name tag read "Darren."

Jay put his hands into his pocket. "Uh, I need to report a case of harassment. Or defamation. I don't know what you'd call it, but someone is trying to destroy my life."

He took in a deep breath and asked, "Your name and address?"

"Jay Wilson. One 'S'. West 87th."

Darren clacked and slapped the archaic keyboard on the counter with a vengeance. The grey plastic encased keyboard looked twenty years old with thick, black keys rising high.

Darren smiled. "I grew up in your building. Second floor. My grandmother still lives there."

"No kidding? Which apartment?"

"2-D. Mary Tibbens."

"Ms. Tibbens! She's got that six-inch white hellhound that tries to kill me every morning."

"Mr. McTickle? I suppose he's a little protective."

Jay let out a mock shiver. "I wake up in the middle of the night thinking about that beast."

Darren laughed out loud and shook his head. He returned to the computer screen. Three times he slammed the enter key before stopping. He stared off to the distance and muttered to himself, "F11? F8? Yeah, F8." With another pound of the keys, Darren returned his eyes to Jay and said, "Okay, well, you have a nice clean record and no open warrants or tickets to pay. That gives you a golden ticket to talk to a detective. I'll call one over."

Jay smiled. "Thanks." He could feel the tension loosen in his body. No bomb threat on his record. That explained his quiet night's sleep without federal agents kicking down his door. Perhaps CityTrust was treating it like a prank after all.

Darren's eyebrows curled up. "Uh, hold on."

He pounded the same key several times. Surely it was the F8 key.

"Interesting."

Jay rose onto his toes to see the screen on the counter. Darren turned the monitor in Jay's direction. "Now it says you have four outstanding parking tickets and four court no-shows."

"Huh?"

"Every time I hit refresh, a new ticket shows up. Look. You're up to six."

Darren hit F8. The screen flickered. "See, there's another one. And these are dates in the past, not new ones."

"Well, I've never gotten a parking ticket," said Jay. "I can promise you that because I don't own a car. Look that up."

Darren replied, "Well, uh...true. That's weird. The tickets aren't tied to any specific location and are missing all kinds of details." He pointed at the screen. "Something isn't right. Maybe IT screwed something up."

Another loud click and Darren's eyebrows shot up. "Whoa. Now you're wanted for a couple misdemeanors, sexual misconduct and arson."

Jay stepped away from the counter. "Uh, you can stop pressing F8."

Darren continued after another peck. "Two felonies of assault with a deadly weapon. A warrant for a bomb threat. This was at CityTrust yesterday? I heard about this."

"You know none of that is true. I'm being framed, that's why I came here," said Jay. After a pause of inspiration, he continued, "Your grandma always said you'd be one to help me if I needed help. Besides, would a guilty person walk right into police headquarters? That'd be stupid."

Darren looked at Jay, his face steady as he processed the logic. "Okay, okay, but I have to sound a silent alarm and arrest you. It's our procedure. I have no choice."

"Don't. I'm the victim here. Would your grandmother send me here if I was truly a felon? Who would put their own grandson in danger?"

Darren's voice fell to a whisper and he barely moved his lips as he talked. "Keep up the act for the cameras. I'm going to give you a long leash before I press the alarm."

Jay begged, "What do I do?"

Darren's mouth quirked. "No one on the force

can help you with this kind of record, even if it isn't real. If it's in the system, it's the undeniable truth. No one debates the system." He paused and then his face lit up. "Grandma knows an old retired detective. Talk to him. Ted Stone. He's old, crusty and possibly senile, but that's all I've got. Get going."

"Thanks," said Jay before he spun and bolted for the door. As the wooden door swung slowly closed behind him, Jay could hear Darren's voice in the background shouting, less than enthusiastic, "Stop! Stop that man!"

Jay couldn't decide whether to stop running and blend into the New York sidewalk traffic or continue running. He bumped a few people, eliciting curses. If he kept this up, he was bound to bump into a boxer heading to his daily workout. His run of bad luck advised him to slow down and not push it.

The subway was filled with security cameras. The kids' park, filled with screaming children, was too wide open. If he entered a store, he could get cornered. He raised his hand and hailed a taxi, hoping to escape anonymous and under cover. Within seconds, he was hunched in the safety of the back seat of a taxi, unsure of his next move.

Dots connected quickly in Jay's mind. Despite his less than stellar impression of the hockey kid, Jay was certain he was the one who was sending his life on an out-of-control spin. There was no other potential justification of a fake rap sheet. This kid was hell bent on revenge. The fake bomb threat was a teaser. Getting services cut was annoying. Deleting his corporate existence and setting the police on his tail was downright terrifying. He shuddered to think of what was next.

Once again, he heard his sixteen-year-old voice cut through his panicked thoughts.

Escape. Run. Hide.

In the lobby of the police station, Karl watched wide-eyed and confused. He spotted Jay on the subway and acknowledged the sign of kismet by following him. Karl meandered close enough in the lobby to sense some funny business between Jay and the officer behind the desk. It was clear they knew each other. The officer didn't even shout an alarm until Jay was well on his way out of the station and it was a half-hearted alert.

Jay was there to get information and he had an insider.

After gathering his thoughts from the shock observation, Karl casually rose to his feet and walked outside. A few blocks from the police station, he stopped under a construction scaffolding protecting pedestrians on a sidewalk and dialed his apartment. The din of construction provided good cover.

"Hello?" answered Scott with a mumble. Karl had woken him up.

"It's serious."

"What?"

"I followed Jay to the police station."

After a short pause, Scott replied, "Well, that's good. The police won't let Jay leave."

"Jay walked in and out. There is a New York exception, you know, when it comes to the police."

Scott's voice returned with a slow hesitation. "What are you saying?"

"Jay is in cahoots with the cops."

"You mean like the mob?"

"I don't see any other explanation. He was a little too chummy in there for someone supposedly being sought by the police."

Scott blew out a breath of frustration. "That's just great. I spent six hours hacking into the government's servers and finally broke through. I just added a rap sheet that would make Charles Manson blush. What was the point of that?"

"Oh my god, Scott. You didn't."

"You bet I did."

"I'm coming home. Turn off your computer. Stop using it until I get back, okay?"

Scott chuckled. "Sure, whatever."

Karl gritted his teeth as he turned off his phone.

"Ms. Tibbens?" called out Jay as he knocked, "Are you home? I'm sorry but it's urgent." He was back in his apartment building standing outside apartment 2-D. Ms. Tibbens lived on the second floor, a convenient single flight of steps from the front door.

Jay could hear the six inch, white-furred demon spawn barking in high pitched yips inside. He stepped back from the door as if the wood slab was not enough of a protective barrier. Frantic scratches at the door stopped only long enough for the dog to reach under the door with a paw. The claws flashed like poison-tipped daggers.

Jay tried to calm himself. He spent the entire taxi ride dreaming up the next disaster being readied for him. Ms. Tibbens would be safe but he couldn't push away the dread of whatever was next.

A faint, high-pitched voice replied, "Just a minute." Several clicks and rattles later, the door opened a crack. The devil-dog shoved it's black maw into the gap, snarled and revealed a mess of crooked, but sharp, white teeth.

"Oh, stop that," said Ms. Tibbens as she nudged the dog away with her foot.

"I'm sorry to bother you, Ms. Tibbens." The snarls stopped, but the yips and barks jumped to a feverish level. Jay shouted over the din, "I'm in a bit of a bind. Your grandson told me that you might know of a detective that could help me."

"You know my grandson? You know, he recently got promoted. He's a hard worker so I'm not surprised." Ms. Tibbens was the master of taking a conversation to places no one intended. It happened all the time in the lobby or mail room. Like a greased pig, Jay was losing control of the subject before he had barely started.

"Well, I just met him for the first time at the station today."

"Oh. What kind of trouble are you in, if I might ask?"

The conversation at the doorway sent the dog into a frenzy. The barking increased in intensity as the hellhound clawed under the door. The beast was losing its mind. Ms. Tibbens turned her head back into her apartment and commanded, "Settle down, dear!"

The dog paid no attention.

"I'm sorry. I seem to strike a nerve with Mr... uh, Mr."

Ms. Tibbens finished Jay's sentence, "...McTickle." She said it again slower, "Mr. McTickle."

Eyebrows raised, she paused for Jay to repeat it back.

"Uh, McTickles."

"Oh, dear no. McTickle. Only one tickle. Nothing more."

"Uh, yes, right."

"He doesn't like you because you're afraid of him."

Jay stiffened. "I'm not afraid of him. He..."

"He's just a poodle, you know. All bark. No bite. Look at him. He's four pounds wet." More grease on the pig. The conversation was going nowhere.

"Yes. Uh, no ma'am, don't open the door."

"If you just say his name, he'll settle down.

He'll know you aren't afraid of him. Try it."

"No, that's okay. Let's try it another time."

She waggled her finger. "Don't be silly. Say his name." Ms. Tibbens opened the door so Jay could see into the apartment. His pulse quickened when he spotted a shadow by the couch. Ms. Tibbens nodded to the shadow and said, "Go on. Call him."

Jay cleared his throat. "Uh, Mr. McChick…"

In an instant, the shadow was a feral ball of white fur, spittle and teeth. Claws clattered and scraped the wood floor as the dog howled, eyes flashing yellow-red pulsing embers. The fiend was faster than lightning.

With a shriek of surprise, Jay spun on his feet and bolted to the stairs shouting, "Mr. McTickles! Mr. McChicken!"

"Now let me look again." Ms. Tibben's kitchen smelled exactly as it should have; freshly baked bread and coffee. The countertops were a museum of every kitchen gadget sold on late-night TV. A towel hung from an oven handle with stitching that read, *Grandmas are moms with lots of frosting.*

Jay raised the ice pack from his forehead. "It's fine. My headache is better. The ibuprofen worked. Can you help me find Ted Stone?"

With a finger on her chin, she crumpled her eyebrows. She was still feeling guilty about the whole incident and had been trying to win Jay over with pastries and grandmotherly concern.

"Oh, dear, it's quite swollen. I think you need to go to the emergency room. Hold on." She yanked a black heavyset phone receiver from the wall and dialed in confident spins. The rotary phone responded with urgent clicks. Lazy tangled swirls of phone cord danced across the floor from the receiver.

"Ms. Tibbens, please. I'm fine. Don't call 911."

She waved her hand. Shush.

"Esther? Yes, I'm fine...oh, yes, the scones were fabulous, that was so kind of you! That's not why I called, but I would absolutely love the recipe..."

Habit called for Jay to check his cellphone. Still no signal.

"...I think I would substitute the blueberry with raspberry. Blueberry stains my dentures, you know..."

Jay rose from his chair without a sound. He was getting nowhere. Even though Mr. McTickle was locked in the bedroom, he was extra cautious with his movement.

"Oh, Esther, I'm sorry. I have a neighbor here. I don't mean to be rude by changing the subject, but do you know if Ted is still living over in El Barrio?"

Jay mouthed to himself, "El Barrio?" Ms. Tibbens nodded at Jay's reaction.

"Oh, I had to check, Esther. I never thought Ted would hold onto that place for so long. For him, I suppose stubborn knows no limits." She chuckled and continued, "I'll come up after the Bunco game for that recipe, all right, dear?"

Dumbfounded, Jay asked after Ms. Tibbens hung up, "El Barrio? Stone doesn't sound like a Hispanic name."

"Actually, he's Italian. Cute, too."

She ripped a page from a small pad of paper by the phone and scribbled on it.

"Here. You'll find him at that address or singing drunken Italian arias at Pinocchio's across the street."

CHAPTER 5

The streets of El Barrio were never quiet. Jay weaved through the clumps of bright colored clothing for sale, hanging from rolling wardrobes on the wide concrete sidewalk. Old men and women sat behind folding tables; their wares in neat lines across the bright tablecloth. Little squares of cardboard adorned their scrawls in black marker. "Two for $1", "Handmade", "Support a vet."

Jay squinted at the address Ms. Tibbens had given him. The street did not exist in any of the maps he had but after talking to a couple locals, they nodded him down this particular street. Nearly every language Jay recognized was blazoned across the windows of the shops. Puerto Rican Cuchifritos were hawked right next to a Palestinian grocery. Above the storefronts, were several stories of windows neatly accented with black, iron emergency platforms and steps. Pots of flowers and vegetables filled every available space. Clothes flapped in the wind, drying in the hazy air. It was the last place Jay expected a well-decorated, accomplished and retired officer of the NYPD to call home.

Pinnochio's was easy to find. The sidewalk tables outside the restaurant were filled with rotund, grey-haired, Italian men singing an aria. Or maybe it was a soccer song. The men were having a great time, encouraged by healthy pours of wine. A waitress, young and full of smiles, bobbed in and out of the gaggle of old men, deftly avoiding the reaches for her rear end. She picked up glasses, poured wine from her bottle, only to stop for a moment to chat, putting a hand on one of the men's shoulders. A loud laugh preceded her return to her well-experienced bob and weave.

Jay caught her as she was about to return inside the restaurant. "I don't mean to interrupt."

The bright smile grew impossibly wider. "It's no problem. Would you like me to find you a table?"

"Actually, I'm looking for Ted Stone. A friend told me he lives on a street across from here. I can't find, uh, Calle Oculto."

She let out a snort. "It's not really a street."

"Eh? It's gone?"

"No, no, it's there. I'm sure it was a misunderstanding until it was too late to fix. You have to see it to believe it." Jay returned a confused glance. She motioned to the building across the street. "Behind those stores is an alley, however, it's shut off on both ends. You can't get in there but through one of the shops."

Jay's face went blank.

"Just head into that pharmacy. Go to the back of the store, like you're going to the restroom, and take the exit. It'll make more sense over there."

◆ ◆ ◆

The cashier in the pharmacy ignored Jay as he walked haltingly through the brightly-lit glass display cabinets toward the restroom in the back. A hand-scribbled placard reading "Open 24 Hours" hung next to an unlit EXIT sign. The exit door was propped open with a brick. A dull grey light beckoned Jay into the dank, wet air behind the store.

The girl was right. It was an alley. The walls' monotony was broken with unmarked service doors. Emergency ladders and platforms rose up to the sky from the bottom of the brick canyon. Each end of the road was eerily punctuated by another brick wall in a different color. The asphalt was worn from years of driving, twin tracks clearly leading up to both ends and directly into the wall. The only thing missing were garbage cans. It felt like Jay had walked into a wizard movie at some mysterious halfway platform between worlds.

One of the service doors was accented by an eyebrow overhang. An intercom hung, rusted and tired, from a box hastily drilled into the old brick. Jay searched the scribbles and cross-outs of the directory to find Ted Stone's name next to #14.

Jay held out his finger to press the intercom and hesitated. It was clear Ted Stone did not want to be found. Jay was lucky the son of an impossibly nice neighbor gave away his existence. Even more lucky, Ms. Tibbens harbored a half-crush on the detective, enough to send birthday and holiday cards to this mysterious address that she gladly revealed.

"Well, here goes nothing," mumbled Jay as he pressed. A short buzz sounding like the static between radio stations preceded a gravelly voice. "Yes?"

"Uh, is this Ted Stone?"

The sound of a frustrated sigh was hard to avoid.

"Who sent you here?"

"Ms. Tibbens. No, I mean, she didn't send me. I asked her how to find you."

"Why are you looking for me?"

"I'm in trouble. I need help. At the station..."

Ted cut him off. "I'm sorry, kid, but there is no charity here. Nor am I available for hire. There's a nice thrift store two blocks east. Find yourself a new blazer for a buck."

"Huh? Why?" Jay looked down at his tattered, grey jacket.

"That way you'll be presentable in an interview. Get a job. Best advice I have for someone looking to get out of trouble."

Click.

How did that guy know he needed a blazer? Jay looked up the metal emergency stairs. Through one of the windows, a man with slicked-back, thinning black hair shook his head in disgust. He stuck his hand out and waved his middle finger.

Blood crept up Jay's neck. The old fool didn't have the decency to even listen to his story. Dread coated his thoughts like molasses, slowing everything to half speed. He was losing his grip on his composure. He was at a dead end.

Don't make a bad situation worse.

Like a cornered cat, Jay slipped from dread to anger. Because of some revengeful nit-wit's technological wizardry, the entirety of the NYPD was hot on his tail. He had no risk of losing his job, because it was likely already lost and he had no reason to hold back. He let the anger flow freely. The fact that he was getting the finger from some old coot ready to move into assisted living was the final straw.

Jay jammed his finger down on fourteen. This time he held it down and looked up at old man with a sneer. The static-buzz was relentless and annoying.

Without looking away from Jay, Ted brought the phone back to his ear with a smile that reminded him of creepy strangers offering kids candy.

The gravel gave way to a deep baritone. "I just cleaned my gun, boy."

"Listen to me, you old fart. I didn't come all this way to be mocked by some senile who spends his days watching *Night Court* in his spaghetti stained t-shirt."

"You know what, kid, despite the fact that my shotgun is dirty, I'm jonesing to use that one now."

Jay laughed. "Don't trip over your slippers

while you're at it."

Ted's smile turned into a grimace. Eyes wide, he slammed the receiver and shouted, echoes bouncing and repeating in the alley, "Kid, you don't know who you're talking to."

"I'm talking to Ted Stone. Former NYPD. One of the most decorated. Unfortunately, the only decoration you know right now is clean boxers!"

Jay punched the button next to fourteen again in rapid fire bursts. "Ha ha! Eat this, grandpa!" Buzz - buzz - buzzzzzzzz.

The service door flew open. Two hands gripped his shoulder and swung him against the opposite brick wall in a quick flurry of thrusts and grunts. Jay's eyes bulged. He could not speak with the air knocked out of him.

Ted's black hair was still neatly in place. A large gold cross pendant sat in a nest of black chest hair. His shirt, white and neatly pressed, was rolled up at the wrist exposing giant hands; knuckles thick and ugly from hundreds, no thousands, of fights. Jay couldn't see the difference between the giant gold rings on his hands and a nice set of brass knuckles.

"Urk," was all Jay could manage. He reached up and tried to pull at Ted's hands and caught his fingers on the oversized gold watch on his wrist. It was as big as a hockey puck.

Ted pulled one hand away without letting Jay move. He wagged his finger in front of Jay's eyes. "Now listen to me, you cockroach, I'm not a grandpa. I hate TV. And I could kick your scrawny, sorry sight for sore eyes across El Barrio before my oatmeal gets cold. You. Don't. Know. Me."

"Urgh." Jay pounded his hands weakly on Ted's arm as he sucked in what precious air he could. The detective's arm was iron and steel.

Through gritted teeth, Ted continued, "Now, when I let you go, you will apologize. You will end every sentence with 'sir'. You will not look me in the eyes, but stare at my feet because that's all vermin deserve."

Jay let out a gasp as he regained his breath. He bent over and put his hands on his knees. The asphalt street started to spin. "I'm sorry. I mean, I'm sorry, sir."

Jay's breaths turned into heaving sobs. The walls were crashing in on him. He was no longer angry, but desperate.

"Some geek kid stole my life. Yesterday, I had a job. A place to live. Now everything's gone. I went to the police and the computer kid had run up a fake rap sheet on me and so now the police are hunting for me. I haven't done one thing wrong. I'm a rat stuck at the bottom of a barrel and the kid is toying with me with a big stick."

Jay put his hands over his face and fell to his knees. "...Oh yeah...SIR."

The gravelly voice returned. "Nice story. I'm tearing up."

"Darren told me you might be able to help. Obviously, he was wrong, sir."

"Darren?"

"Yes. Front desk." Jay looked up.

Ted scratched at his chin. "Dammit. Darren knows better than to send you to me. I only threatened him once and that was the last I ever heard from him. Why would he risk my wrath again for you?"

Ted paused to connect eyes with Jay. Then he slowly pointed at his shoes. Jay obliged and returned his head back to the ground.

Ted continued to talk to himself. "Darren must have had a weak moment."

Jay grunted. "Forget it. Never mind. I don't know how a police detective who retired before computers existed could help even me. It's like throwing rocks at a tank."

"Your daddy didn't teach you about respect, did he?"

"Didn't mean to offend, sir. Honestly. But this kid is a technical whiz. He shut off my power. Bounced all my checks. He even erased my HR records at work. I need someone who can get a step ahead of him. Every corner I turn, he's already there setting fire to any way out. I need someone who can find him in this web of wires and blinking lights."

"Ha. You sound like my old CO, back in the day, whining about cockroaches with automatic weapons against all of us with our measly little handguns. I tried to tell him, cockroaches have little brains. Eat, poop and run from the light. A total waste of space. Your guy; he sounds like a cockroach."

"Totally. He put sexual misconduct on my rap sheet, sir."

Ted burst out in loud shouts of laughter, holding his hands to his belt to keep his pants from falling from his potbelly. After gathering his breath, he replied in a serious tone, "More than forty years on the force taught me one thing about cockroaches."

Jay looked up.

Two decades of age seemed to fall from Ted's face. "There is nothing, I mean *nothing,* more satisfying than the crunch of one under your heel."

He pulled Jay to his feet. "Come inside kid. Let's hear about your little infestation."

Scott's cackle was at an unusually high pitch that morning.

"I got it, Karl." Scott leaned forward and set his laptop down gingerly on the coffee table in his apartment. "Expect lots of bouncing checks up ahead. I reassigned Jay's bank account numbers to some poor kid who had less than fifty dollars saved. If he writes a check, not only will it bounce, but it'll be a crime of forgery."

Karl scrunched up his eyebrows in disbelief. He took a break and pushed his chair from his desk across the room. "I didn't know you could even do that. Again, the agreement is that you stay only if you clean this mess up and cover your tracks."

"Yup. I've been working that non-stop. I

promise you, everything will be untraceable. We'll be good."

Karl stared without saying a word.

Scott rose from his usual slouch and stretched his arms. "I dropped Jay's credit rating to the lowest possible number. In a moment of inspiration, I checked to see if I could hack Jay's landlord. Easy. I reset Jay's account status to show he missed the last six months' rent. Checks will start bouncing and his credit score is abysmal. They'll toss his stuff to the curb before the week is over."

"And why is this so important to you?"

"We need some copies of his signature among other things."

"I thought you pulled it from the DMV database."

"Sure, but it's too low resolution to recreate faithfully on new documentation. Plus, I need a few examples so it isn't obvious I'm reusing the same one."

Karl slapped his head. "I think you need to burn a couple weeks out of town until things blow over. If the cops are in cahoots with Jay, they could come bursting through that door anytime."

"Oh, come off it. I searched all the email servers of the police, major internet providers and the text message databases of Manhattan's finest telecom providers. Nothing. Unless they are making old-school voice phone calls like someone from 1950, we're safe. My name comes up nowhere and your precious address is also coming up clean."

"That's no guarantee."

"You're just like my father. He's never satisfied."

Karl rolled his eyes and sat at his desk with a slump. "And you sound like my five-year-old nephew who promises not to shoot you in the face with the nerf gun."

"Touché," said Scott as he continued his cackle. "I'm going to get some exercise. If the landlord is like most that I know, Jay's stuff will be next to the nearest dumpster. You know what that means?"

Karl nodded slowly. "Dumpster diving." He held up his hands in defense. "Scott, no offense, but I can't see you climbing over the side of a tub without the risk of breaking your neck."

Scott stiffened. "That's not nice."

"I'm being realistic, not mean. We don't need the police to rescue you and start asking questions. I'll do it if it means we get this wrapped up sooner. I want this done."

"Awesome! Then I'll have more time to finish up here. Just get me something that has a few copies of his signature. Old addresses. Old employers would be so bonus. Just grab anything of his history. Tax forms would be gold."

"When will this stop, Scott?"

"When Jay calls off the dogs and ceases to exist. At least in the US of A. I'll stop when I know we're absolutely safe."

Karl furrowed his eyebrows. "Layman's

terms. Not making sense again."

"I'm going to get him deported. That's my final task before calling it over." Scott returned to excitedly clicking away at his laptop keyboard. Without looking up, he continued, "So, what do you think? Will Jay's surname Wilson pass for someone from Eastern Europe? Or should I make him South African?"

Karl face brightened. Scott could make the worst of deeds fun. He laughed, scratched his chin and said, "I think that Mr. Jay Wilson shall hail from Paraguay!"

Scott giggled. "I hope poor Jay speaks Spanish!"

"Right now?" asked Jay. He was standing outside Ted's apartment peeking through the door only open a few inches.

He could hear the clatter of Ted pulling a drawer open and fishing through the contents. "I'm retired, kid. I've got a little time. You have an appointment to attend to first?" He slammed a drawer shut.

"No. Sorry."

Another drawer was the jackpot. Back in view, Ted palmed a small, beat up notebook that was no larger than his hand. It was spiral bound at the top with a stubby pencil shoved into the misshapen coils. He flipped through the pages, paused to read one and grunted to himself. "I remember that cockroach."

He ripped out the page, crumpled it and tossed it to a small trash bin by door and continued to no one in particular, "Another interesting thing about cockroaches. Put 'em in a confined space and they'll eat each other."

Jay raised an eyebrow. "I don't follow."

Ted growled, "The last guy I collared was killed in maximum security by a couple guys who didn't appreciate his taste in little boys. Saved the state a few bucks. Gotta love that. Let's go."

"Where are we going?"

"Are there clues here in my apartment, kid?"

"I doubt it."

Ted waved his notebook and rolled his eyes. "Then we probably shouldn't start here. Ideas?"

"The police station."

"Would the cockroach be there?"

"No."

"Then we probably shouldn't start there, either."

Jay paused. The bank he worked at was not an option. Security at the front entrance be on high alert, even if he had a retired detective in tow. He was terrified of even stepping out of Ted's apartment. They agreed to find a place for Jay to hide, but not after Ted got some answers.

After shaking his head, Jay said, "Maybe we should swing by my apartment before getting started. I need to grab a few things if I'm going to disappear. I don't know if it'll be safe to go back there until things are sorted."

Tod nodded in assent. "Actually, your apartment is a good place to start. Are you the packrat type?"

"Why?"

"Last I checked, computers can't erase paper, right? Let's collect some old-fashioned paper evidence of your existence while you can."

To Jay's delight, Ted finished grilling Jay on the events of the last few days as their taxi pulled up to the curb outside his apartment. If there were a bright-hot interrogation light in the cab, Jay was certain Ted would have used it. Every detail, mindless as it was to Jay, was flipped, poked and prodded and then minutes later when he thought he was moving on, Ted would bring it up again. A break in the questioning existed only so Ted could lean over, pull his notebook from his back pocket and scribble a date, name or location with his short, golf pencil.

Ted seemed satisfied. He no longer cast suspicious glances. He reveled in every detail and seemed to brighten as Jay unfolded the sequence of events that led him to Ted. He wasn't sure if the old detective enjoyed stories of self-destruction or was building an appetite to find his antagonist.

Before exiting the cab, Jay looked up to his bedroom window, almost expecting someone with binoculars to be looking back down at him. Ted's questioning dialed up the paranoia meter in his brain. He let Ted exit first. His gargantuan frame caused him to scoot, grunt and push himself out the too-small cab door. Like Yoda, he appeared to be saving his quick reflexes for when he really needed them.

Before they left El Barrio, Jay changed his clothes again. This time, he wore an ancient NYPD baseball cap from Ted's old softball team and aviator sunglasses that seemed to be a prop from a classic 70's cop TV show. The only thing missing to complete the picture was a bushy mustache. Despite the constant change of clothes, he could not avoid the feeling of people watching. Ted offered the small comfort that his years of experience would spot something suspicious before Jay.

"Nice neighborhood," said Ted as he kicked at the pile of clothes, boxes and furniture piled outside the apartment entrance. "Most landlords keep the furniture and toss the rest down the garbage chute. It's good to see a little old-time courtesy by tossing it out to the curb."

Jay cried out, "This is my stuff!" He ran his hands over some of the furniture, checking for damage. A sheriff's eviction notice was posted on top of one of the boxes. "I never miss my rent. This is wrong!"

The passersby on the sidewalk didn't give a sideways glance to Jay or the motley pile of furniture covered in mounds of clothes, still on hangers.

Pedestrians wove neatly through the mess like river water around rocks. Just another day in New York and everyone was too busy getting wherever they needed to be.

While Jay angrily punched in his entrance code at the door, Ted opened the boxes and peeked inside with his pen, holding the flap aside, as if it were homicide evidence. He mumbled, "Empty. Curious."

Jay punched his entry code in again. The speakers responded with a loud buzz, reminiscent of a wrong answer in a game show. The door handle rattled but would not budge under Jay's frustrated slaps, yanks and punches. He returned to Ted and stared at what was left of his life, stacked ready for a Goodwill donation pickup.

Ted flipped open a couple more boxes. Empty.

"It's awful nice of your landlord to leave out moving boxes."

"No," replied Jay. "They're from my storage closet." He paused, wiped sweat from his brow and continued, "Wait. Did you say they were empty?"

Jay opened a box marked TAXES in his familiar black-marker block letters. Empty. He tossed it aside and tore open another marked BILLS. Also empty. Pedestrians waiting for a light change to cross at the corner stared at Jay's antics in half-interest.

"Stop Jay. I think it's obvious what's in the rest of the boxes." Ted pulled Jay back with a strong hand and continued "...a whole lot of nothing."

"This isn't the time for Mr. Snarky," sighed Jay. "Why would someone steal old files and leave my clothes and furniture?"

Ted wrote in his notepad. He paused to chew on the end of his pencil, stared into the distance thoughtfully and shoved it back into the metal coils. "These cockroaches are good."

"Nah, I'm sure it's just one guy."

"You said he was fat, right?"

"Immense."

Ted pointed down the sidewalk with his thumb, as if he were hitchhiking. "Then why is a tall, skinny guy walking off with your papers? Please, do tell me it's your accountant."

Jay's eyes widened.

"Okay, cockroaches may scurry fast but they always run to dark corners. So predictable. Let's go."

Jay hesitated. His instinct was to run the opposite direction. Ted was already in hot pursuit, moving at a pace that defied his age. He looked at his belongings one last time and followed.

The oversized pile of paper in Karl's arms started to slip as he hurried away from Jay's apartment. The fact that he was stealing started to sink in. His shirt stuck to his chest; drenched from nervous sweat. The whites of his eyes darted around, sensitive of watchful or curious eyes. Glancing down at the mass of paper in his arms, Karl concluded there was no way he was going to make it home by subway without culling back the huge stack or finding a suitable bag. Even worse, he was going to draw attention to himself. He didn't want to create a memorable scene in case folks started to ask questions.

Karl stopped at a garbage can, flipped through the papers as quick as he could. He shoved a handful of unimportant documents inside. Empty coffee cups and paper plates covered in pizza billowed out the top of the trashcan and served as a spring to what he pushed inside. The papers rose back up to the lip of the garbage can, fell down the side and caught a gust of Manhattan wind. The paper in his arms shifted as he reached out and he nearly dropped his whole stash into the street.

A pedestrian in a blue suit stopped to help by stomping on several of the papers blowing away.

"No!" shouted Karl before he realized his rudeness.

Startled, the man's eyes widened and he held out his hands. He spoke in a clipped tone. "Sorry. Was just trying to help." Before Karl could apologize, the man marched briskly on as if he had run into a crazed homeless man.

In a panic, Karl shoved as much as he could into the garbage can saving only the tax forms. He forced everything he could into the narrow opening, arms pumping like pistons. Feeling eyes on his back, Karl turned and froze.

Karl spotted Jay. He must have arrived just

minutes after he left with his papers. Jay gesticulated wildly at his pile of evicted belongings. Standing next to him was a tall Italian man with broad shoulders. He chomped lazily on a short pencil like an unlit cigar. Gold glittered from the multitude of rings on his hands as he slicked back his long dark hair that fluttered in the wind. A pendant sat on his chest, resting on the dark, curly hair rising from his unbuttoned shirt. It was a hitman.

Karl's brain screamed at his muscles to move, but he was frozen in headlights like a midnight raccoon on Kentucky highway. Turning in his direction, the hitman's eyebrows furrowed on his sun-worn face and then cleared with realization. His face darkened and then narrowed. The man seemed to take in every detail. Karl casually turned on his heels and walked. He fought every urge to look over his shoulder. In his hands, wrapped in white knuckles were a rubber-banded collection of tax forms. It was what Scott wanted most and was all he had left.

"Hey there," shouted a gruff voice from the distance.

Karl burst into a sprint, weaving through pedestrians and cars in the street. He used his long arms to push aside briefcases, groceries and hold up cars honking in frustration at the green light. He weaved, slowly through the cars and taxi drivers eager to get through the intersection. Catching his breath at a busy corner, Karl dared himself to turn around to see if he was still being pursued.

The hitman was deceptively fast, moving in what appeared to be a slow jog; striding painfully on two gimpy knees and bad hip. It seemed as if he was swinging his arms to minimize the impact of each step. His teeth cut into his lower lip with a grimace and the sun caused the sweat on his face to glisten. His eyes, however, never lost him; a dark, relentless stare.

The traffic light turned red and the hitman had a clear crosswalk to gain in pursuit. Karl thanked Scott's foresight to evict Jay in broad daylight because no hitman would shoot someone in a busy intersection; at least one that had some sense of self-preservation. Karl didn't want to find out. He spun on his heels, hugged his papers tight to his chest, and ran into the sidewalk traffic. The hitman would never catch him stride for stride, however, Karl wanted to duck out of view as quickly as he could.

After several turns to shake his tail, Karl burst into the lobby of the first available office building that didn't have a glass-windowed lobby. Inside, a bored security officer sat behind a desk, his head barely visible over the high counter. Without looking up from whatever video was playing on his tablet, he pushed a clipboard forward for Karl to sign.

Karl looked at the list of folks who had signed in and copied a name from earlier in the day. He asked, "Are there restrooms that I can use before I go up?"

The officer pointed around the corner. "Second set of doors before the dock door."

Karl slipped around the corner and started to breathe again. He found the restroom and committed himself to wait thirty minutes. Hidden in the stall and still clutching Jay's tax forms, Karl muttered, "No more, Scott. This has to end."

◆ ◆ ◆

Scott slapped his forehead. "The hitman saw you?"

"For a second, yes," said Karl back in their apartment. "Do you realize this means the mob is involved? No single hitman could be influencing and collaborating with the police. This is organized crime." Karl stood at the window and flicked the blinds open to look down to the sidewalk. Jay's tax forms, beaten, sweat-stained and torn, sat at Scott's feet.

"Does he know where you are?"

"There is no way he followed me."

"Karl, he's a hitman. Worse, a mobster. He doesn't need to follow you. He just needs to know who you are."

"I was a block away. Shouting distance. The best he'd do is make out the color of my clothes and that I run like a gazelle when I'm frightened."

"Not funny. Hitmen don't like humor. You're absolutely sure he was mob?"

Karl scanned the street outside, his heart still pumping double-time. He had never been this afraid. This was worse than sitting in the high school principal's office finding out he was going to be expelled due to Scott's antics. This was much, much worse.

Karl answered, "Absolutely. An Italian built like a tank, wearing brass knuckles like rings."

Scott walked over to Karl at the window and put his hand on his shoulder. "The good news is that the mob has a data center."

Karl rolled his eyes. "I know they call it organized crime but that's a little too organized for the mob."

"No, I mean it. In all my days, I've wanted to hack the mob and figured everything they did was off the books. They're old-school. However, these last few years, I bet they've modernized. We're a million steps ahead of them. Nothing to worry about."

"I suppose you're right. They're cavemen who discovered the wheel," said Karl sarcastically. "We are the epitome of the modern man."

"I like what I'm hearing."

Karl snapped the blinds shut and pointed at the tax forms. "I stuck my neck out to get these papers. It was only so you could get this over with. Finish this. You promised. Get Jay out of the country, the mob out of our hair and then we're done." He shoved his hands into his pockets.

"Once I scan signatures, I'm going to have some fun with this information. Like the guys in *The Godfather* leaving behind a bloodied horse's head, I say we leave our mob friends a message they will find impossible to misunderstand."

CHAPTER 6

Simon had a thing for Hawaiian shirts. It wasn't well received by the others in his mob family, but at eighty-six, Simon didn't care. He also had a thing for lunch. A styrofoam container sat on his desk, top open, exposing a greasy, double-cheese meatball sandwich. The soggy bread was barely visible under the bright red sauce.

Out of necessity, the office was windowless and the walls solid concrete. The heavy coats of yellow paint failed at brightening the space but was another essential feature. It was easy to clean after meetings that ended violently.

Simon smacked his lips continuously as he searched the desk drawer for a napkin large enough to cover his coveted shirt. The fading yellow shirt hung over his shoulders loosely. Palm trees dancing with a lady in a grass skirt and coconut bra cut across in a diagonal pattern. Simon called it his "Do-I-Look-Like-I-Care" shirt. All the other good-fellas wore suits; dapper and meticulous. Simon was lucky he could still dress himself. Heck, he was lucky he was alive. If he was blessed enough to wake up in the morning, it meant he could savor another lunch. Life's little treasures were lunches. Today, it was Angioletta's famous meatball coronary.

A confident knock at the door broke Simon's lip-smacking. He barked, "What?" Without missing a beat, he opened and searched another drawer.

A deep voice on the other side of the door replied, "A moment, sir? Urgent news."

Simon found a cloth napkin, smiled and started smacking his lips again. He tucked it into his undershirt, smoothed the white cloth over his chest and leaned over his lunch.

Another knock.

"What?"

The door opened. Simon didn't look up. He was too busy ogling the meatballs like he did the coconut bras when he was in his twenties. Two people stepped into the office quietly. One wore a black suit, slightly oversized and long at the waist. The other was a young girl, not quite twenty, wearing jeans and a brown t-shirt that read, "Bring Back Firefly." Her blonde hair was straight and neatly parted at the top of her head.

Long-suit continued, "Sir, we need to discuss what the kid found."

Simon held up a finger, asking for a pause, while he devoured a giant meatball with his other hand. He chewed happily, mouth open and smiling. The twosome waited patiently in the doorway. He leaned back in his chair, wiped his face and let out a guttural burp.

"All right," nodded Simon. "Let the pretty one talk."

The girl didn't pause to breathe. "Someone has been trying to hack our systems. I've been watching these intrusion attempts for the last few hours. They keep using the same anonymizer servers so I could pattern the round-robin IP addresses back to a local ISP. They're getting lazy. I set up a honeypot and I've located the central office and am narrowing it down to a specific switch. I'm close to figuring out who it is."

Simon's mouth hung open. His eyes were glazed over. He turned to the man in the suit and said, "This girl is so pretty I can't understand a word she's saying."

The man fought the smirk growing across his face. "Not only is she pretty, she's brilliant, sir."

The girl interrupted. "Gentlemen, I want to give you a little bit of context so you'll understand. I'll summarize the complicated bits. Our hidden servers have been breached by a hacker for the first time in our history. The mob is now in a cyberwar. Someone just fired the first shot."

Faint music burst from the girl's pants. The tinny voice sang with a country twang, "Burn the land, boil the sea, you can't take the sky from me."

She pulled a phone from her back pocket, glanced at the screen and smiled. "I have better news. There is no need for the switch information. I have names and addresses now. Karl Gil. Scott Whedon. But this third person, Jay Wilson, brings up a lot of questions. These two hackers seem extremely interested in Jay's information. I implanted a sniffer on their switch and this name comes up a lot."

Simon leaned back over his meatballs and, without looking up, said, "I don't care who is who. Get Johnny. Kill those three men in a tub."

CHAPTER 7

T ed let Jay fall asleep in the booth of Julio's. The dive was located in a dark corner of El Barrio and was empty with the exception of two locals debating the merits of the latest signing of the New York Red Bulls soccer team. Gordy's was now off-limits and this was perfect cover for Jay and Ted. They had finished a quick burger, while waiting for Mike.

Jay twitched and murmured in his sleep.

He was back in Louisiana.

It was Tuesday night at the food pantry in downtown New Orleans. As usual, he was waiting in the darkness for the pantry to close. He was hungry but he couldn't care less. In fact, nothing mattered except Tuesday nights. He was under a spell and it bore the name Jenni.

The other days of the week were a blur; a nuisance that got in the way of the joy of Tuesdays. Those nights he didn't have the urge to escape. He didn't need to run. He felt safe.

Jenni came around the corner with two large bags in her hands. "I've got some good stuff."

"You always do."

"Oh, but this time, I got pop-tarts!"

"Never had one."

"Are you kidding me? Here, I'll show you how to eat them."

Jenni opened a foil package and handed one of the pop-tarts to Jay.

"You break off the outside bits. They are dryer than cardboard. Totally gross." He watched her well-manicured hands with nails painted deep purple. Like unzipping, she skillfully pried away the outside border of the pop-tart in seconds and let it drop to the ground.

"The rest is filled with fruit stuff. Probably fake fruit, but it's good anyway. You try it."

Jay clumsily broke the pop-tart in half.

Jenni giggled. "That's okay. You'll get better with practice. See the filler? That's the good stuff."

The crust was dry, but the pastry was a flavored sugar bomb. After devouring half the pastry, he smiled with cheeks full.

"Yeah. I thought you'd like it."

Jay struggled to chew and swallow. He held up his finger, asking for a moment to finish. He motioned for water.

After setting the overfull bags on the ground, Jenni fished for bottled water. Jay crouched and collected the crumbled, dry edges of Jenni's pop-tart from the sidewalk.

"Oh, my god." Jenni covered her eyes in embarrassment.

Jay took a swig of water and gulped. He popped the handful of dry edges from the sidewalk into his mouth. The subsequent burst of sugar coursing through his veins felt good. After another swig of water, he turned to Jenni with a broad smile. "We have a winner. Love the pop-tarts."

Jenni was silent. Her eyes were brimming with tears.

Jay looked around for the source of her angst. "What's wrong?"

Her lip quivered. She covered her face with her hands. "You must think I'm a horrible person."

"Huh?"

"I can't believe I did that."

"Did what?"

"Showed you how to throw perfectly good food away. That was vile!"

"As long as you save it for me, I'm good." He tried to calm her. His time with Jenni was precious. He long moved past needing Jenni for food. He needed her in ways he couldn't describe. Seeing her upset flipped his brain into a panic.

"No," said Jenni. She straightened her posture and declared, "I'm never doing that again. I'm eating the whole pop-tart from now on."

"You'd do that for me?" teased Jay. "I'm honored and humbled." His humor helped cut through the thickest of moments.

Jenni tried to stifle her laughter through her

tears. Her time with Jay was a relentless onrush of emotions, experiences and enlightenment. Every moment was discovery of a world she never saw but lived alongside. It was electric and addictive. No other boy compared to Jay Wilson.

◆ ◆ ◆

Mike poked Jay awake in the booth at the bar. "Took a while to find this place but even longer to find you. Where did you get those horrible clothes? I barely recognize you. Regardless, up and at 'em, bud. You're not going to enjoy what I have for you."

Mike concealed the screen of his phone against his chest and emptied his highball in a single swallow. He motioned to the bartender for another by rattling his ice.

"There hasn't been much to enjoy lately. What does it matter?" Jay rubbed his eyes, still slumped in the booth. He glanced at the mirror behind the bartender. Ted sat at the back wall, reading the *New York Post*, his brown eyes just over the top of the front page. Ted glared. Jay returned his eyes to his hands. Ted insisted that he not be revealed to Mike and wanted him to avoid even the minor subtleties of eye contact.

Mike let out a sigh and held out his phone. He tapped it to start a video. Shaky from walking down a hallway, grey carpet rolled by in a blur. "Hold on, you'll see it in a minute."

Jay squinted. The camera struggled to focus on a video monitor. It was from the CityTrust lunchroom. Jay could hear the clanging of trays and silverware over the murmur of the lunch hour. His employee badge picture came into focus on the screen.

"Oh great."

"Hang on, there's more. It was quiet after the bomb threat. Things went back to normal after it was confirmed to be a prank. You were off the hook but then this was on the screen today."

His face was replaced with large white text reading, "Wanted for multiple felonies. Report any information on Jay Wilson's whereabouts to HR and the police immediately."

Jay shook his head and rolled his eyes. "Well, I guess it's not so bad that I was evicted. The police would have been waiting there for me now. I did go to the station and the phrase 'multiple felonies' is being modest. I barely escaped."

Mike nodded somberly.

Jay raised an eyebrow. "What are you not telling me?"

"I can't risk meeting you anymore. Our co-workers at CityTrust know we're friends. Someone could follow me to you."

Jay stiffened and glanced at the door of the bar. Mike held out his hands. "Don't worry. I was extra careful coming here. I had to take a major detour to get your stuff into storage."

In the bar mirror, Jay could see Ted drop his

newspaper and look outside. He rose to his feet, lips pursed, and strolled to the restaurant door. Chewing on a toothpick, he pushed open the door and leaned out to look up and down the sidewalk. Satisfied, he returned his attention to his paper. However, he did not leave his watchpost, leaning against the wall like someone waiting for a cab.

"Well, I don't want you to get into trouble, Mike. You've risked so much for me already. Plus, I've got some...help."

"Really? Who?"

"I'm not at liberty to say."

Mike furrowed his eyebrows and looked away.

"It's not that I don't trust you. The less you know, the safer you are."

Mike nodded. His usual ice-blue eyes were dark with concern. "Do you have a place to stay?"

"Not yet. But I have some ideas."

By the door, Ted cleared his throat. Two policemen walked by the bar window cradling their coffees, steam rising like miniature campfires. Ted watched them intently.

Jay turned to Mike and extended his hand. "You're the best friend one could ask for. I'll let you know when this blows over. Either we find this guy, or I'll be crossing the river Styx."

Mike shook. "If anyone asks about you, I'm not saying a word. If you need someone to back up your story, send them my way. Share something from our time back home so that I know they're legit."

"You bet. Now go before those two cops decide a cold beer sounds better than warm coffee."

Mike nodded silently and left as if weights were attached to his arms and legs.

Ted and Jay moved to sit at the end of the bar as it filled with patrons punctuating their workday with a drink. The NY Yankees game on the TV was not going well for the locals and the shouts and curses provided perfect cover for their conversation.

Ted shook his head and growled, "Are you sure she can be trusted?"

Jay rolled his eyes. "I'm beginning to think you don't trust your own mother. Yes, as I said, we can trust her."

"My mother left me in front of an orphanage when I was three."

"Oh," said Jay. He looked at his hands.

"Don't be. The fact that I don't trust anyone made me a better cop."

"Makes you."

Ted's eyes glinted with gratitude as he pondered Jay's compliment. His gruff voice returned, "Use the bar phone to call her. Once we're done, we can't come back here."

Jay nodded, rose from his seat and retorted, "That's too bad. I'm going to miss the black-purple mold in the bathroom."

In the darkness of the back of the bar, Jay punched in the all-too-familiar number. After a few rings, syrup oozed out of the phone's receiver. "Good evening, this is Jenni."

"Hey. It's me."

"Well, I'll be." Jay pictured her hands at her mouth in surprise. "Aren't you the eager beaver calling me back so soon and from a strange phone number?"

Jay felt the heat rise up his neck. Jenni knew exactly how to control a conversation even when someone else instigated it.

"I wanted to hear your voice."

"That's sweet."

"It's completely true."

"Yes, but there is something else. Are you still having troubles?"

"I know this is a stretch, but can I come over?" The bar erupted with cheers.

Jenni's voice rose a pitch after a short pause. "Line drive. Jeter."

He waited.

"Am I going to regret this?" asked Jenni. "How bad is it?"

"Really bad. I have nowhere else to go. I'd rather us catch up under better circumstances, but I've run out of options."

"I'm going stay up until the game is over or until I finish my wine. After that, I need my beauty rest. Whatever you need to talk about, you've got six innings or two glasses of wine worth."

Jay was more than relieved, he was ecstatic. He was going to see Jenni.

He blurted, "What if I picked up another bottle on the way?"

"Cart and mule, Jay."

"Oh, right, yes. See you soon."

CHAPTER 8

Kaylee loved her job. She had a blank checkbook for all the technology she desired and it was her digital playground. Simon, and his small army of goons, were happy to keep her well funded as long as they got a healthy payoff.

Her office was a computer room nestled under the largest chop shop in Manhattan. Cosa Nostra was organized and exceptionally careful. No one trusted outsiders of the mafia to their darkest secrets, so she had to build the computer room herself.

Kaylee preferred to do it herself, anyway. She was meticulous. There was only one way to set up a computer room; her way.

She had the family muscle dig the trenches for the fiber optic cable runs outside the building so that even the telcos had no record. Just like the old days, legitimate businesses provided a front to nefarious mafia activity. Instead of a bakery front for a bookie, it was a large insurance company that provided her secret network gateway to the rest of the digital world.

Kaylee pulled her hair into two long pigtails. She liked to switch her appearance up and keep the goons' rapt attention. She had long gotten used to the stares of the men ever since she was a young teenager. She was brilliant and had a lot to offer, but the only purpose those stares seemed to reinforce was that she existed only for men to ogle.

It didn't take long before she learned that it could be turned into a weapon. Tight clothes. A flirtatious smile. A giggle at a dumb joke. Those were just as powerful as a pistol, bat and dagger. She was practiced and skilled. She could turn off a man's rational, functional brain in seconds.

She built the computer room with short skirts and tight tank tops. Once she had her base of operations; the firewalls, routers and racks of processing power was able to deliver profit.

Like someone taking apart an engine to learn how it works, Kaylee took apart the digital world. Week by week, she unlocked doorways that flipped old mafia practices into its digital counterpart. Old bookies sitting in the back of restaurants were replaced by online apps that accepted credit cards or even bitcoin. The young goons who used to break legs to collect payments were out a job. Kaylee simply transferred the money owed via digital means. Not only was she increasing revenue, she was slashing costs.

In a few short years, Kaylee became the young

queen of New York's Cosa Nostra.

But there was a new puzzle. Scott Whedon and Karl Gil. These individuals somehow broke through some digital front doors and landed in her trap. She purposely left a server with weakened security behind one of her firewalls. Fake data was posted as a honey pot. In this case, it was a honey pot to attract hackers, not bees.

Over the past day, she watched these hackers work. They were skilled. Of course, the mob servers were safe. Kaylee's security designs were brilliant and impenetrable because she had the mind of a hacker herself.

In front of her, an oversized monitor flashed data across multiple screens. She formed a digital profile of Scott and Karl from their virtual fingerprints left on servers all over the globe.

Scott was the primary one behind the attacks. Over the years, Scott purchased custom, Chinese-built processors to mask his activities. Once Kaylee identified the supplier, she hacked the laptops of the supplier's designers and downloaded the schematics of everything Scott ordered.

She had his decryption key. She could see everything. Like a digital god.

Karl, however, seemed to be trying to build a legitimate career. He wrote apps but didn't do a great job of it. He seemed to make a living from his low billing rate by avoiding taxes. Karl was a nuisance.

Kaylee returned her focus to Scott. Thanks to

the decryption key, her screen flashed thousands of anonymous postings made by Scott on internet forums, chat rooms and blogs.

Scott was a raging lunatic. He posted manifestos and conspiracy theories from every imaginable angle. Not only did he push these theories, he planted information in legitimate sources to inflame and reinforce them.

Kaylee read with fascination and horror. Scott pushed conspiracies of a deep state designed on creating an anarchist society. He fanned fears that the government was executing a decades-old plan of mind control through cell phone towers. He pushed to build platoons of militants in the United States to fight off a potential government takeover. He made it look like the corporate executives of Fortune 500 companies were all in on the plan.

Scott was the ultimate internet troll.

Now he was trying to get into Kaylee's servers and try to muck up what she had spent years building. It was not happening. He was going to get more than just a wrist slap. This was cyberwar and Scott will be the first casualty. Scott's death would be well-deserved because even to the Cosa Nostra, he was a stain on the world.

She texted Johnny.

SENDING SCOTT AND KARL'S ADDRESS

After a few more swipes, she sent a map location.

SENDING JAY'S ADDRESS

This address was harder to get. His most recent address was an apartment, but it was missing in multiple locations and inconsistent. What was consistent, was his prior address. A house shared with someone named Jenni Delacroix.

She sent the second map location to Johnny.

Of course, Johnny never acknowledged her texts. There was never an "OK" or "10-4". Just silence. It drove her crazy.

CHAPTER 9

J ay shifted his weight from foot to foot on the stoop of Jenni's front entry. The crinkle of the cellophane-wrapped flowers mixed in well with the creaks of the front deck floorboards. Her house was nestled in a neighborhood that had not succumbed to the onrush of apartment buildings blocking the sky. Lawyers, doctors and politicians lined the street in an elegant call back to days when humans did not outnumber the pigeons in New York.

Jay's throat was dry. His eyes darted down the dark street confirming the black outline of a large Chevy. Somewhere inside, Ted was watching.

"Well, look what the cat left me!" Jenni played with a button on her blouse as she ran her eyes disapprovingly across Jay's latest disguise; a scuffed face, blackened shirt and torn pants. Standing in the doorway, her nails were perfectly done, a subdued red matching the pout of her lips. She was slim at the waist but bore incredible, over-exaggerated curves highlighted by her tight capri pants.

Jay pulled his eyes away. "Like I said…"

"…you're in trouble." Jenni finished. She nodded and pulled the door completely open. Warm golden light rolled out across the steps. "What are you hiding back there?"

"Oh," said Jay, "these are for you."

"Such a gentleman." She held the flowers up to the light with a thumb and index finger. "I love carnations."

"You do?"

Jenni didn't answer and motioned Jay inside. "You look like you could use a drink. I finished the wine but have something stronger."

Fabric-covered lamps sat on each end of the couch of Jenni's living room. They provided enough light to walk without bumping a shin into the dark, ornate furniture but not enough to read the titles of the multitude of books. The walls were lined with bookshelves, tucked back in the shadows as if they were hiding secrets. The Yankees were on the TV with the sound turned low.

Jenni walked in, swinging her glorious hips with every sure step. She carried two tall glasses of iced tea.

Jay asked, "Long Island?"

She smiled, "Only the best."

Jay sipped. It was mixed perfectly, of course. He sighed and laid back in the couch.

Jenni sat her drink on a tiny armchair table next to the TV remote and an empty wine glass. "So, do tell, what is the news?"

"There is a cop outside. Well, a retired one."

"I was talking about us."

"Oh." Jay's neck grew warm.

Jenni chuckled and tossed her hair back. "I was just teasing."

"Did you miss me?"

"The nights are certainly much quieter without someone else around."

Jay cringed. She was dodging the question. He was careful not to press on. His presence in her living room was a significant step in the right direction.

"I ticked off the wrong guy and now he's trying to ruin my life."

"What did you do to him?"

"Nothing!"

Jenni didn't take her eyes off Jay as she took a sip of her drink. Silence always worked. She was a master of the conversational thrust and parry.

Jay continued, "He overreacted. I didn't want to miss the train and was in a hurry. I'm paying for coffee and the next thing I know some fat kid goes off the rails."

"So, what's he doing, chasing you?" chided Jenni, her voice a half giggle.

"I don't know how to explain it." Jay looked up to the ceiling and ran his hands through his hair. "It's like he's dismantling my life one piece at a time. No. It's more like he's erasing it."

Jenni's face was blank with confusion.

"Jenni, I woke up yesterday and I was no longer a CityTrust employee. I went in to sort things out and someone, posing as me, called in a bomb threat. I...I panicked. Mike helped me figure out who did this, but all hell broke loose when we found him. I went to the police, thinking this will all get settled only to find I'm on New York's most wanted list with an unbelievable rap sheet. Not just a bomb threat. Really bad stuff."

Jenni leaned forward. "CityTrust fired you?"

Jay blew out a breath. Out of everything he said, she latched on that one thing. Getting fired from his last job was what brought on their last argument. He vividly remembered his suitcases sitting neatly by the door just a few feet away from the living room. He didn't really want to leave, nor did she ask him to, but deep down he knew it was the right thing.

Jenni deserved better than him. Plus, a jobless live-in boyfriend was not going to be his occupation. He was not going to live his entire life dependent on others. It was a promise he made to himself when he was very young.

Two years ago, they made a pact to build his career from the ground up. His commitment was to stop chasing impossible shortcuts and grind it out. No more moonshot failed investments. No more wasted time in interviews for jobs he was never qualified for. Jenni's commitment was to carry the financial burden but to treat it as an investment, not a handout.

Regardless, Jay dreaded the prim and proper cocktail parties with guests posing the proverbial *What do you do?* question. He could almost hear the whispers around the room. *How cute. Jenni the lawyer has a mail room boyfriend.* The shame was worse than the daily career grind that seemed to never end.

"No, they did not fire me," answered Jay. "They have no record of me working there. Can't even badge in. It's like I never existed. Sure, Earl and some folks in the office can vouch for me. But why stand up and help someone who supposedly called in a bomb threat? My cellphone no longer works. I was evicted today. My stuff was piled up on the sidewalk and you know I *never* miss a payment."

Her face tightened up with concern.

Jay couldn't stop babbling. "I have no place to live. Thank goodness for Mike as he was able to arrange for someone to put my stuff into storage. Tonight, 1 had to tell Mike to stay away because the police are on a man hunt and they know we're co-workers. We were chased by drunken and armed vigilantes from Gordy's! All I have is thirty eight dollars in my wallet and a retired cop from the Great Depression who doesn't know the difference between a cell phone and a TV remote."

A low voice growled through the window. "Hey, show respect for your elders."

"Ah, oh!" shrieked Jenni. She pulled her legs up into her chair and covered her mouth.

Jay hung his head. He continued, "I'll say this a

different way."

He looked into the blackness of the window but could not see Ted.

"All I have is thirty eight dollars, but two people, who shouldn't give a damn about me right now, have opened up their hearts just enough to give me a chance. I can't figure out whether to thank you or say I'm sorry."

Jenni took the cue, straightened her blouse and stood. "Jay, dear, aren't you going to properly introduce your friend?"

Ted towered over Jenni. He hunched to clear the threshold into the living room. "Hello, miss. My name is Ted. I'd just as soon you forget my name when I leave."

Jenni smiled. "Then don't leave too soon. You two have piqued my curiosity with all this drama. It isn't often that someone can steal my attention away from the ball game."

Ted leaned over to look at the TV. "Who's up?"

"Blue Jays. Top of the seventh. But we had a good inning and now the stretch is going to probably kill our momentum."

"I stretch every inning. Those seats are torture devices."

Jenni laughed and motioned at her chair. "It's more comfortable there. Plus I don't have to hold binoculars to see everyone's cute butts."

Jay cringed. She claimed her flirting was out of habit, but there was a hint of pleasure even when feelings were hurt.

After some pleasantries about the game and a trip to the kitchen for a beer, Ted had a question. "A tan Buick," asked Ted. "Do you have a neighbor with one?"

Jenni thought for a moment and shook her head. "No."

"It drove down your street four times this last half hour. I left my car to get a better look at the driver. He didn't see me, but I saw him. I'm certain it was Johnny Gjerdes."

The name rang familiar. After a moment, Jay's face lit up and he said, "Mob. He was big in the news, wasn't he?"

"Years ago. Johnny is not someone to take lightly." Ted turned to Jenni and asked, "Your neighborhood doesn't seem to be a place well-suited for wise guys."

"No. In fact, two doors over is George Chan. He's NYPD. I can't envision the mob and the cops sharing a barbecue at our neighborhood parties. I know most of this neighborhood and it's mostly young mothers waiting for their work-addicted husbands to come home."

Ted grunted. "Mob or NYPD, sometimes they're the same thing and you need to figure out who is paying who. But one can never underestimate the observational power of bored housewives. Nothing escapes their prying eyes."

The announcer on the TV broke into a high-pitched tone over the crowds loud cheer. In silence, they watched a replay of the Yankees double play to start the eighth. A commercial broke the reverie.

Jenni spoke first. "Should I be concerned about this Johnny person?"

"Depends on whether it is a coincidence or not. The guy we saw rifling through Jay's skirts and blouses was definitely not mob. But at this point, its safe to say there are no more coincidences."

Jay set down his glass and rose. "I'm not going to wait and find how the mob got involved. This is insane. I should never have come here in the first place. Ted assured me that no one was following us over here. How could that kid sic the mob on me?"

Ted bristled. "There was no one on our tail, kid. I'd spot a tail even if I didn't have mirrors on my car. Johnny is here looking for something and it's good luck that we're here."

"Jay, it's a little too late to question your judgement," said Jenni. "What's done is done. Let's be smart about what's next."

Jay's necked burned. His judgement. A frequent topic of argument. It was difficult to build a bridge between old money and an orphan. Jenni and her family were famous for their philanthropy for the plight of the homeless. Despite their big hearts, they would never truly understand.

Jay tried, at times, to help Jenni see. The psychology that comes from the experience of a three-year-old orphan devising tactics to ensure a decent meal in a lunchroom filled with dozens of older kids is not easily explained. Eat fast, as food can't be stolen from your stomach. Eat last, because everyone's bellies are already full and least likely to eye your plate. Eat fast, eat last. Survive. Even twenty seven years later, it was a hard mentality to shake. Some call it judgement. Jay called it instinct.

As if punctuating the conversation, headlights cut through the curtains and moved across the walls at a snail's pace. Ted rose and walked to the side of the window and pushed a curtain aside. The lights bobbed gently, hung in place and snapped off.

Ted flipped the catch on his holster and crouched in the darkened corner. He motioned to Jenni to turn up the TV volume and stay in her seat. With the relaxed grace of a southern belle, she sipped her drink and bumped the volume up a few ticks. She casually tucked one leg under the other.

Jay, on the other hand, set his glass down on the side table with a loud rattle as it wobbled into place. He squeezed his hands together, wringing them in nervous turns. He fought every urge to look to the entry way on his left. He and Jenni breathed in shallow breaths.

Ted held a finger to his lips and pointed at the window. A dark shadow, backlit by the streetlights, moved into view and stopped. Jenni took another casual sip of her drink.

The shadow slinked along the side of the house. Ted rose, pulled out his pistol and shuffled quietly along the bookshelf into the kitchen to the back door. The din of the crowd's cheers on the television drowned out the floorboards creaking under his feet. Motionless and hidden by the fridge, Ted waited.

A shadow hovered in the back-door window, lit by the blue-white moon. Ted held his breath. The outline was of a stocky man with a hunch like a seven-foot kindergarten teacher. The doorknob turned slowly, creaked at a half turn, and then stopped. Someone's storm door slammed shut down the back street. The figure turned to its side and revealed an outline of the person's face. Short forehead. Oversized nose. Receding chin.

But the hat, confidently tilted forward, gave Ted the clue he needed. It was Johnny. Ted adjusted his grip on the pistol to clear the anxious sweat in his palms. The doorknob slowly returned to its resting place. Without looking behind him, the figure stepped away from the door with cat-like reflexes and was gone.

Their breaths returned, short and halting. Johnny had impeccable timing. Some called it good luck, but a good run of luck wouldn't last fifty years. Johnny had an amazing sense of foreboding and it served him well. The cockroach weaseled out of every potential sting operation and court charge. Ted had a chance to catch Johnny on simple breaking and entering and Johnny sniffed it out.

After the car pulled away, Ted returned to the living room. Jay and Jenni were still in their chairs.

Jay was frozen in a wide-eyed stare, his pale face resembling a Roman statue. Jenni still held the remote casually, but her knuckles were white.

"My apartment keys," said Ted as he tossed them to Jay. "Take them and get out of here immediately. Both of you."

Ted turned to Jenni. "Jay knows how to find my place. Backtrack every turn, in and out of buildings, jump a couple taxis. Eyes in the back of your head."

"Is it serious?" asked Jenni. Her voice was a high-pitched whisper.

Ted nodded. "Very."

"Where are you going?"

"I'm going to tail this cockroach. He's a special one to me."

CHAPTER 10

The FBI tower in New York was built in the sixties and had not changed since its construction. The yellowing concrete, with an orderly grid of darkened windows, was a perfect false facade for the advanced technologies and minds housed inside.

It was public knowledge what agencies worked on each of its forty one floors. Underground, however, was one of the FBI's better secrets. One of the largest data centers and network hubs of the world quietly hummed, listening surreptitiously to the world's network traffic; storing away data neatly and methodically.

From his desk above ground and on one of the more public floors, Tyler Brown watched his co-workers huddle over a photograph-covered table in the briefing room. The shades weren't quite drawn on the meeting room window and he could not resist staring. He had been a brick agent for the FBI for a few months and he was still glued to his desk.

He was lured to New York because it had plenty of action but he was getting none. The pros kept asking him to google everything under the sun "because no one else knew how to use the google." In due time, Tyler kept telling himself, in due time he'll get his chance to join the agents on the big cases.

His fit physique cut through his white linen dress shirt. His ritual of visiting the gym at the end of every day paid off. If he had any pet peeve, it was the implication that his inky black skin meant he was born ripped and cut. It was just another day of having to constantly prove himself in face of a world designed to make him invisible.

The loud clop-clop worn by the shoes of the assistant special agent in charge warned him to turn his attention back to his computer. Chuck didn't appreciate agents that weren't running at any speed lower than top gear.

"Got another one for your inbox." He tossed a folder into his wire basket.

"Thanks."

Chuck ignored Tyler's lack of enthusiasm. "Put this on top of your pile. Deportation order."

"What do I need to research?"

"Nothing. Grab your roscoe and go find this guy. Paraguayan mob. The last thing we need is a turf war on top of a turf war."

"Paraguay has a mob?"

"Mike Tyson is a singer?" Tyler couldn't remember a time his CO wasn't annoyed.

He turned to shut down his computer and hide his blush. "Ok. I'm on it."

Chuck pointed at a redhead a few desks down. "You will assist Hot Stuff. Bag and tag. Report back to me on progress before the day is over. Voicemails every two hours. Can you do this?"

Tyler heart was pumping double speed. He replied loud and sharp, "Yes, sir."

Tyler looked over at the red head. She stared at him with her hazel eyes, arms crossed with a smirk on her face. "Ready, kiddo?"

"Uh," said Tyler as he rose. Her smirk put him right back into his first-year jitters. He was crashing from his high of finally getting a real assignment. "I'm Tyler Brown. Just joined the force in February."

"Yeah, I know. I'm Hofstra. Not Hot Stuff."

"Right, you aren't."

She raised an eyebrow.

"I mean, of course you are. I just know better."

She let out a chuckle. "I like you already."

She straightened the grey skirt of her suit as she sauntered over to his desk. Her white blouse was unbuttoned far too low to ignore.

"Who's the target?"

Tyler opened the manila folder on his desk. A single piece of paper was inside. "Jay Wilson. Thirty. Five foot seven, 163 pounds."

Hofstra snorted. "That's half of New York."

"Blonde hair."

"Ok, we're down to five percent."

Tyler pushed the paper forward and pointed.

"What does the red FOND stamp mean?"

"First offense, but no historical files available. Strange for someone from Paraguay. There would at least be visa paperwork and flight data."

Hofstra put both her hands on his desk and leaned forward to read the report. Water cooler talk warned of Hofstra's tactics. Wicked smart and knew how to get what she wanted. She was a fast riser and got results. She was only a few successful assignments away from a significant promotion.

"Well, this isn't much to work from," said Hofstra as she closed the manila folder, "so let's go to the basement."

"B-b-basement?" said Tyler.

"Yes, the basement. The kids down there google better than you do. Do you have a better place in mind?" She crossed her arms and tapped her shoe. Tyler's mind was buzzing. He had always wanted to see the wizardry in the basement. Even better, this was his first real case so he was already on the way to the elevator.

"Let's go."

The basement smelled of stale french fries and the week-old clothes found at the bottom of a hamper. Despite the stench, the area was meticulously clean. Monitors, flashing text of all colors, filled every open space on the front wall. In the center of the room was a collection of neatly organized desks filled with keyboards and mice. No wires were seen anywhere. No paper either. Three young men, hunched over their desks, never stopped their fingers' dance across the keyboard when they talked. Their eyes never left the monitors that surrounded them either.

"Paraguyan Mob. No such thing." The youngest of the basement dwellers ironically had the longest, majestic, bushy beard. His lips were not discernible amongst the mess of mustache, neck hair and beard that extended to his chest.

Tyler asked, "Are you absolutely sure?"

"Yes. I know that there is no mob that is Paraguayan-based. I checked the police and governmental records of not only Paraguay, which isn't much, but also INTERPOL and the CIA database. Organized crime over there looks to be nothing worse than government bribery and midnight goat stealing."

Hofstra held up her palm to Tyler and asked, "Is there a chance that Paraguay could be an operative location for a mob that is based anywhere else in the world?"

"Yes, there is a chance."

"But that's what I asked!" said Tyler.

Bushy-beard lent a dismissive eyebrow at Tyler and returned his gaze to Hofstra.

"We've got a guy flagged for deportation," said Hofstra, "but his file is light. Usually I get a rolling file cabinet's worth of paperwork from intelligence when any mobster lands in the US."

"After lunch, I can look him up for you."

Hofstra leaned forward, palms on desk. "I'll buy lunch."

"I appreciate the offer," replied Bushy-beard. He motioned to his co-worker loudly clacking away. "We've got a Magic game on pause from yesterday that needs to resume. We'll be quick."

The man wearing an oversized Rage Against the Machine baseball hat snorted. "Yeah, he'd rather not delay the inevitable. Utter destruction at the hands of Tormar the Plainswalker."

Bushy-beard shook his head. "If I win this match, you can eat my mana because I'll not only achieve the impossible but show that brilliance can indeed overcome relentless bad luck."

Hofstra let out a breath and turned to Tyler. "We'll have to come back later."

It was Tyler's turn to hold up his hand. He turned to the guys, "Can I play?"

The rolling click-clack of typing stopped in unison. Rage Hat smiled as if he had fangs, "If you know the rules, of course. You begin with me."

Rage Hat slid the wireless keyboards and mice under his desk and in the return motion pulled out a large black portfolio the size of a poster. He laid it on the desk, pulled the zipper around the entire edge and opened. Tucked away, in neat pockets and clasps, were playing cards with pictures of orcs, wizards and every monster imaginable. Large, twenty-sided dice the size of a fists were snuggled away in the embedded netting. Rage Hat unclipped a thick deck and handed it to Tyler.

"That's a good starter deck. Stacked to beat me. It'll give you a fighting chance."

Tyler smiled as he riffled through the deck, examining each card with a cursory glance, "Go ahead, Hofstra. I think I can handle this long enough while you two dig around."

Hofstra smiled and turned to Bushy-beard. "Jay Wilson."

"That doesn't sound Paraguyan." His fingers flew across the keyboard.

Hofstra chuckled. "Congratulations, Plainswalker, you have clue number one. When you smell something fishy, it usually is dead fish."

After some typing, Bushy-beard said, "There is no recent activity for us to locate Jay at this moment. But I have something interesting. I'll throw it up there." He stopped typing and pointed at the monitor on the wall.

Hofstra was overwhelmed by all the screens flashing data. "What am I looking at."

"Monitor sixteen, center. This guy has a helluva rap sheet. But it's all crimes committed here in New York."

"Okay, so?"

"They are logged as if he were a citizen, not as a foreigner. He has a bank account and received a paycheck from CityTrust. But there is no record of him ever being an employee of CityTrust. None of these crimes show any hint of a need for deportation or review of a visa. These are some serious crimes. But, look at monitor seventeen, just to the right."

"All the fields are blank."

"Exactly. Kind of hard to book a guy on a rap or give him a paycheck if he has no social security number. No driver's license number. No address. But there are consecutive registrations for elementary school records in Louisiana, Oklahoma and Texas all in a span of one year for a Jay Wilson with the same birthday. This data is not fake. Who moves their kid between three schools, much less states, at that age? You would think our glorious NYPD would hold a guy tight in a cell on the first offense if everything about him came up blank and was a foreign national. He's halfway real, halfway ghost."

Tyler looked up from his hands full of cards. "So, how is that even possible?"

Bushy-beard ran his fingers through his beard. "It isn't possible. It's like someone deleted this data to cover their tracks, but wasn't thorough enough. Or, this Jay Wilson is not Paraguayan mob, but an uber-spy. He could have wiped enough of Jay's information to protect whatever mission he's on. We know Jay Wilson is a real person and a citizen, but we don't know if *this* version of Jay Wilson is the one that the FBI wants to arrest. Is this a stolen identity? Or sabotage?"

Hofstra crossed her arms. "Occam's razor. The simplest explanation is usually the right one. When was the last time we had a case involving Paraguay? Never. Even worse, who would steal an identity that half exists and is full of blanks. Someone is messing with Jay. This deportation order is starting to feel like a cover. The question is *why and for what*."

All the typing stopped. A red-headed, freckled boy that resembled Opie from the Andy Griffith show spoke, in a high-pitched voice, "Then that means whoever is messing with Jay, is really good."

"How good?" asked Tyler.

Rage Hat laid all his cards down and pulled a wireless keyboard back on top of the game board. "Better than us, and there is no one better than us."

Bushy-beard turned to Hosftra with a look of concern on his face, "I think we'll take you up on that lunch."

CHAPTER 11

"Oh no," said Scott. He typed furiously on his laptop. Sweat ran down his temples. He repeated, at an even higher whine, "No, no, no, stop." Then like a punctuation to his sentence, he yanked the wires from the side of his laptop. He stared at his screen, breathing heavily.

The hair stood up on the back of Karl's neck. "What's going on?"

Scott's face was clammy-white. He pumped his jaw as if he were going to speak, but nothing came out but grunts.

"Scott? Are you okay?" Karl rose from his chair and sat on the glass coffee table in front of Scott.

"I screwed up."

"Yeah, tell me something I don't know."

"No, I mean, I really, really screwed up." Scott chewed on his lower lip and stared into the distance. He needed to quiet the alarm bells clanging in his brain.

"I want you to take your stuff and leave. You're not welcome here anymore."

Karl ran his fingers through his hair. It was greasy from two days without a shower. Neither of them could sleep. Karl couldn't bear to look out the window in fear of being watched.

Scott ignored Karl. "The IP address was a public address. Like a neon sign saying *hack me*."

"You're not making sense. And you're ignoring me."

"I assumed the mob would be low-tech. Why would I make such a stupid assumption?"

"Who cares?" Karl stood and pulled a large printer paper box out from under his desk.

"You should care. I got in and poked around. Took my time."

Karl raked Scott's paper off the coffee table and into the box. "Here, let me pack for you."

"It was almost too easy. I decrypted the password file in minutes. Next thing I know, I had root access."

Karl walked to the pile of clothes under the window. "I'm going to put your clothes in garbage bags. I want you to leave tonight, Scott. Stop ignoring me."

"So, I poked around a little more. Next thing I know, someone is port-scanning me. I'm lucky I noticed it. It was masked and my firewall didn't alert me. Someone installed a replacement firewall on this," said Scott as he tapped the laptop on his belly, "in seconds. If I hadn't noticed the slightest slowdown in my PC, everything would have looked exactly the same. This could be the ultimate trojan horse. This software has been running for a while."

With a frustrated huff, Scott pushed his laptop aside. No lights were blinking, as it was powered down, and wires were splayed across the couch in a tangled mess. "I'm listening to you, Karl, but I need you to understand this first. My entire laptop was copied. Someone hacked me. They laid a trap."

"Are you saying that those mob servers were a honeypot?"

"It was bait."

"For who?"

"Us."

Karl threw his box, full of Scott's papers, to the wall. "You've got the mob going after us? Are you mental?"

"I'll fix this," said Scott. "I just need a little bit of time."

"No! No more. You're leaving now. If you have anything in my apartment after dinner, it's going down to the furnace chute."

"Come on, Karl. I didn't mean for this to happen."

Karl held up his hand. "The more you talk, the less time you have to pack. I don't want to see a trace of you when I get back from Number One Chinese."

"Oooh, could you bring back some spring rolls?"

Karl's glare could have killed.

"Give me a balanced deck this time."

Rage Hat grumbled as he reached into his portfolio. Tyler smiled inwardly. He was glad that his free time spent as a kid at Hobbits and Heroes Comic Shop was not a complete waste for his professional career. Tyler frequented it when he needed a break from his training. It was the one safe place where no one was jockeying for a position on a class curve, comparing track times or other inter-recruit sabotage. It was only at Hobbits and Heroes that folks of all backgrounds came for one thing; to be kids again and have fun.

Tyler riffled through the new deck, noting the unique characteristics of the creatures and spells. The card game was classic cat and mouse. Attack and counterattack. Feints and strikes.

"Ah! Guys look at this," said Bushy-beard. He nodded at the large monitor at the front of the room. "I found this in a backup archive from CityTrust's cloud-based security software." Jay's CityTrust badge was oversized. With a flick of a finger, he zoomed in on the text underneath the picture on the badge. The blocky, black text on the badge showed Jay's hire date.

"Looks like we've removed the possibility of Jay being a foreign mobster. You can't get a job without a social security number," said Tyler. "But a badge doesn't prove Jay was an employee. Anyone with access to their security system can make a badge."

"Maybe this will," answered Bushy-beard. The monitor flickered as it played a video of employees entering CityTrust. He froze on a frame showing Jay passing through security. "Right here, that badge was scanned for the very first time. This was Jay's first day at work and it matches the badge's start date. But wait, there's more."

The video started again and continued to show Jay after passing the gate. Mike came into the frame, high-fived Jay and swung his arm over his shoulder as they walked into the elevator laughing.

"Oh my," said Tyler. "I hope that guy still works at CityTrust. We now have a link to finding Jay. If Jay's a mob national or a victim of stolen identity, we need him in either case."

Rage Hat added, "Jay hasn't been back in the building since he was deleted. All the videos are clean. I'm going to run a facial match to CityTrust badges for this other guy. Might take a while, but we can pass it through our passport and driver's license databases. We'll figure out who he is."

Tyler interjected, "I did some digging of my own." The basement dwellers stopped typing to listen. What could this brick agent possible contribute as Watson to these technical Sherlocks?

"I found a social security number tied to Jay. He got a GED in New Orleans; one of the states you guys said he went to school. I ran it against our social security database and it's the only number skipped and unassigned in the entire population since the inception of the program."

Rage Hat and Bushy-beard replied in unison. "Deleted."

Hofstra unbuttoned her blazer and hung it over the back of a chair. "Gentlemen, it looks like we're going to be here a while. I'll order dinner while you figure out who and where this nice looking, blonde metrosexual is. I think he's going to be our next source of clues on Jay."

"I bet this place is booby-trapped," said Jay as he rattled the key in the door. His attempt to be jocular was not working. Jenni was silent the whole way to Ted's apartment. The unrecognizable address in El Barrio, the access through the store and the blocked alley seemed to put her on edge.

"This whole place gives me the creeps." Her eyes darted left and right in the dark, empty hallway. She saddled up against Jay. "Just get inside."

After a satisfactory click of the key, Jay opened the door with a vigorous shoulder push. He ran his fingers along the walls, searching for a light switch. The faint smell of incense filled the air.

Jenni let out a short gasp when the lights came on. Beautiful knotty wood shone from the arms and legs of two chairs in the center of the living room. They were covered in blankets decorated with patterns of Egyptian hieroglyphs, black against the natural brown and green hue.

A TV hung over a cedar long table, decorated with trinkets of every imaginable culture. A South African mask sat next to an orange-gold statuette of a fat elephant wearing a headdress. Jay recognized it as the hindu diety, Ganeesha. Painted Russian jewelry, ornate flowers on a black background, were staged on hand carved and polished buckthorn stands.

Lamps were smartly tucked away out of view, the indirect light lending a casual comfort to the surroundings.

Jenni cooed, "Who knew Ted had taste?"

Jay nodded and peeked into the kitchen. Light blue and white subway tile lined the ornate granite countertop that was filled with swirls and imperfections that captured your gaze. Spices, lined neatly on the miniature shelves by the oven, shone under even more hidden lighting. Fresh produce filled a basket in the center of the small eating table.

Jay opened the fridge. "I think we have the wrong apartment. There are more vegetables in here than a farm market."

A loud rap at the front door prompted Jenni to jump and let out a quiet "Oh!"

Jay held a finger to his lips and crept to the door to peek through the peep hole.

"I think it's safe," whispered Jay.

Jenni returned a questioning gaze.

"This guy has to be a century old."

He pulled the door open a few inches. With Jenni behind him, they peeked through. Jay mustered up courage to keep his voice from wavering. "Ted isn't here. Come another time."

A tall black man stood, hunched as if he wanted to avoid bumping his head on the threshold. His short-cropped afro was peppered grey. Under his arm, he held a large drawing pad. His bloodshot eyes darted between Jenni and Jay.

"You kids the J and J?" barked the old man. His face quickly broke into a disarming smile. "Ted told me you'd be here enjoying his hospitality."

Jenni laughed, visibly relieved. "Now that's just cute. Yes, we are, and to whom do I owe this pleasure?" She pulled the door open.

"Elmer Nattipatrick," said the old man as he took Jenni's hand in his wrinkled, calloused grip. He kissed it politely and nodded to Jay. "Ted tells me that we've got a cockroach to exterminate."

While Jay went to get water, Elmer took his time setting up his drawing pad. The paper, yellowing on the edges, hung from an impossibly frail, wooden stand that unfolded in his experienced twists and turns. From his pocket, Elmer pulled out a wood box, carefully opened it to expose multiple charcoal pencils and sat it gently on the coffee table.

"Excuse our surprise and caution," said Jay, "Ted didn't tell us you were coming."

Elmer let out a grunt. "When Ted's on the hunt, he doesn't leave time for pleasantries. He mentioned that you had a run in with a kid at a coffee shop. Twice."

Jay nodded. Jenni ran her finger along the frames of pictures lined neatly on the wall. "Are these Ted's relatives?"

"The sketch artist is usually the one asking the questions, but I'm happy to oblige while I scritch and scratch." Elmer pulled out a short charcoal pencil and examined it closely. "I can't see that picture from here, but it's likely to be his family. He doesn't have friends."

"That's terrible," said Jenni, "everyone should have friends."

Elmer turned to Jay. "Ted said the kid was a ginger and overweight. Straight or curly hair?"

"Curly. Really curly."

Jenni didn't look away from the pictures. "These are really old. I think Ted is the little boy in this one." She pointed at a large picture, faded from black and white to brown and white. There were two young boys standing in Sunday clothes under the watchful eye of their parents.

"Yup. I recognize that picture. It's one of the few pictures that Ted has of his younger brother."

"What happened?" asked Jenni.

"Killed. Never finished college. My turn. Was the kids' face round or oblong?"

"Perfectly round. Cheeks so big they almost blocked his ears. Why was he killed?"

Elmer paused and looked at Jay and Jenni. "You don't know about Ted's family?"

"We haven't known him long."

"Well," said Elmer, "there are certain hazards to Ted's occupation. The mob don't take it lightly when someone successfully locks up one of their own."

Elmer continued drawing as he talked. "Ted was engaged, too. It was right about when I first met him. Real smart and the ladies fell over each other to spend time with him. He owned the world and he was committed to the force."

"I remember when he bagged Vinny De Luca. Famous mobster back in the day. His capture was big news. Ted couldn't have been twenty five. Vinny always eluded capture. Ted rolled the dice and rammed him with his police car, sent Vinny into the Hudson and fished the guy out. Like I said, smart and willing to play with lower odds than anyone else would."

Jay turned to face the picture. "Then they killed his brother?"

"Yup. Ted was famous all over New York for catching Vinny. It was in the news for weeks. He made the most of it. He was young. Who would fault him for enjoying the time in the spotlight? But things got dark quickly. He loved his little brother."

"His fiancée," asked Jenni, almost too afraid to hear the answer, "what happened to her?"

"Pushed her away. Same with his adoptive parents. He said things he shouldn't have said, but he did it on purpose. Estranged. Haven't spoken for most of his life. He couldn't bear to have it happen again to someone he loved."

Elmer quietly returned to his charcoal.

Jay put his head in his hands. "Now he's living a quiet life, happy in retirement. I bang on his door and mess it up. I can't believe this."

"There is a big heart, " said Jenni as she put her hand on Jay's shoulder, "in that Ted Stone."

Elmer smiled in agreement. "Kids, I haven't seen Ted this happy in two decades. Whatever you two have done..." He seemed to choke on his words.

"He's got a mission now. He's doing what he does best. You should have heard him when he called me. He sounded twenty five years old. I had to slow him down to make sense of his babble."

After pulling out a yellow handkerchief from his back pocket and blowing his nose, he continued, "He needs this more than anyone. Every year, on September eighteenth, we celebrate his engagement. It has been forty one years. I was there for the first celebration. I thought it was an odd, even grim event to celebrate."

Jenni gasped, "You're breaking my heart, Elmer."

"We have a steak dinner. A bottle of Bordeaux. Dessert. The whole works. Every year, we hoist our dessert port with full bellies; toasting family, loved ones and friends. While Ted has very few of those, he is proud that they're alive and enjoying life. His ex-fiancée has two kids and four grandkids, all of whom he couldn't be prouder."

"That man," cried Jenni, "simply gave us the

keys to his apartment when we had nowhere to hide."

Elmer picked up a new charcoal pencil. "Well, you won't hide long. Ted Stone loves to hunt and is one of the best. But," said Elmer with a pause, "he only hunts one thing."

Jay smiled, ear to ear. "Cockroaches."

Number One Chinese was Karl's happy place. If there were ever a new tenant, they'd never be able to remove the odor of half a century of Mandarin cooking from the walls, furniture and fixtures. Piled inches high on his plate were noodles upon noodles of happiness. Sadly, the salve didn't work as well as he had hoped. With every bite, he silently cursed his predicament.

Scott wound a tight knot for Karl and this was the last one he was going to untie. He considered turning Scott in. He was certain he could prove his own innocence in court, but he couldn't bear the thought of waiting in jail for months for an uncertain conclusion.

But even that wasn't going to be easy. While Scott irritated him, he could not turn on his only friend. Scott would never even consider such a thing for Karl if the tables were turned. Betrayal almost felt as bad as going to jail. It wasn't in his DNA.

Worse, this was New York. A visit to the police would be a gamble. Any detective he talked to could be under mob influence. Worse, no information in the police could be trusted to be held confidential. If he shared Scott's activities, he'd be putting his own life at risk if it got to the mob. The odds were high that the corruption was stacked against him. It was a risk simply not worth taking.

Karl motioned for another order of egg rolls. His fork slipped from his grease-coated fingers and clattered on the plate. Two gentlemen, sitting in the corner of the restaurant, looked up at him for a moment and then continued their hushed conversation. Fear cast suspicion that they were monitoring him.

Karl imagined himself begging a mob-boss to let him live. Crying at his feet, at the base of an ornate throne; crafted from dark mahogany and brass-riveted, red upholstery. He couldn't push aside the fantasy-based perceptions but the reality was there. The mob kills. There had to be some way to talk and sort everything out. A simple mistake should have a simple resolution.

But who could call off a paid hitman? His brain worked every angle for an opportunity.

After two egg rolls, he settled on Jay.

Jay got the Italian on their trail so Jay was the one who could call them off. Unfortunately, Scott was quite effective in wiping Jay's existence. He was probably extradited to Paraguay already, looking for a safe place to sleep amongst the streets. He had no family to rescue him. Scott was sure to dig into that.

Mike, the dapper blonde who secured Jay away safely at the Running-a-Ground, came to mind. Scott poked around and discovered that he was a co-worker at CityTrust and dropped the matter when he found his involvement was innocuous. Mike was probably his best chance at finding Jay.

Karl leaned back in his chair and burped. He had a plan and he had to act fast. Finish dinner, ensure Scott was out of his home and then find Mike.

The best part was that Karl knew exactly where to look.

Scott rarely walked at night. He was a few blocks away from Karl's apartment headed in no particular direction. His mind was a jumble of anger and frustration and he hoped that the random hullabaloo of a Manhattan evening would calm him.

Deep down, he was sure Karl wouldn't kick him to the street. It was a threat he'd heard before but never followed up on. But he had never seen Karl this angry.

It was Jay's fault. Scott seethed. He wished for Jay to miraculously step on to the sidewalk in front of him so he could strangle him with his own hands. He let the joy and satisfaction of Jay's imaginary gasps for mercy wash over and help resolve some of his anger.

In front of him, he heard some chuckles. A man with two women were dressed for a night out.

They were enjoying a smoke and were likely headed for the popular live music joint around the corner.

Both of the women's eyes darted at Scott and looked away. Their low murmur of conversation was peppered with shrieks of laughter.

While Scott couldn't understand what they were saying, it was obvious they were laughing at him. Unknowingly, they were throwing gasoline on Scott's already hot temper.

Scott walked into the threesome's private space. He leaned in, only inches apart and asked, "What's so funny?"

Scott's blood was pumping endorphins fueled by unbridled rage.

The man blew out smoke and used his other hand to push Scott away. "Hey man, back off."

Scott poked his chubby finger into the man's chest. "Is this your idea of entertainment? Stand there, trying to look cool with your smokes and laugh at random people all night?"

One of the ladies stepped back and scolded Scott. "What is your problem?"

"My problem," said Scott, "is that you can't mind your own business." He turned and shoved her. With a yelp of surprise, her high heels hastened the lady's fall to the ground. She laid, stunned by what happened, and watched with wide eyes.

Scott turned back to the man and continued with his poking. "How does that feel, you elitist,"

Poke.

"Soul-sucking,"

Poke.

"Pile of puke?"

He punctuated his question with a two-handed shove. His girth, rather than true strength, powered the man several feet back into a crowd of onlookers. Behind him, he could hear the quiet beeps of someone making a phone call.

A dozen onlookers circled; attracted by the verbal melee. To Scott's eyes, it seemed as if there were more phones than people. Faces were lit by the small screens, eager to consume the street side entertainment and elated to have something to post on social media that will certainly garner several coveted likes.

A voiced shouted, "Looks like we found some Manhattan crazy!"

Scott spun and looked for the source of the voice. Spittle built in the sides of his mouth. "Who said that?"

"I'll pay you twenty dollars if you let us kick you in the nuts!" The laughter cut into Scott's psyche. He started swinging, blind with rage.

"Look at the cute boy dance!"

Scott tripped over someone's outstretched leg. He lost his balance and stumbled over the curb. Butt-first, he landed in the street. His hands could not break the fall and his palms were torn to shreds by the asphalt.

A taxi braked with a screech, narrowly avoiding Scott. Angry honks broke the stunned look on Scott's face. He grabbed the bumper of the taxi and pulled himself up. Laughter filled his ears. He slammed the top of the taxi's hood, leaving blood splatters.

He screamed at the growing crowd, "You have no idea who I am! I am Deetwuh!"

The crowd noise transformed from a laugh-track to raucous peals of laughter. People were hugging their stomachs. Some were busy typing on their phones. A young woman, shouted, "Did he say he's Beelzebub?!?"

"He's crazy."

After wiping away sweat, Scott's face was streaked with blood. His pallid complexion shone bright in the streetlights. He wanted to crush the torment, but the growing crowd was a threat even he couldn't handle.

"Are the police here yet? Someone needs to pick up this nut-job."

Scott ran into the intersection. Cars honked and added to the crowd's rancor.

He howled at the crowd, "You will pay. All of you. YOU. WILL. PAY."

CHAPTER 12

J ohnny Gjerdes was getting sloppy in his old age. He no longer drove his car in circles and cutbacks. His tan Buick didn't suddenly accelerate into highway traffic and off onto an exit ramp unseen. Ted had no trouble tailing him and was surprised that Johnny shook the habit. Ted was ready to accelerate at every off-ramp, but it never happened. It was just two old guys cruising the New York night.

Johnny had no reason to be worried about a tail, even if he had known Ted was following him. Four times Ted snapped cuffs on Johnny only to have him return his gesture with a same wry smile and say, "Well, now isn't this inconvenient?"

While cockroaches like Johnny were resilient, Ted was persistent. Retirement from the force didn't mean he didn't use his free time to watch the activities of the New York underground, ever-watchful, patient and observant. Why have a cup of joe on the street, if you could have a cup of joe on the street next to wise guys? No one suspected an oversized, ancient Italian to be a threat. Johnny had old eyes and the new guys wouldn't recognize Ted. It all worked out for a nice retirement where he had plenty of time to lay branches and leaves over a trap. Progress on building his cockroach trap was slow, but there was no consideration of giving up. It was a long game.

Ted still felt he had plenty of time, until Jay showed up. Now he was tailing Johnny just like he did thirty years earlier. He called his old friend, Elmer, to meet up with Jay and Jenni and to draw up a head shot of the kid from the coffee shop. The kid was the key. Johnny was leading him, hopefully, to another clue as to what this key unlocked. Years of experience told his gut this kid was not with the mob. However, Johnny's presence was an unavoidable but happy circumstance. If he could help Jay and wrangle one more cockroach, it'd be time well invested.

The further they drove into Manhattan, the harder it was to stay on top of Johnny. The New York street lights rarely gave Ted enough time to skip across an intersection without setting off a handful of taxis into an attention-getting, profanity-laden, honking tirade. Johnny was going to shake him the longer this chase went on.

Johnny's brake lights signaled his intention to turn off to a quiet street lined with low-rise apartments and restaurants. Ted took his time and slowly rolled around the corner. A restaurant valet whisked away Johnny's car and, instead of walking into a restaurant, he turned to face the featureless apartment building across the street. He lit a cigarette and pulled out his cell phone.

Ted pulled in front of Rubio's Wine Bar, a couple storefronts away. He handed a couple bills to the young valet and barked, "I know my odometer reading. No joy rides, boy."

The boy stammered and looked at the battered Cadillac, the grey-silver paint matching the spots of exposed metal underneath, "Uh, ok, sir."

After telling the host he was waiting for a friend, he kept a watchful eye on his old nemesis from the bar's vestibule.

Johnny strode through the traffic to the apartment building entrance and scanned the resident listing at the intercom comparing it to a paper in his hand. Part way through, he hesitated and quickly turned back to the sidewalk.

In the bright lights of the apartment lobby, a resident checked for her mail in the massive wall of mailboxes and turned to leave the apartment. Timing perfect and at a full, confident stride, Johnny walked towards the entrance. He politely held the door open for the resident who was leaving and after a pleasant nod, ducked inside.

At the wall of mailboxes, he returned to his head bob comparing the information in his hands what what clues he could find on the mailboxes. After a few minutes, he stopped, folded the paper and inserted it into his breast pocket. He pulled his hat down over his eyes and disappeared into the apartment building.

Ted smiled. While it was obviously not a nest of cockroaches, Johnny was after someone he did not know. Someone was going to be surprised and it wasn't going to be the birthday kind. No cake, but probably some fire.

From his chest pocket, Ted pulled out his notebook. He flipped the cover and scratched down the address. Fourteen stories with the usual eight apartments on each floor. One hundred and twelve doors to knock on. If Johnny didn't get to this person first, Ted figured he'd get down to a half dozen possibilities before sundown tomorrow. By the time Elmer had a drawing of the kid, Ted will be able to convey his memory of the person stealing Jay's papers and get that drawing, too. They'd have two faces to use during their search and would have this part of the mystery solved.

There was always the shortcut of accessing the apartment building records in the manager's office. Depending on the intelligence of the person between him and that file cabinet, it could be a quicker option. The files would be a treasure trove of resident information compared to what outdated scribbles existed at an intercom or on the front of a mail slot.

"Sir," asked a pleasant voice behind him. It was the hostess of Rubio's. "Would you like a drink at the bar while you wait?"

It was a long drive home and it was late. Ted decided to start first thing in the morning when he was sure Johnny was out of his way.

"No, thank you. Are you open for breakfast tomorrow?"

The hostess raised an eyebrow. "No, just lunch and dinner. I'd recommend the Super Mercado on the corner. Esmeralda in the back makes great huevos."

Ted smiled. "Excellent."

Ted heard laughing from inside as he pulled his apartment key from his pocket. He paused for a moment and listened. The low murmur of conversation calmed him. Ted leaned forward and put his forehead on the frame of the door and closed his eyes. He could not remember the last time someone laughed in his home. Elmer's familiar voice rumbled at an easy pace; deep, measured and methodical.

The click of his door opening unfortunately broke the revelry inside. Ted stood in his doorway to take in the scene and a smirk came across his face. Jenni was wearing loose-fitting pjs adorned with hearts and wine glasses in various shapes. Her legs were curled up under her. The highball in her hand was filled with white wine.

Jay's head was in her lap as he laid lengthwise on Ted's couch. His loose-fitting, adidas-striped athletic pants contrasted with his oversized led zeppelin t-shirt. Jenni was caressing Jay's hair as she listened to Elmer talking and drawing from Ted's favorite chair.

Elmer sat ramrod straight; putting the finishing touches on his charcoal drawing in an easel. The face he drew looked like a cartoon. A baby-faced young man, thick curls around his rotund checks, was eerily looking back from under Elmer's practiced hands.

"Clearly you're losing your touch, Elmer," said Ted. "It took me a little while to recognize what you were drawing."

"Suck an egg," replied Elmer without looking up, "and get me a beer."

Ted snorted and nodded to Jay. "You?"

"That'd be awesome. I only saw wine in the kitchen."

Ted furrowed his brow. "Wine? The stuff I set aside as a gift?"

Jenni gasped and looked down at her glass. Ted raised a hand. "I should know better than to tease a lady. I'm glad you found the bottles. Ms. Tibbens keeps bringing them over for me and I have no place to keep it all."

She raised an eyebrow. "You do know what it means when a lady brings wine over, Ted?"

Ted ceremoniously rolled his eyes. "Beer. I have cheap or expensive. You have a preference?"

Elmer grunted, "Cheap."

Jay raised an eyebrow and shrugged in acquiescence. "Cheap." He continued, "It's very generous of you to let us stay."

Ted wordlessly left and returned from the kitchen with three cans of beer in one hand. He tossed one to each and fell dramatically into his other favorite chair. "You're welcome. But, don't expect much from the host tonight. These old bones are rusty. But, remember, you are in hiding. I would avoid getting out much until we get this sorted."

"This guy, " said Elmer as he tapped the sketch of Scott, "has got to be mob if what you say is true."

"How did you come to that?" asked Jay.

"You said you'd done nothing more than offend someone trying to buy coffee. Maybe threw a verbal insult or two? But you don't owe anyone money. Your family isn't even from around here. There is always a motive and I struggle to see normal people escalating a passing offense into this level of destruction."

"Right."

Elmer turned to Ted. "This is like Conor, ah, um..."

Ted finished his sentence. "Murphy. Conor Murphy."

"What did Conor do?" asked Jay.

After a swig from the can, Ted answered, "Nothing. That's the sad thing. Conor happened to be in the wrong place at the wrong time. Conor was buying a used car. He was in the street, dickering with the seller when a couple wise guys mistook him for the building's landlord. A landlord who had stopped making protection payments."

Elmer shook his head in disbelief. "He went missing. A few days later, Conor was found in a garbage dumpster; bludgeoned to death."

"Elmer and I investigated this case for a long time. Every lead came up dry. We knew it was a mob hit, but we could never make a connection between Conor and the mob. One day we were circling the building, looking for any possible angle we were missing. The landlord came out and questioned what we were doing."

Elmer added, in a sorrowful baritone, "It was eerie. Conor looked exactly like the landlord. It was like the ghost of Conor Murphy had walked out of the pictures we had in our files. Of course, Ted made the connection right away. It was a simple case of mistaken identity."

"Did you catch the guys who killed Conor?," asked Jenni.

Ted's face darkened. "No. Cockroaches are hard to catch and much harder to keep bottled up. But we were able to give Conor's family some comfort and closure. Sad as it sounds, it meant a lot to them to know it was a mistake and that Conor did not harbor a second life, secret to who he loved most."

"You two make a great team."

Elmer chortled. "I just take Ted's lead. He has incredible instincts, except when it comes to the ladies. That's where I come in."

"Very funny, El. If I remember right, I was the one who introduced you to Sylvia."

"Sylvia practically introduced herself. She always had a thing for men in uniform. That doesn't count. What does count are all the cockroaches you've locked up."

"Was never enough."

Elmer turned to Jay and Jenni. "Ted was the best. He got so many awards and commendations that he stopped showing up for the ceremonies. Mob hated him. Guys on the force claimed Ted could smell 'em blocks away."

"El, you do realize they call that racial profiling today."

"Hey, it worked most of the time. Everyone is just a little too uptight and too careful. I think it comes at the cost of common sense. Even worse, these days if it isn't on a computer, it truly doesn't exist."

Elmer turned to Jenni. "You should have seen me at the pharmacist a couple days ago. My name was misspelled in the system. One 't' was missing. The pharmacist refused to refill my prescription! The idiot. How many Nattipatricks do you know? How many Elmers? We had a very long discussion. I can be very persuasive."

Jenni could barely stifle her laughter of the poor pharmacist who had the luck to get tied up with Elmer. "Did they figure it out?"

"I left with nothing. But I had the last word as I pointed at the gentlemen's precious degree hanging on the wall and declared that it had no more value than as toilet paper when it comes to common sense!"

◆ ◆ ◆

Patience was one of Karl's strongest suits. Today, in order to locate Mike, it was the matter of waiting a shift out. No problem. Karl had all the time in the world.

Enjoying a now-cold latte, Karl sat across from the CityTrust building. New York's bustle flowed past him, a menagerie of faces, fashion and purpose. Everyone in New York walked, but as a necessary evil. Karl walked because New York provided just as many interesting sights as his childhood walks in the forests of Washington. Nature was beautiful, but people were more interesting.

While there was much to watch, Karl never took his eye off the employee entrance of CityTrust. According to Scott, Mike was a call center agent. Karl could not wipe the smirk off his face as he reminisced on that point. He and Scott loved to torment call center agents when they were younger. Their teenage technical hubris was reinforced by the poor souls on the other end of the line as they struggled to keep up with Scott's technical thrust and parry.

Karl tried to picture what Mike might look like. He imagined an adult who never outgrew his boyish looks. Forever doomed to be marginalized as someone who could not contribute more than a quick fix to a simple problem and was forced to follow a script that was mind-numbing for both the caller and the agent.

Karl's phone beeped, just like Scott said it would, alerting him to Mike's exit badge scan. When a tall, dapper blonde stepped into the human river of the Manhattan sidewalk, Karl did a double take. Mike's swagger was almost over the top. He dipped and bobbed between the walkers with a grace of Gene Kelly. His back, ram-rod straight, lent an Englishman's elitist nuance to every move. The only thing missing was a black umbrella swinging in his hand.

"Call center agent?" muttered Karl as picked up his latte and worked his way out of the gated seating area of the coffee shop. He never took his eyes off Mike's figure. He was easy to track. There was only one person in Manhattan wearing a light blue mod-suit highlighted by yellow shoes, socks and handkerchief.

The B train was Mike's likely destination. It only took a few sips of latte for Karl to calculate the odds that Mike probably hailed from Brooklyn. As if he willed it, Mike paused at the crosswalk and when traffic cleared, walked directly toward him. Karl finished his drink, tossed it in the garbage and waited. Not as a snake coiled to strike, but as a father ready to lecture his son's post-curfew arrival.

"Jay isn't safe, but I can help." Karl's tone was casual as he strode alongside Mike, matching his pace, stride by stride.

Mike cast a sideways glance, almost to make

sure he wasn't about to be mugged by a homeless person, but kept his pace.

Karl kept an even tone. "We both have friends who are in trouble. I think we can help get them sorted."

"I think you have the wrong person."

Karl hesitated. His instincts fought his logic. This guy was probably an executive. His impeccable dress reinforced it. If he had waited a few more seconds, a kid would have stepped out wearing a hoodie back at CityTrust and fit his call center agent profile. He cursed himself for acting too quickly. Now he'd have to wait another day for another shift to end.

"Sorry," said Karl and he slowed his pace and moved to the side of the sidewalk to collect his thoughts. He could not take his eyes away from the Englishman in New York. Something was not right.

The back of Mike's neck was bright red under his blonde locks. As if on cue, his foot caught the back of someone shoe in front of him. He shuffled and fought for his balance, arms outstretched, to break his fall.

After muttering an apology, he unbuttoned his jacket and walked, stiffly. The swagger was gone. The doubt in Karl's mind was washed away by the adrenaline in his gut. It definitely was Mike.

His prey seemed to visibly ease the closer he got to his train. Karl boarded the same car and waited until the B train doors closed. It wasn't going to be easy to convince Mike to get Jay's cronies off their tracks, but it certainly would help that Mike would have nowhere to run and would have to hear him out.

Karl slithered through the crowd on the train and gently forced a spot open next to Mike. Without looking up, he whispered, "I'm not going to drop this. We need to help each other."

Mike ignored him, cleared his throat and buttoned his blazer. Eyes forward and unmoving.

"This whole thing has escalated beyond rational. This needs to stop." Karl fought every urge to grab his impeccable jacket and shake reality into him. This was his only chance to talk. After this, Mike was likely to seek protection.

Desperation caused Karl to stumble over his words. "If you don't talk, Jay is dead. Dead. Ignore me and you'll regret this moment. The rest of your life. You have his life in your hands and you act like I'm begging for quarters."

Nothing. Not even a blink. Changing tactics, Karl shrugged, passive and disinterested, and turned to move to the back of the car. It was a last-minute gambit from his hours spent at the poker table. Sometimes fear was enough equity to get someone to fold a good hand; especially when you had nothing but bad cards in your hand and you desperately needed a win.

"Wait." Mike's voice was almost a whisper. "What is it that you want?"

"I want to forget all this happened. Both sides to walk away and call it a draw."

Mike's face went from confused, to shocked and back to confused. "I think that's fair." said Mike. "Will you restore what Jay lost?"

"I can't do it personally but I'll do everything I can to put things right. You have to trust me. Just call off the mob. If I'm dead, I can't help fix this."

"The mob?" asked Mike. Then he paused for a long time, staring at Karl, until understanding washed over his face. *Somehow he thinks the mob is on our side. Makes no sense but if it gets Jay out of this mess, I'm going with it.*

Mike continued, "Ah, yes, well. Like you, I don't have full control of the situation but maybe I can influence it."

CHAPTER 13

"Thanks for agreeing to a walk. I really needed the fresh air," said Jay. Despite the cold, cutting breeze, the pathways of North Central Park were filled with a menagerie of well-dressed, scarf-tucked residents walking their miniature dogs. Joggers wove in and out, music blasting from their ear buds underneath their wool hats. A rag-tag homeless duo pushed and pulled at an overstuffed grocery cart, filled with black plastic bags. Both had multiple layers of worn jackets and oversized boots tied together with old belts and shoelaces.

"I don't like being out in the open anymore. I can't relax," said Jenni.

Jay watched the couple fight against the stuck wheels of their cart across the uneven pathway. They never talked or met eyes. Every tug or shove was met with an assured counter-balance by the other. They had been doing this a long time and it looked like a dance of a long-married couple.

Jenni continued, "Darling, please pick up the

pace. I'm freezing. Ted was pretty clear. We get a few minutes of fresh air and then back inside."

"Come here." Jay pulled Jenni close as they walked. She smiled half-heartedly due to her teeth chattering. Jay was overheating in his wool cap, covered by the hood of his winter jacket. A scarf covered his nose and mouth and dark Ray-Ban sunglasses filled in what last bit of skin might be showing. "Let's get a coffee first and then head back."

"Mmm, coffee sounds wonderful. Nothing against Ted, but I can't drink more than a cup of whatever brand he keeps in that pantry."

"Cop coffee. Serves one purpose. Keeps you awake."

"Ugh. No wonder they are so grouchy."

Jay smiled and nodded at the couple with the grocery cart. "Do you know that homeless couple?"

Jenni returned her gaze to the couple and squinted. "They look familiar, but no. They probably stop by the pantry occasionally, but they look pretty independent. Unlike Louisiana, the homeless here could populate their own city."

"I don't know how you squeeze the time in to volunteer."

"Like my dad said, if it's important to you, you find the time."

"They don't even say thank you."

"Some do, but that's not why I help. Whatever their circumstance, no one seems to care. It's almost as the world has decided that being homeless is the choice of the lazy. Far from lazy, they're doing everything they can to survive."

"Right. Despite this mess I'm in, it's nothing like the days of trying to find the next meal or even a place to sleep. There is no hope. There is only the focus on surviving. One day at a time."

Jenni squeezed Jay's hand. "You had it worse than that. You were only a kid and your caretakers failed your trust."

Jay winced. "It made me stronger."

Jenni paused. She wasn't sure if this was the time to prod a little further, brushing away detritus carefully like an archeologist unearthing a thousand-year-old fossil. In Jay's case, there was something buried deep that even a decade together could not reveal. "There are some people in your life that will never break that trust."

Jay pulled down his scarf to talk. "I keep telling myself that. But it's hard to shake the kid in me who suffered betrayal after betrayal. Believe me, Jenni, I know I don't sound rational at times. How I *feel* doesn't follow logic. Far from it."

Jay stopped to collect some courage and said, "I've never told you this before."

He looked down at the ground and removed his sunglasses. Jenni's eyes never wavered. She would not dare make a movement or sound in fear of breaking Jay's thoughts.

"The last family I lived with, the Flourintales, was the final straw. The mother, Darlene, was great. She helped me with homework. I was so far behind for my age and had a lot of catching up to do. She was a former teacher, so I basically had a live-in tutor.

She would make this amazing spaghetti sauce once a week. It would take her most of a day. I'd sit in the kitchen with my homework and she'd go between me and that sauce she was cooking. I swear the smells bumped my IQ up a few points."

Jay rubbed his cheeks. His eyes darkened.

"Every day, when her husband Jake got home from work, she'd change. Turned into a bundle of nerves and talked in a whisper. She'd never leave my side until Jake was passed out drunk out on the patio or tucked away asleep. I'm talking about a mother goose with her goslings. She'd literally squawk if I wandered out of her sight. She was scared of Jake and I couldn't figure out why.

There must have been a school holiday or something, but I was home while Darlene was grocery shopping. Jake was working. I had the whole house to myself, yet I wanted to be outside. They had a great stream for fishing a few blocks away. I had nothing to my name, but there were fishing rods in the garage so I grabbed one and headed out.

The fishing was great. It was warm and I found a great spot in the shade of the bridge over the creek. A few cars rumbled by, but I didn't think much of it until one crossed, stopped and backed up. It was Jake's car. His shift must have ended early due to the holiday. Jake stared at me from his window for a long time, never said a word, and then drove home."

Jay's blue eyes were swimming in a mix of shame and anger. His lip quivered.

"A few minutes later, he stood over me on the bank of the creek. I never heard him approach. He asked me if I had friends with me and I did not. Apparently, there was a better place to fish, just under the bridge and he led me there. I never said a word while he gave me a speech about how much I owed him and Darlene. I was using his fishing rod. Food was expensive and he could have rented out my room instead. The foster care subsidy never covered the costs of taking care of me.

He said there was a way that I could make things right. Jake said I had to close out the tab. That's what he called it. Closing out the tab."

Jay's voice turned to a whisper.

"Right there under the bridge. He made me do things. I was old enough to know it was wrong, but too young to know what to do about it.

Darlene tried to protect me, but all along she *knew*. In so many ways, she hurt me more than Jake did. I don't expect you to understand, but you need to know something got cut out from inside me that day. Jake took something that I never got back. I'm broken and part of me can't be fixed."

Jenni curled her hand around Jay's arm and leaned her head on his shoulder. When the time was right, she'd have something to say but she knew there was no better salve right now than silence. They sat at the park bench and watched their breath form clouds in the cold air.

The homeless couple with the cart negotiated up two risers of concrete steps and returned to their slow progression across the park. A policeman strode into view. After a verbal check-in on his shoulder speaker-mic, the policeman talked and motioned to the homeless couple to return the way they came. Jay and Jenni couldn't hear the conversation, but it was clear the couple did not want to turn around.

"Let's get out of here," said Jay.

"I had a bad feeling about coming to the park. We should never have left the apartment," replied Jenni as she turned to go back the way they came. "Let's skip the coffee. My heart can't take this."

Their abrupt turn nearly knocked over the policewoman that was behind them.

"Oh, pardon me," said Jenni in her most pleasant voice. Jay returned the sunglasses to his face.

The policewoman looked at the couple with interest. While interracial couples weren't unusual anymore, they still caught glances everywhere they went. It was unnerving at first, but they grew used to the stares. Jenni used to joke, "They're trying to figure out who asked who out first."

"Is something wrong?" asked the policewoman. Her cold blue eyes never wavered from Jay's.

"There appears to be a little incident brewing over there with those...poor folk. Best leave them be," replied Jenni. Jay was amazed at Jenni's calm. His own heart was pounding through his rib cage.

"Sir, can you remove your scarf?"

"Why?"

"Please remove your scarf."

Jay went numb. He willed his brain to concoct a viable excuse and the best he got was to not convey any nervousness or unease. The chances that this policewoman would have seen Jay's mug shot was pretty low, despite Ted's warnings. Stirring up any concerns might cause the officer to pause.

He pulled his scarf down. "What's the problem?"

Her pupils dilated, but she kept her composure and casually moved her hands to her waist. He was found and it was too soon. Ted said that their story had to be solid before approaching the police. Police custody meant that the mob would know where he is. *The police are fixed.* Ted beat it into his brain. *You are not ready for the police.*

"I'm going to have to ask both of you to drop to your knees and put your hands to your head." She called out on her speaker-mic and turned to look for her partner. "10-10P, North Central Park."

Left with a fraction of a second, Jay bolted, pulling Jenni behind. They cut through the thick brush along the path and scrambled down a small hill for another cluster of cover. The officer's shout a second later, gave Jay the confidence they had few seconds of cover before splitting up.

"Get back to Ted, but not until you know you're in the clear. They aren't looking for you. I've got to disappear and quickly," whispered Jay to Jenni.

"Where will you go?"

"No idea. I'll figure it out as I go." Jay pulled his hat, jacket and scarf off. Anything to disrupt the officer's fresh mental picture of Jay.

Jenni spun in circles, looking in every direction and stopped. "This might sound crazy."

"I'm listening."

"I know a few guys that live close by. They come to the pantry sometimes. One is a Vietnam vet."

"They'll take me in?"

"They live in the sewer."

"Oh. That's strangely frightening and brilliant at the same time. Get out of here."

Jay bolted.

"I love you, Jay!"

Jay couldn't hear anything over the blood pounding in his eardrums. His footfalls fell in loud smacks on the wet pathway as he raced for the closest manhole cover. Up ahead, a loud "whoop-whoop" of a warning siren preceded two police cars screeching to a halt, blocking the main gateway out of the park.

Jay spun on his heels and scanned the area. The conservatory blocked most of his exits. A small crowd lingered around Lasker rink. Hoping that Jenni had not gone that way, he stepped off the path into the brush and thin trees and ran amongst the shadows. The safety of the darkness of Huddlestone Arch in the distance beckoned at him from across the quiet park street.

Inside the arch, Jay put his hands on his knees and caught his breath. Like a workhorse in the winter, the plumes of his breath shot out in a forceful blasts. Behind him, he could see four police officers walking around Lasker rink, calmly scanning the crowds for his face.

In the other direction, the forest pathway was still dark along the Loch, a babbling creek. Two more police cars screeched to a halt, this time in front of Huddlestone. Jay shrank into the shadows. It was hard to discern if it was to isolate everyone in Lasker rink, or to prevent him from entering the woods of North Central Park. He wasn't going to wait to find out and slipped away.

The woods were eerily quiet, with the exception of his panting and rustle of his clothes. He ran along the creek in a steady pace. The area was familiar to him and that was to his advantage. Ahead would be a small pond and a pathway along it leading to the potential safety of the 103rd metro stop.

The open road between him and the pond slowly came into view. A police car crept slowly by; the officer's head craning out of the open window to scan the woods. Jay flattened to the ground and held his breath. The car stopped at Glen Span arch as if Jay would just stroll casually into view. He waited and willed the police car to move on.

Behind him, voices shouted. Branches snapped and a dog barked excitedly. Several more dogs joined in, almost shrieking with anticipation. They were hot on his scent and he had little time.

Taking a gamble, Jay bolted in a crouch, across the street behind the police car. He heard an officer shout, "Hey!" The dread of being discovered only lasted a second as adrenaline kicked in.

There was no place to hide. Between the dogs and being outnumbered, he had to avoid being surrounded in the park. He lengthened his stride and willed his body to breathe deep, taking in all the oxygen he could muster.

The quiet forest devolved into the loud chaos of barks and shouts. The New York city rumble and honks grew louder as he raced to the city street of Central Park West. He thanked his luck when he found that no police cars were waiting for him.

The buildings across the street would be a trap. The dogs would eventually follow his scent if he returned into the park woods. Down the sidewalk, a manhole cover gleamed in the newly rising sun. The sewer. His scent would be lost quickly in the morass of New York's waste.

Jay flipped the lid to a nearby garbage can and looked inside. Filled with food wrappers, coffee cups and bottles; he had nothing to create a disturbance. With a grunt, he tilted the entire can on its side and rolled it down the pedestrian crossing into traffic. Loud honks and shouts were his signal that there was sufficient distraction before returning to the manhole.

He yanked the manhole cover open, descended into the darkness and slid back the lid hiding him from the world above. The stink in the darkness never felt so welcoming. He was safe.

He tried to quiet the mantra repeating like an earworm. *Escape. Run. Hide.*

CHAPTER 14

"**G**ot something!" shouted Bushy-beard as he flipped some data up to the large monitor for everyone to see. "While Jay's cell phone account was erased, all tower queries are still logged and I was able to pull a filter of the cell phone's IMEI."

Hofstra was exasperated. It had been an uneventful and boring day of technical outbursts with immediate setbacks in the virtual hunt for Jay. Her hair was down, pumps off and jacket tossed askew. She didn't even put down her ice-coffee. In a tired tone, she muttered, "English please."

Tyler was already standing over Bushy-beard, taking in the data on the huge monitor. He spoke in a rushed tone, "An IMEI is a cell phone's serial number. Not all records of Jay calls were deleted. Our blessed basement-dwellers are stitching together some logs which will give us a recreation of Jay's last calls and movement. Its not perfect, but it's the best thing they've been able to dig up all day."

Rage-hat giggled. "Oh, yes, this is the best." The printer in the back of the room came to life, loud fan and rollers spitting out paper. He pointed. "Have at it, secret agent people."

Hofstra scanned the colorful printouts. The last burst of activity on the long list was filled with text messages and calls to one single number. She asked, "Who owns this number? The one receiving all of Jay's messages?"

Bushy-beard replied, "Last page."

"Michael T?" she asked. "Can you give us a surname?"

"That's it."

"T?"

"Are you sure?"

Rage-hat put his face in his hands and answered, "We only print things that we're sure of. If a tree is going to die for us, it better be for good reason."

Hofstra smirked. She was starting to find their quirks endearing. The good news softened her mood.

Tyler fidgeted as if he were in line to enter a bouncy house. "Let's hit the street. Unlike this Jay guy, Mr. T has loads of information at our fingertips." He held up a printout. "If his credit card is any clue, Mr. T has moved from gold-chains and tank tops to haute-couture. Hugo Boss is his best friend and he visits him frequently."

Hofstra practically cooed. "A man with good taste? Can't wait to meet him." She pulled on her jacket and shuffled on her pumps with practiced ease. "Well done gentlemen. We'll be in touch."

The basement-dwellers never stopped typing. "Oh, we're not done. Whoever did this to Mr. Jay Wilson failed to cover all of their tracks. There are more clues out there and we're not done looking."

A gleeful chorus of boyish cackles followed Hofstra and Tyler's exit to the elevators.

Scott couldn't put his finger on what was odd about the note he was reading. Last night, he assumed it was for Karl. It had been slipped under the door. Scott noticed it when he got home last night and tossed it in with the rest of the mail piled on the kitchen counter. His name, written in the careful script of someone from his grandparents's era, caught his eye. It was the first clue that something wasn't right.

The message inside was straightforward. A courier had a package for him and missed a chance for delivery. The courier would be returning tomorrow and asked him to be available between five and seven o'clock. There was no letterhead of the courier's business name. No number to call. Just two sentences. The note was signed, "Johnny."

The stationery was unique in its thickness and quality. There were imperfections, like threads in linen, that lent an air of sophistication. This was one high-end courier.

Scott bandied about in his mind what could possibly be on delivery. He had ordered nothing recently. He was always careful to do cash-on-delivery because anything purchased with credit or bank transactions was traceable. He was paranoid for the very reason he was able to easily get so much information on everyone else.

Unfortunately, some of his compatriots online were just as careful as him. It was not unusual to have couriers deliver dedicated ASIC hardware for brute-force cracking of passwords or video cards retrofitted to power the incredible processing requirements of solving decryption keys. All couriers, however, left a note with the building manager in the lobby.

None made it to his front door.

This package was exhilarating in its mystery but also frightening in its secrecy. His brain was overclocked, working every little thing he had done recently that could result in this special delivery.

CHAPTER 15

Rotting rocks. Jay couldn't explain the smell any better than that. It wasn't overwhelming, nor was it particularly onerous. It just hung, thick in the air, and grabbed at your lungs and stomach in dull punches.

The walls were beautifully lain brickwork, encircling him in a perfect radius as far as his eyes could see; an oversized pipe of exquisite masonry. It was hard to envision men constructing this beauty so far underground and how little those above knew of the scenes below.

Jay had been walking for hours. The dim light from holes in manhole covers and sewer downspouts lit his way. He thanked his luck that it was still light outside, but he didn't have long to find an escape. Once the sunset arrived, he would be trapped in the darkness. Jenni said there would be homeless living down here, but he didn't spot one hint of inhabitants and was running into dead ends.

He would be under suspicion arising from a

manhole on a busy street so close to where he disappeared. He told himself, just a few miles further. It was better safe than sorry. He slogged along, splashing in the ankle-high frigid water, with no feeling in his feet. The only dry piece of clothing on him was his scarf, which he wrapped around his head to retain the only remaining warmth he had.

Jenni's voice, childlike, rang out behind him. "Fried chicken tonight! I came out as soon as I could."

With a loud splash, Jay spun on his feet. The sewer was empty. He remembered that voice from when Jenni visited him behind her house. Not quite in full womanhood, her voice was high-pitched and unpracticed. They were both sixteen.

Of course, she's not down here. I'm hearing things. He continued his slog, one foot in front of the other and embraced the exhaustion. He wanted to hear more of Jenni's voice and let the scene unfold in his memory.

Jenni fed him in secret, almost every night, the summer he ran away from Darlene and Jake. He sat behind the detached garage of Jenni's home, tucked in an opening of their wood pile. Being the teenagers they were, they had cleverly restacked the logs in a way that Jay could hide inside just like their childhood game of building forts from furniture and quilts. These days, the floors were not lava but a safe respite for an underaged runaway. Jenni provided everything he needed; bedding, a flashlight and, most importantly, food. When her parents were out, she'd sneak him inside for a much-needed shower.

Jay heard his own voice reply to Jenni, "My favorite. I smelled it a couple hours ago and it has been driving me crazy!"

Jenni frowned, "Sorry. I have to be careful."

"Don't be sorry at all. I really don't deserve this."

"Are you kidding me? This has been the best summer ever!"

"Uh, well."

"No, no," Jenni held up her hands. All summer, she'd been working hard to help Jay forget his last foster family. "I didn't mean it like that. But you have to admit; me, you and Mike are making the best of it. I still crack up in bed thinking about when we broke into Hallorans!"

"We're lucky we never got caught. You should never have come with us, but I have to say, I love my new wardrobe." Jay pointed at a neatly stacked set of bright clothes resting on top of a cardboard box. "Someday, I'll have a decent job to actually buy these clothes."

"Mike would love to help you get that arranged."

"A job?"

"No, buy more clothes!"

"He's so stylish. I envy him. It's so clear what he's going to do with his life. Designing suits, maybe?"

"Primping models before getting on the catwalk?"

Mike's voice made Jay and Jenni jump. "More like a perfume salesman at Belk's." He slipped into their hideaway, laid out his school backpack on the floor and sat on it neatly.

Jenni laughed and put her hand on Mike's arm. "I seriously doubt that. I've seen your designs. Those sketches are brilliant. You promised me that one dress, remember?"

"You'll be the first to wear it. I haven't forgotten."

Jenni and Mike continued their banter while Jay devoured his dinner. Mike asked, "Jay, you remember when we first met?"

A greasy thumbs up was acknowledgement.

"Well, I might need your help again."

Jenni's curiosity was piqued. "With what? Can I help?"

"Too risky for you. There's a fabric store down on Palisade Street over by Hallorans. I need as many scraps as you can get. You're looking at the new costume designer for the senior play!"

"Get out!"

"Yeah. Just don't tell anyone. I only agreed to Mrs. Broussard's repeated requests for help if she'd keep things anonymous. My dad would kill me if he found out."

"What does this have to do with Jay?"

Mike cracked a broad smile. "Jay lived in the fabric store last summer."

"No way." Jenni turned to Jay. "You are full of

surprises."

Jay wiped his greasy fingers with a napkin. "It's a pretty funny story. There was a pizza shop next door. They would sell me a leftover pizza that was never picked up by a customer for a buck. I'd check in every once in a while and would get lucky. The manager there was so kind. A whole pizza would carry me for days.

There was a picnic table out behind the strip mall. I guess it was for employees to eat lunch. If there was extra pizza that day, I'd bring that pie around back and enjoy a bit of my good luck and carefully pack up the rest for later. After eating there a few times, I noticed a pattern at the fabric store next door.

First, they never locked the back door during the day. There was always a wedge holding the door open. I came back at night and it was still propped open. It was only after the night cleaning crew finished did they kick the wedge out and let the back door lock. Like clockwork, the crew finished at eleven p.m."

Mike chortled. "I worked at Halloran's a few shops down. Saw the same thing but from a different vantage point. We had two sixteen-year-olds casing a fabric store at the same time!"

Jay continued, "Our motives were different, but the target the same. After a while, I'd just wait until it was real dark and slip in the back of the store around ten thirty. There were a few good spots to hide until the cleaning crew left. Then I had the store to myself. There was a shower and a kitchen-ette. I had everything I needed. I had to make sure to leave by six in the morning before people came to open the store. It was a good arrangement. I just wasn't expecting to see Mike."

Mike took the cue and continued, "I'd slip in after I finished my shift at Halloran's at nine. I'd have to wait a couple hours, so I just took a nap in the same hiding spot every time. Once the coast was clear, I'd go to the fabric aisle, check out bolts of new arrivals and cut what I needed for my projects. There was no one to catch me shopping at a fabric store and tell my parents. Tongues wag in our town, you know, if anything seems out of the conservative worldview of what boys or girls should be doing."

In the excitement of telling the story, Jay interjected, "He was sleeping in one of my hiding spots. Remember, there were still people cleaning the store when we snuck in. There was a huge box that held foam corners for packing. I lifted the lid and jumped in."

"You stepped on my face!"

"As soon as I felt your hands grab my leg, I ab-solutely freaked. Here we were, screaming of fright, wrestling each other in a giant box filled with foam corners."

"I thought you were a store manager or the police."

"So did I!"

"Jay put me in an armbar and covered my mouth. I still kept screaming through his fingers, but I don't know, maybe all that foam was a bit of a sound barrier. None of the cleaning crew ever heard us. I figure they were vacuuming or polishing the floors with some loud equipment."

"I whispered in Mike's ear that I wasn't stealing anything and promised to leave right away. It was all a misunderstanding. Mike pulled my hand off his face slowly and said the same thing. We kicked the box open and let the light in. Picture a well-dressed kid, still wearing his Halloran's name tag in a tangle with someone who resembled Pig-Pen from *Peanuts*."

We sat there, silent. Between the adrenaline and fear, my brain was frozen. Mike broke the silence."

"Yeah, I asked if Jay was waiting for the new Lucienne Day pattern reissue. Classic, iconic designs. Been waiting for months."

Jay snorted. "After a while, I knew we'd be friends. When I saw that you left money behind, it stuck with me."

"Money wasn't the issue. My dad was the issue. And you, Jay, didn't steal a thing. Enjoyed a hot shower and even cleaned up after yourself in the kitchen. That's when I told you about the pantry. Had I told you about Jenni, maybe you would have shown up sooner."

Jay playfully punched Mike's leg. "Your biggest mistake, Mike, was not mentioning Jenni."

In the darkness of the sewer, Jay tripped. He held out his hands to break his fall in the shallow water of the sewer and jarred himself awake from his daydream. The cold water cut away at his sanity, biting in numb waves at his arms, legs and core.

◆ ◆ ◆

"We can't talk out here," said Mike. He looked over his shoulder and scanned the crowd, pausing and squinting for effect. Mike and Karl had left the B train and were waiting to jump to another connection. Mike was doing everything he could to buy time. He was enjoying the theatrics and Karl was buying every bit of it. "Pigs are everywhere and are hard to shake."

Karl nodded and wiped sweat from his forehead. "Lead the way."

They had been walking for some time. When Karl approached Mike outside CityTrust asking him to have Jay call off the mob, it took several minutes to gather his wits.

Mike needed more time to think and jumping between trains to shake his imaginary followers was going to give him plenty of time to try to piece together the increasingly overwhelming puzzle.

As promised, Jay disappeared. Mike tried reaching out to Jenni to no avail. When dialing Jay's number, he didn't even get a single ring. He knew the service was disconnected but wanted to keep trying anyway in the odd chance he'd answer.

When he least expected it, this guy shows up and tells him that Jay's life is on the line. He was so young he probably couldn't rent a car. It met no line of logic.

Like changing channels and unsure of what he wanted to watch, Mike flipped from thought to thought looking for inspiration; a thread of an idea. He recalled seeing Jay's victimizer at Running-a-Ground and the picture in his mind snapped into focus.

This guy was the one who helped the fat kid to his feet and escape. He was sure of it. Mike pondered and pulled at the thread. Perhaps this was the same person who shattered the store front glass. Mike tugged more. Why do something so brash and attention getting?

The threads came together into a neat pattern.

This guy likely saw him and Jay snapping pictures and acted without thinking. These two kids were not only in cahoots but were protecting each other. Suspicion and fear mixed with panicked adrenaline as Mike returned his gaze to his follower. Was this sidewalk solicitation just another step in not only destroying Jay, but himself as well?

One fact was immutable. This guy was connected in a personal way to the coffee shop kid who ruined Jay's life. The challenge was to find a way to turn the tables to Jay's favor.

Karl followed several feet behind. His hands were tucked into his pockets and his eyes downcast.

As they switched trains, Mike mulled over his options. He could lead his follower right to the police, but he would likely run as soon as he wised up to the eventual destination.

It served no purpose to lead his follower to his own apartment. At some point, his facade was going to be revealed. Plus, the less Karl knew of Mike, the safer he was.

The voice of the train operator announced the next stop in a bored tone. It was Jay's stop. There was no sense leading his follower to Jay's apartment as the place was likely surveilled by the police due to his bogus rap sheet.

The creases of deep thought fell from Mike's forehead. Jay's apartment was perfect. His follower likely had no idea that it would lead directly to the police. If his follower would confess, the police would drop their pursuit of Jay and turn from foes to friends.

Mike nodded curtly to Karl across the train car. Karl nodded back somberly and understood. They would step off at the next stop.

Hofstra was on the phone with the basement dwellers as Tyler drove. The start-stop traffic of Manhattan tied knots deep into his neck. Every time they got close to Mr T's signal, he would dart in a different direction.

"He's definitely trying to shake us," said Hofstra. "Rage-hat says he's jumping trains, but based on his speed right now, he's in the station and hasn't boarded another train."

Tyler spoke through gritted teeth. "Amazing that he doesn't realize how easy it is to follow someone with their cellphone on and how maddening we can't keep up through this traffic."

Hofstra patted his leg. "We don't have to nab him right this second. We'll trap him once we know where he's is trying to go. Patience improves our chances."

"Right."

"Is this your first pursuit?"

"Sort of."

"Sort of?"

"I interned with the IRS."

Hofstra laughed loudly and punched him in the arm. "Did you chase down an overweight CEO?"

Tyler smiled. "As a matter of fact, yes. Last year, I was working out when I got a call that someone we'd been looking for was spotted in my neighborhood. I ran into the locker room, snapped my duty belt around my sweatpants and literally walked across the street."

"You're making this up."

"I wish," continued Tyler laughing. "He was eating at a small cafe. I'll never forget the look on his face. He never took the fork from his lips when I walked up; a tall, black man in sweat pants and hooded t-shirt with FBI issue around my waist. I flipped my credentials and he looked at me full of skepticism. It ticked me off and I got more forceful with my tone."

Hofstra winced. "You are kind of a baby-face. I mean that in a nice way."

"Right," said Tyler. "I think it had more to do with my unbelievably awesome tan. Anyway, the guy had the nuts to shout, 'I'm being robbed!' and bolted from the restaurant. I couldn't believe he did that. After processing the fact that he was running away, I turned to go after him. What do you think the patrons did?"

"Oh my god. They swarmed you?"

"You bet. Not only did two men try to get me to the ground, a lady who I swear was Betty White, kept hitting me with her purse. She must have kept shop tools in there. It hurt!"

Hofstra shook her head half in amusement and embarrassment. "I hope you eventually nabbed him?"

"Oh yeah, I managed to break free and made chase. Imagine me running after a three hundred pound, impeccably dressed man in my sweats. Even worse, I had two men chasing me chasing *him*."

"I'm so sorry."

Tyler turned to Hofstra. "How so?"

"To have to deal with that … default perception."

"Sadly, I deal with it every day. It can be a bit exhausting to have to constantly prove that I'm not the stereotype that sits in people's minds. That particular day, however, I learned another lesson."

"What's that?"

"Black men are much better off wearing a uniform."

Hofstra chuckled. Tyler had a way about him that was disarming.

Her phone rang. "Yeah?"

Her face brightened. "You guys rock. Good work. I'll let you know how it goes down. Could you alert ICE for me?"

Tyler raised an querulous eyebrow. Hofstra put her phone back in her jacket. "Mr. T is headed to Jay's apartment."

"That makes no sense. It's sloppy. If we don't think Jay's really Paraguayan mob, why call in ICE?"

"We need the manpower and we can't sequester and question Mike on the basis of speculation. The original order to deport Jay is still in effect and this will give us the opportunity to ask questions first and apologize later."

"That's a heck of a way to do a grab and go. I'm not sure ICE will appreciate being used."

"Who cares? I want to talk to this guy." Hofstra flipped the visor in the car and checked her hair and straightened her blouse. She caught Tyler watching.

"Mr T shops Hugo Boss," said Hofstra as she reapplied her lipstick. "Never know. He could be the one."

It was Tyler's turn to laugh.

The charcoal sketch of Scott would have been

a carnival-drawn caricature if the paper size had been bigger.

"What creative muse possessed you to draw that cartoon?" asked Ted. The Buick's twenty-year-old shocks rocked the two gentlemen in lazy bobs on the highway as they talked.

"Ha," said Elmer in a dry rattle. "Indeed, I asked Jay twice about every feature and he swears this is the guy from the coffee shop. I had some fun drawing this one up. Could have been a Disney character."

"Well, he couldn't be any different than the guy I chased from Jay's apartment. I need you to draw that one up. We've got two people tangled up in this. Neither of them look or act like made men. I'm sure Johnny was looking for this guy last night at the apartment building." Ted tapped the drawing of Scott.

"We need to find this kid before Johnny does. This unique face will work to our benefit. He's going to be memorable to anyone we question."

"Yes," chortled Elmer shaking his head, "it's better than starting a sketch with 'He was a large black man!' I never get much more to work with beyond that, no matter how much I try."

"Let me guess. Black kinky hair. Muscular. Lots of gold. The best one was when that one lady said, 'He looks like you, sir.'"

Elmer shook his head. "When we finally nabbed that guy, he wasn't even close to looking like me. She should have said he looked like Sammy

Davis Jr. and we would have had better luck."

"Indeed."

Elmer folded the sketch and inserted it in the front pocket of his shirt. "So, are we casing the apartment building?"

"No time. We need to be more efficient."

"Ah. I suppose we have no risk of losing our jobs now. We can finally break the rules. I was tired of bending them."

Ted smiled. "The brass would never have dared to even threaten to fire us. Captain Feeley's career rode on our success."

"Good times."

"Yes. All my body parts worked."

"I could drink five cups of coffee," retorted Elmer, "before even thinking of the restroom."

"My joints didn't creak."

"We could have a shootout and still have enough buzz to enjoy the night life," said Elmer. "Nowadays, I'd have to nap after a briefing."

Ted nodded at the concrete apartment building as he pulled the oversized Buick to the side of the road. "This is it. Johnny was there."

Elmer blew out a breath. "So how efficient are we going to be? Sneak inside and question the residents? Threaten the landlord? Kick down doors?"

Ted deadpanned, "Yes."

"Then let's get to it." Elmer let out a couple grunts as he scooted out of the Buick. The sidewalk was empty with the exception of pigeons crowding spilled garbage around a waste bin. Out of years of habit, they took their time to take in the surroundings with a few seconds of silence.

The front door to the apartment building was locked and no one was in the lobby. Without speaking, the two men leaned against the wall by the door and continued their banter in a low voice.

"Three minutes," said Elmer.

"Five minutes, no more."

"The wager?"

"A six pack."

"I sense your confidence waning, Ted. A full case."

"You and I must not be living off the same pension."

"Nah. I just don't lose."

A young couple laughing and holding hands burst through the door from inside. They didn't give the old men notice.

Elmer smiled as looked up from his watch. Ted caught the door and they slipped in. "I win. None of that cheap beer either."

The lobby smelled of week-old ammonia. A door next to the mailboxes read "Property Management".

"I'll get the expensive craft beer stuff everyone is crazy about if you don't flub your lines here."

Elmer smacked his lips loudly. "Then let's get it done." He tapped his watch. "Nap time is in thirty minutes."

The property management offices looked to be a former storage closet. Half the room was filled by a desk covered with stacks of paper. The dusty odor of carbon called their senses to a stack of curling, old white, blue and pink triplicate paper. A laptop rested precariously on a riser of manila folders. Barely visible behind the desk was a kid barely out of college.

Elmer stood with his feet apart, hands joined behind his back at military attention. Ted chewed casually on a toothpick and stared in silence.

The kid tapped frantically on his computer. He hit the delete button once for every two keys he punched in. "Erm. Sorry. My boss tells me I always have to submit this form before answering questions with the police. It'll only take a second."

The toothpick rolled easily from one side of Ted's mouth to the other as if someone were rowing inside.

Elmer turned to leave. "Sir, I'll alert the precinct that we're getting a stall."

Ted nodded slowly. He held his stare on the frightened kid behind the desk.

"No. Please." The kid held up his hand. "This computer isn't working quite right. I'll fill out the form later."

Elmer stopped in the doorway, his back to the office. He kept a watchful eye out as residents milled in and out of the front entrance. He assured the kid with a curt nod, "Good choice. Ted doesn't give much sympathy to folks who don't cooperate.

I hate driving people to the hospital. Traffic is bad enough without an emergency to deal with."

Eyes wide, the kid snapped his laptop shut. "You know what? What do you want to know? I bet my boss never reads those forms anyway." He rose from his chair and knocked a pile of papers onto Ted's feet.

The kid's eyes widened and he stopped breathing.

Now that Ted had the kid's full attention, he pulled the sketch from his blazer pocket and held it out. "This man is a resident here. I need his name and apartment number."

The kid didn't hesitate. "I don't know his name, but I think he's a freeloader. He's living with Karl Gil on floor fourteen."

"Freeloader?"

"Mr. Gil has a one-bedroom apartment and I'm pretty certain they aren't lovers."

The river of humanity was flowing unusually heavy in front of Jay's apartment. The slow pace helped Mike's nerves. His brilliant plan was coming apart quicker than he could muster up another escape route. The goal was to walk Karl into the hands of police surveilling Jay's apartment. He was certain someone was waiting inside. It was likely a bored rookie cop catching up on the news with his smartphone. They had no idea the gift Mike was going to deliver.

First things first. The lobby door to Jay's apartment. He didn't know how to get in. How was he going to weasel around that?

"If I may ask, where are we going?" Karl was walking directly behind Mike.

Mike's harsh shake of his head ended the conversation. He was focused on the sidewalk traffic. He begged silently for someone in front of him to turn for Jay's apartment up ahead. It was going to come down to timing and unbelievable luck. He took no notice of the fact that the street was full of unmarked SUVs with obscured, black windows.

The SUVs screeched into the intersection in front of them and stopped traffic. A litany of honks preceded the doors of the SUVs opening in unison. Men and women, wearing blue with "ICE" in large, white letters on their back, shuffled out of the vehicles.

Tyler pulled his car in behind the SUVs. "The ICE are fast. We had a head start and they beat us."

"Ever since immigration control became part of Homeland Security, their funding has been beyond ridiculous."

She shoved the door open. "Let's go."

Mike quickened his pace and never heard the ruckus in the intersection. He was certain the pizza guy walking with his bike, outfitted with a pizza warmer, was making a delivery to Jay's building. Perfect luck.

"Up ahead. The next building. Stay with me,"

said Mike. If the pizza guy got too far ahead, everything would fall apart.

Karl stopped. His face was ashen, eyes agog. The sidewalk traffic had stopped as well.

A loud voice commanded, "Homeland security! Hands in the air!"

"What's wrong?" asked Mike. He turned and shook Karl's shoulders in a panic. They had to get moving or his plan was going to come completely apart.

"I said, hands in the air!" The air rushed out of Mike's chest from the impact of being tackled. He was pulled to his knees after his hands were quickly cuffed. His vision was clouded with purple stars and fog. It took a few shakes of his head to regain his bearings and comprehend what had hit him. Agents surrounded him. Their dour expressions did not bode well.

A drop-dead gorgeous redhead stepped into his view wearing an impeccable blouse, skirt and jacket ensemble. It was as if Moses parted the red sea.

"Sorry about the suit," said Hofstra as she scanned his outfit and the tears at his knees.

"It's okay. It was my everyday James Brown. It was time to move on. Very much last year," replied Mike. He continued after a dramatic pause, "I can't but notice that the Herrera fits you well."

"Oh," blushed Hofstra. She unconsciously tugged at her jacket as she collected herself. "Thank you, Mr. T. It has been a long day and she's holding up well."

"Indeed," Mike cocked a confident eyebrow. "Call me Mike."

"Kat."

Clearly uncomfortable with the banter, the ICE agent tugged at Mike and said, "We'll have these two ready for questioning at HQ."

Tyler could not hide his smile as he turned to Hofstra. "Somehow, I get the feeling that if I let you drive, we'll beat ICE this time?"

There was clearly something strange going on in 14B. The well-worn carpet did nothing to quiet the squeaks as Ted and Elmer shifted their weight outside the door, but it didn't matter as the voice inside was at a fever pitch. The thick door muffled the voices.

Ted motioned to Elmer to finish his coffee. With a dramatic swig, Elmer emptied his styrofoam cup and handed it to Ted without a word. In a practiced motion, Ted put the cup to his ear and leaned against the door to free both of his hands. He pulled his notebook from his jacket, untucked the pencil from the spiral-bound wire and flipped to a blank page.

Elmer watched Ted's scribbles. After decades of working together, they had an unspoken code. CFBN, "Call For Backup Now". 3PWG, "Three Perps With Guns", or IHBP, "I'm Hungry, Butterfingers

Please".

The cup sticking from Ted's ear would have looked ridiculous if his forehead wasn't so crumpled and knotted up in concentration. Elmer could make out some of the conversation. It was one-sided. Most likely a phone call.

"I don't understand," said Scott. "You're being held where? US Immigration and Customs Enforcement? On what charge?"

Ted wrote in his notebook. "ICE. Downtown. Friend? or family?"

Scott's voice continued, "Dude. Don't call your parents. I can fix this. I don't care if they say they're only questioning you to find out about someone else. They will do anything to trick you. Give me any information that you can. Do you know the name of the highest-ranking person you've seen so far?"

Ted crossed out "family" in his notebook and underlined "friend".

"Well, I need something to work from. FBI? Holy crap. Her name is cat? Is that with a C or a K? Never mind. Close enough. Find out who they are looking for. It makes no sense they'd grab you. Give me an hour to hack something up. Thinking of kicking me out now? You need my help."

The scribbling continued. "KAT from FBI also involved."

Elmer raised his eyebrows in surprise. He mouthed, "FBI?" Ted nodded.

"Oh, one other thing, please tell me you

ordered a package. I'm getting creeped out. It looks like a private delivery service." Scott paused to let his friend speak. "You're not expecting a courier package at all? Something fishy is going on. The delivery notice was super unofficial, but high class. He's coming early evening tomorrow." Another pause. "You tried to settle with the mob? Jay's friend? You were with him? Karl, what have you done? Don't you understand now? This is why ICE is involved."

It was Ted's turn to look surprised. He wrote, "MOB. Roommate tried to deal." He scratched a big arrow pointing at "friend" and wrote "KARL". Elmer followed Ted's scribbles with rapt attention.

Scott continued with a high-pitched squeal, "I had this under control and now you had to mess it up! Never mind. Like I said. Give me an hour." The call ended with a loud slam of the cell phone on the countertop.

Ted pulled his head away from the door and let the cup fall for Elmer to catch. He pointed to the elevator as he put away his notepad. It was time to go and think this through. There were so many threads, tangled full of misdirection and shortcuts. If there was one thing Ted wished he had told his younger self in the force, it was that patience painted a far clearer picture before action. He needed some time to put things into neat logical boxes. There was much here to ponder and he had to get it right the first time.

CHAPTER 16

J ay was frozen. His thoughts were a numb, jumble of molasses. He didn't think to mark his path in case he needed to backtrack. His clothes were not only wet, but frozen stiff against his skin. The sewer tunnel, thankfully, presented a shelf wide enough to walk safely above the low babble of water, but the tunnel ended at an impassable grate. He could go no further and he had a maze of tunnels behind him.

A dead end.

Again.

With hands shaking uncontrollably, Jay struggled to climb onto the dry shelf to collect himself. He couldn't lift his legs onto the ledge, so he buckled over at his stomach and shifted his weight back and forth like a freshly unearthed worm struggling to burrow.

The dead ends were agonizing, like seconds ticking off on a dreaded countdown. Nothing coherent could form in his mind. A haze of colors, emotion and sounds washed across his thoughts in broad brushes. He laid on the concrete shelf shivering. With hands no more useful than clubs, he pulled off his wet jacket and sloughed off his wet shoes and socks. The cold air bit, mercilessly, at Jay's extremities.

"Nuh nuh nuh," mumbled Jay as he clawed at his clothes. In the dark corner of the shelf, by the grate, Jay spotted a pile of branches and garbage. He pulled himself, inch by inch, into the rabble. His instincts willed him to find a hole and cover himself.

Death would be a gift to his agony of spirit and body. In the cloud of his vision, he saw Jenni standing next to the grate wearing a summer dress. This time she wasn't sixteen. It was the summer after high school graduation. She had bloomed into a stunning young woman that turned many heads like a diamond glittering against black felt.

She stood, hands on her hips, almost as if ready to lecture him on his latest failure. Regardless, deep in his chest, he felt warmth. "Jenni."

She leaned forward and wagged her finger. "Darling, you done it again. Buying the cart before thinking about a horse. No matter, this is not the time."

Her back straightened and she looked down on him, eyes soft and understanding.

"You hear me? This is not the time, Jay Wilson!"

Jay's mind snapped to the warm, sticky heat of Louisiana. He willfully let his mind wander into the deep recesses of his memories.

Despite the oppressive heat, Jay's neck and face burned with embarrassment. He was there to apologize to Jenni.

"It was a little white lie that got out of control."

Jenni looked back at her house to see if her parents were watching. She opened the front gate to her yard and motioned for Jay to walk around back. Jay was eighteen and no longer under the grip of state rules for minors and juveniles. He was his own man now and walked unhidden.

They sat overlooking a small Elizabethan garden. An ancient, manicured southern live oak hung over their gazebo, branches stately and protective. The fragrance of gardenia was sweet and refreshing.

Jenni's arms were crossed and her face passive. She was hiding the anger the way southerners were taught; maintain appearances and reputation.

In a soft tone, Jay spoke. "I did it for you. When you told me you were accepted to Tulane, I got desperate. You're going to graduate from one of the top law schools here. I can't go scamper off and lose a semester or two getting a GED."

He rubbed his face slowly and selected his words carefully. "I only said I had a high school degree in my application so I could get in. I was going to finish my GED while at Loyola. By the time my freshman year was over, I'd be golden. I had no idea they'd double check every little fact."

"Our relationship is not a competition, Jay."

214

Jenni stared out at the garden as she spoke. "When are you going to understand that the high road, while arduous and longer, is the road worth taking? Why the shortcuts? You had a full-ride scholarship. You were set. All you had to do was wait and finish your GED."

"Right. So you're going to tell your future Tulane friends you're dating someone who hasn't graduated from high school? Your parents are going to be totally okay with your drop out, runaway boyfriend?"

"I really don't care what they think."

"Sure, for now. Just wait until you run into handsome trust fund law students asking to study. They'll pull up in their BMW and drive you three blocks to the library just to show off their old money. I give you one hour after moving in before they start circling. *That's* who I'm competing with."

"That's not fair, Jay. You're saying that I'm just a butterfly, flitting from flower to flower."

"No, I'm not saying that. Your heart is so big, you let a runaway crawl inside. I don't know where I'd be, had I not met you. When we became friends, it was a heaven I never could imagine. But now, I feel like the clouds are dissipating. No matter how hard I try to hold on, it's nothing but wisps and puffs. You are the most perfect person I've ever known and I'm going to lose you if I stand still."

"I'm far from perfect. I'm not going to stray. You have to trust me, Jay."

"I...I can't. I can't leave things to hope and

trust. I'm going to earn you. The clock is ticking and you'll eventually come to understand that. I'm going to win over your parents. Not through talk, but by my accomplishments. I'm going to win you over, too."

"You already have." Jenni put her hand on Jay's cheek and played with his hair. "Why can't that be enough? You have nothing to prove."

"My life is quicksand. Nothing stays the same. When it's good, or when it's bad, it always changes. I can't explain it, but it's filled with continual panic that I will go under. That's me since the day I opened my eyes and screamed at the world."

Jenni raised her other hand to cradle Jay's face. "I love you, Jay. For once, hold someone's hand and have some faith."

"This is the only time I wish I had a chalk-board in my apartment," huffed Ted as he paced in front of his couch. Elmer sat while Jenni dashed to the kitchen. Everything about her was frantic. Ever since she lost Jay in Central Park, she was in sixth gear. It took Ted and Elmer's joint persuasion to keep her inside the apartment and focused.

Ted continued, "It's easier to work through this when you can actually see what I'm thinking."

Elmer chuckled. "All these years and I thought it was because the chalk dust boosted your IQ."

"Don't you have a whiteboard pen in this junk drawer?" asked Jenni from the kitchen as she open and shut drawers in a clamor.

"Oh, my purse!" She cleared Ted's white kitchen countertop with a wide sweep of her arm. "I did this a lot when I was a kid, despite Mom swearing I was going to use permanent marker one day and regret it. And voila!" She pulled out markers from her purse and motioned to the men to join her in the kitchen.

Elmer smiled and winked. "I suppose you have a hammer and tape measure in there, too?"

Jenni didn't bat an eye, and replied in a dead serious tone, "Just a tape measure."

She popped the cap and handed the pen to Ted. He hesitated before he put the pen to the counter.

"Go on," said Jenni, "life is boring if you don't take chances."

He went to work. Four words were written in each corner of the white counter in large block letters. MOB. FBI. ICE. SCOTT.

"Anyone else?" asked Ted.

"I don't mean to be impolite," said Elmer, "but you factor into this picture as well."

Jenni crumpled her eyebrows.

Elmer continued, "We need to know as much as we can. Just so we can help."

"What is it that you need to know?"

"You and Jay broke up recently."

"Yes."

"This isn't out of personal curiosity, but the circumstances of your breakup..."

"Don't be shy, Elmer." She pulled up a stool and sat at the counter. She paused to collect her thoughts as she straightened her blouse and tightened her braids in her ponytail.

"Well, Jay left me." Jenni looked up at Ted and caught a look of surprise. She continued, "He told me that you, too, were left at an orphanage?"

Ted nodded.

"Perhaps then, you have a deeper appreciation for what still is a mystery for me. I come from old money. Black old money, if you can believe it exists. My grandfather, my *pepere*, built a law practice as a free person of color in New Orleans. Many folks don't realize the culture of New Orleans at the time had enslaved blacks and free blacks in co-existence. Regardless, he built something that has not only survived three generations but overcame the impossible hurdles and setbacks of a black man in a white world.

As a young girl, I'd listen to my *pepere's* stories. He told of black soldiers that were denied disability pension. Businesses refusing to provide critical services even when a black person's life was on the line. Through all those horrible stories, he never lost his temper. He never raged about the injustice. Calm and collected, he fought on without the cry of a victim.

When I first met Jay, I saw a bit of my *pepere*. Like I said, I can't appreciate what Jay's life has been like. I know he lived in an orphanage for most of his childhood, learning to fight for himself at the youngest age. Jay was never adopted. When I met him, he had run away from a foster family.

I'm not trying to paint a sorry story, but it's important to know that Jay is always waiting for fate to deliver his next setback. Just as things get good, it's like he wills something to go wrong. That was the argument. He needs to stop bringing problems on himself and accept what good may come. But he knows of no other way to life."

Jenni let out a sigh and straightened her back.

"He was working as a bank teller for a local bank. This was before his job at CityTrust. After finishing a shift, his drawer cash balance didn't check out. He was short something like forty dollars. Jay was upset at the implication from his manager that he had stolen it. Here is Jay trying to work himself into a career in finance, starting at the very bottom, facing the implication he'd steal a measly forty dollars. It was insulting and demeaning at the same time.

Jay, being Jay, lost his temper. Said the wrong things. Quit the job. He was already frustrated with me, because I have been pressuring him to build a career. I was only trying to help him from himself.

He misread me. It was as if I was disappointed in him because he wasn't meeting my black old money expectations. Far from it. But he left me and I think the pause, the space we really haven't had since high school, is helping us understand each other a little better. Strange, I know."

"Absence makes the heart grow fonder," said Elmer.

"I've also heard that absence helps the heart forget. I need Jay back," replied Jenni.

Jenni grabbed a red pen, drew a heart and wrote, "JAY + JENNI" in the middle of MOB. FBI. ICE. SCOTT. "There. We have everyone."

"Good grief," said Elmer trying to break the somber mood. "Jay's an international man of mystery. What organization is not after him?"

Ted put the pen to his temple. "Let's start with that. Why would ICE be after the same person as the FBI? There is something called jurisdiction after all."

"Perhaps the jurisdiction isn't clear yet," said Elmer.

"My father does a lot of litigation for the banking industry. I saw a presentation from the FBI on cyber-defense," said Jenni. "They're big on protecting national interests; particularly financial institutions. National security, according to the FBI, includes financial stability. The FBI are well known for their capabilities in cyberspace as a result."

Elmer shook his head. "Whether it's the mail, the phone or the internet - jurisdiction generally is about the type of crime, not how it is carried out."

Jenni blew out a breath of frustration. "I don't know how you guys figure anything out with so little information."

"We don't. That's the problem," said Ted. "We

need more information. Which of these four are our best chance for gathering insight but present the least risk? Always start with that."

Elmer answered, "I'd stay out of the way of two departments arguing over jurisdiction!"

Jenni crossed out ICE and FBI. "That leaves Scott and the mob."

"Wait, that's it. Terrorism falls in a grey area and might confuse jurisdiction," said Ted, eyes bright with realization. "That could be the root of this. I've always joked that all of our branches will report to the Department of Homeland Security someday."

"Back in our day, organized crime was terrorism. Same issues, too," replied Elmer. "Random, senseless violence. If you saw an Italian with weapons you knew someone was about to be killed."

"Wow, Elmer, listen to yourself," mocked Jenni, "racial profiling?"

"Well, all I can say is that most smart Italians avoided carrying guns and stayed away from the dark corners of restaurants in New York. They knew the stereotype and avoided reinforcing it out of personal safety. Unfortunately, that's something our brothers today can't quite figure out."

"True that," replied Jenni. "But look at Ted here. He's the largest, scariest looking Italian I know and he's packing heat. Apparently, he hasn't figured it out either."

Elmer nodded, "It takes one to know one."

"That might be all we need," said Jenni as she

brightened. "Ted, do you think you can impersonate someone from the mob?"

"A cockroach? Of course, I can."

"Sure seems like intimidating Scott is a low-risk, high-yield investment."

"Like a call center agent from CityTrust relentlessly buzzing my intercom when I'm trying to read my morning newspaper?"

"Paid off in spades. It found Jay the biggest heart in the Barrio." Jenni put her head on Ted's shoulder, "and I really mean that."

The cell cut into Mike's psyche as the minutes ticked by. No bigger than his cube at work, the floor to ceiling glass cube was icy to the touch. The fan in the ceiling was silent, but the breeze was enough to push the unbearably cold air deep into his bones.

The air smelled anti-septic and the bright, florescent lights shone its relentless rays into every corner of the cell. There were no shadows. No place for anything to hide. A single table with a chair sat outside Mike's glass cage. Behind it was a short privacy wall and another glass cell. The design of the room was clear. Interrogation. He scanned the room repeatedly for a burlap kit that would be unrolled, ceremoniously like in the movies, to reveal knives, pulls and other torture devices. He promised himself that when he got out, he'd stop watching war movies.

Mike was unaware that the clock on the wall was purposely set to run quarter-speed. He watched the secondhand saunter along the clock face and felt the tendrils of doubt and uncertainty creep up to the back of his neck. The agents said nothing about why he was being held, but he was certain it was because of Jay.

Worse, he could not shake Kat from his mind and it broke his focus from the crisis at hand. The moment he saw her for the first time on the sidewalk, an apparition amidst the swarms of black-clad ICE agents knocking him down, he sensed the intervention of fate. All he knew was her first name and wanted to know more. If any good would come of this obvious mix-up, he hoped to see her again.

And of all the days he chose to take the easy path on fashion, she entered his life wearing Herrera, of all things. He felt ashamed; no different than tossing together Wranglers with Izod for a punk gig at CBGB. He knew better.

The door to the interrogation room opened. An officer, clean-cut and emotionless, entered the room and walked around the privacy wall, ignoring Mike. A few seconds later, Karl appeared into view and was escorted to the door. He appeared relaxed and relieved. After a shake of hands, the officer let Karl out on his own and shut the door behind him. He then turned, stood at attention and stared at Mike.

Guilt, for something unknown, washed over his body. He was certain he had done nothing wrong but couldn't avoid feeling like he did.

Mike swore the officer blinked every three seconds. The clock said ten seconds. How could the clock be wrong. He wasn't sure.

He really wasn't sure of anything anymore.

The white kitchen countertop in Ted's apartment was filled with colorful scribbles. They had spent the afternoon working every angle of how they'd accost Scott. Ted already had changed his clothes and Jenni helped find the right hair product to add "that mobster shine" to Ted's thinning, but jet-black hair.

"These cockroaches always get away on a technicality. We've gotta be lock-tight on pulling this trickery off. No loose ends," said Ted. His face was a permanent scowl when he was concentrating.

"We've gone over this enough. I think you have this down pat," said Jenni, "I'm worried we're losing time. Jay could be anywhere. The police didn't get him, but we don't know who did. New York isn't exactly filled with people willing to give a lost soul some money and a place to sleep. My hope is that he did find safety with the homeless vets. I don't know exactly where they are, but they do come to the pantry every once in a while. I've alerted our volunteers to call me as soon as they see one of them."

"Excellent. If we only get one chance, we need

to get this right. Jay's a survivor. Back on point. If Scott is this magical hacker, what would be his profile? He's obviously pissed at Jay and doing everything he can to destroy him from the comfort of his living room."

"My grandson told me that many hackers are driven by ego; not money." said Elmer, "A lot of the hacks that make the press bring no financial benefit. It's a bragging game to establish a pecking order of who is the best in their trade."

"That makes no sense. Ego doesn't pay the bills," Ted retorted.

Jenni jumped in. "I was friends with a computer guy for a while at Tulane. He would work through the night if there was a problem at work, but he was always cheerful the next day. Drove me crazy. He said that working with computers are like intricate puzzles. Every puzzle he solved added to his knowledge banks and was like a game won. He was always giddy after those long nights. It was a rush for him.

He was super-competitive with his co-workers, too. Strangely enough, none of them wanted to rise into management and get promotions and more pay. They wanted to be the smartest and wanted their co-workers to know it. He wanted to be the alpha-geek. The one everyone had to go to in order to get something done or fixed. He was a priest at the technology altar."

Elmer asked, "Still, what benefit is it to be known as the smartest if you don't get something for it?"

Ted held up his hand. "It's human. No different than the gambler who keeps playing, despite never winning. One little win along a lot of losses is a dopamine rush. A thrill. Think about the wise guys who could have succeeded in less nefarious trades, doing amazingly stupid stuff. Remember, Freddie Tomasatti, Elmer?"

"I could never forget him. Worked for the mob for years as their top hitman and his only pay was room and board. Spaghetti every night was enough."

Elmer shook his head in disbelief and continued, "Said he killed people because it felt good. His last words on the electric chair were, "This is going to be a helluva ride!"

Ted said, "Why do guys climb mountains when they could die? Jump out of planes? Write on their kitchen countertops? We're human animals and we feed on the rush."

"So, we gotta play to his ego," said Jenni. "Whatever you do or say in Scott's apartment, Ted, you gotta play to that."

"No way am I sucking up to a cockroach. The only thing lower than a cockroach is whale dung. I'm going to go with what works every time."

"What's that?" asked Jenni.

Elmer answered for Ted. "Fear."

CHAPTER 17

J ay felt the heat, radiating like prodding fingers from the steel barrel that housed long-burning embers. A dull yellow-red glow danced across the brick and concrete sewer walls and revealed a small, square room filled with piles of boxes and garbage bags.

Three men huddled around the barrel. Each wore multiple layers of sweatshirts and jackets, scuffed and torn, but repaired with duct tape and yarn, jagged and multi-colored.

One of the men turned to Jay. He was bald except for a half ring of jet-black hair encircling his head just above his ears. His eyes, clear green and sharp, did not fit his filthy and scarred face. "You alive?"

Jay was curled up under a pile of blankets, cardboard and jackets. He squeezed his hands and wiggled his toes. They responded, weak but present.

One of the other men, who bore a shock of

unkempt blonde-grey hair, bobbed gently over the fire. He tugged and swirled a lock of hair in his fingers. Jay remembered the game he played as a young kid, where he had to rub his stomach while patting his head. The kids giggled and laughed at each other's failed attempts.

This man, however, seemed deep in thought; his rhythmic bobs never-ending. He broke into a smile without breaking his repetitive motion and said, "Alive, yes. Huh. Alive. Ooh, ohh."

Then his face fell blank as he returned his gaze to the fire.

Jay let the heat caress his face. He willed it into his bones, deep, full and yellow. He craned his neck closer, burning what little energy he had left and his lids lulled him back to sleep. The heat, burning his face, reminded him of the fierce summer sun of New Orleans. His deepest sleep always sent him back to happier times and he was willing to ride along.

Jenni, Mike and Jay stood outside a truck dock in the thick, humid Louisiana night. Mosquitos buzzed loudly, eager to savor their fresh teenage blood garnished with hormones. Jay brushed them away, protecting himself and Jenni. With help from moonlight, Mike fiddled with the side door trying to get his key to catch. "You just have to jiggle it the right way."

A nighthawk cried out and made Jenni jump. Jay pulled her close. Her body was trembling and it was a thrill Jay had never felt before. The summer had been one delight after another. Holding hands for the first time. Her head on his shoulder while he read books aloud at night. Now she curled her arms around his chest, shrinking in his embrace. Her perfume was intoxicating.

"Hurry up, Mike. Someone could drive by here anytime," urged Jenni. She was not a rule breaker. Adrenaline, sourced by fear, made her eyes wide and observant.

With a click and rattle, the doorknob turned. "See? Nothing to it. Let's go shopping." Mike pushed the door open.

Halloran's wasn't known for its cutting-edge fashion, but they had a few sections of the popular labels. In the darkness of the store, Mike guided them to the men's section. Mike's idea of a good time was to try on expensive clothes in his free time. He worked at Halloran's for a summer before his manager wised up to the fact that Mike spent more time in the dressing room than helping customers.

"The employee discount was pretty pathetic, so it's about time I collect my paycheck," said Mike. He voice was filled with glee. "Don't let me forget to get a pair of those gorgeous suede penny loafers from the shoe section before we leave. Here, Jay, I present to you the glories of Izod." He spun on his heels and spread his arms like Willy Wonka opening the doors to his chocolate factory for the first time. "I'll leave you lovebirds alone."

Jay turned to Jenni. "Dress me. I can't wait to

burn my old clothes when we get back. You two are awesome, yet again, for helping me out. I promise I'll have things sorted before school starts again. I just couldn't stay with the Flourintales."

"Stop apologizing, Jay. But you can't hide forever."

"Just until I'm eighteen. Seven more months. No more foster families. No more taking and never giving back. Too many people have helped me my whole life and I've given nothing in return."

"You're a kid, Jay. Taking is what kids do."

"I don't want to owe anyone anymore."

"What is it that they'd want? They are foster families because they want to help, right?"

"Most do. It's hard to describe. You get a room and a seat at the dining room table. It's incredible generosity. But I can't take without giving something back. Then it ends and I'm off to the next family. The debts grow and I have no ability to pay one off before the next. It just accumulates. But then there are families that aren't what they appear to be. I seem to get the pick of them, too."

"What do you mean by that?"

"Some aren't foster parents because they want to help." Jay clenched his teeth. "Sometimes they want more. I'm fine returning favors, but not that way."

"You're not making sense."

Jay stared into the darkness. "They hurt me. That's all I can say. It's one thing to bounce from family to family. It's another to be trapped. It's not important what happened, but that I got away and I'm never going back. Good or bad. I'm on my own and it's better that way. For me and for them."

Jenni was quiet.

"Sorry," said Jay.

"There you go again. The apology tour. However, it is adorable and cute. You have a good heart."

Jay shook it off. "Just pick out my clothes."

"Anything?" asked Jenni, "I can pick anything out for you?"

"Sure. No suits, however."

Jenni giggled. "Let's start with a polo shirt. A size too small to accentuate your best feature."

"I thought my best feature was my wit."

"Yes, but," said Jenni as she outstretched her hand on his chest, "this is just as nice." Jay's heart was pounding. His face felt hot. He was thankful the store was dark. His thoughts raced.

Her other hand snaked around his neck.

It was the signal he wanted.

The clock outside the glass interrogation cell was mesmerizing. Mike couldn't look away. If he closed his eyes, the air-conditioned breeze cutting from the vent above stole his focus. Shivers, unstoppable and almost painful, would start. So, he stared at the clock, willing away the torment of sitting in bright silence; cold, hungry and confused.

He tried to meditate. He couldn't lay down

because his hands were cuffed behind his back. After pulling his legs into a lotus position, he returned his gaze to the clock. Time marched along at a measured pace; pulling at memories from places in his mind that he had tucked away to never be painfully recalled again.

In the darkness of the closed Halloran's department store, Mike seethed. He hated working at Halloran's. In fact, he hated everything about southern Louisiana. The oppressive heat was bad enough, but the fact that everything interesting going on in the world was happening everywhere else, was worse.

Every night, he flipped through magazines filled with pictures of cutting-edge fashion and drew, in the secrecy of his bedroom, his visions of style. He was ready, if one of his parents knocked, to pull his textbook over his work in one swift motion.

When his dad caught him sewing, it was the final straw. He was so engrossed in his work, trying out different collar styles in the mirror, that he did not hear him come home from work early and descend down the basement stairs.

"Say what, boy?" His dad was dressed impeccably in his navy uniform and worked at the base in Belle Chase.

Mike's arms fell. In each hand, he held a collar. He wanted nothing more than to hide them away in the boxes under the sewing bench. "Uh, hey there, Dad."

"What's going on here?"

"Nothing. I'll come up in a sec."

"Are you sewing?"

"Kind of. Just fixing a shirt for my band concert."

"Oh." His eyes scanned the fabric draped across the bench. He descended a couple more stairs to look at the drawings scattered along the floor. "What are these drawings?"

"They are Jenni's. She left them behind. I'll pick it up." Mike held his breath, hoping his father would not think twice and leave.

"Nah, these are your drawings, boy. I can tell." His back stiffened. "This whole scene here is causing me some real concern."

"Dad, I'll pick it up."

"Shut your mouth." Instinctively, Mike stood at attention, dropped his collars and put his hands behind his back at attention.

"Yes sir."

His father walked around the room, calm and in silence. His decorated uniform shimmered in the sun's rays cutting through the basement window. His shoes, impeccably shined, clomped loudly across the drawings on the floor to the sewing bench. As he turned, he ground his heels into the paper; tearing and ripping what he could. As he calmly looked around and pulled fabric from the table, examined it and let it fall to the floor. All along, he continued his destructive pacing.

"A man's place is not here unless it is to fix the

sewing machine for his sweet mother."

"Yes sir."

"I don't think you understand me."

Mike hesitated.

"Last I checked, there were no daughters in this family. I thought I was raising a young man. "

"You are, sir."

He walked slowly to the steps and before ascending, he looked Mike in the eyes. "Don't bring shame on this family, boy." His voice was halting. "It's not right."

He ascended the stairs, in a measured pace, but leaving loud footfalls even as he exited into the kitchen upstairs.

Crying, Mike ran his fingers across the glorious texture of one of the suede shoes kicked asunder during his father's inspection. He hated him for making him cringe at doing something so simple. He couldn't enjoy any of it without clouds of guilt. Some days those clouds blocked the sun. Today it rained. His blood was a flash flood of anger washing away guilt.

It was that moment that Mike decided he was going to run away with Jay. At seventeen, the world was going to rotate on his terms.

In the ICE interrogation cell, Mike's tears felt warm on his cheeks. Just like living under his father's watch, the cell rediscovered the guilt and fear that he had lived without for over a decade. It was Jay who helped him steal away in the night and discover the joys of living to his true self. Now, more than anything, Jay needed his help. This cell was nothing compared to what Jay endured.

He wanted nothing more than to get his hands out from behind his back. His shoulders screamed in agony. These days, he no longer stood at attention when spoken to, but he never lost his fear of men in uniform. The beauty of their discipline and precision spoke nothing of the unforgiving heart that beat underneath. Once again, he felt the guilt, despite doing nothing wrong, wash over him. With gritted teeth, he promised Jay that he would soldier on and never betray him. Bring on the interrogation. He was ready.

Outside the interrogation room, Hofstra and Tyler would not relent. The ICE officer was to start the interrogation without them. The room was a buzz of field agents pecking away at computers, chatting on phones and laughing as they mingled near the water cooler.

"I called you, because I thought this might fall into your jurisdiction," said Hofstra, "but after receiving information from our investigators, we have proof that this is not international organized crime. I already communicated this to your department head and they agreed."

Hofstra was bending the rules. She sent an email to ICE but did not wait for a response. The basement dwellers did indeed find proof of Jay's citizenship. They called with the good news while she and Tyler were on the way to the ICE detention center.

Jay had a birth certificate, but it never left the hospital where he was born. According to old hospital and police records, Jay was born to parents who provided fake names on his birth certificate. The parents snuck away with Jay as soon as they were able.

Bushy-beard was convinced Jay was the son of criminals but had reached an informational dead end. However, it was undeniable that Jay was a US citizen.

Hofstra continued adding to the web of doubt building in the ICE officer's mind. "This is now an FBI case. Stolen identity. These are not your suspects. Not until I'm finished with them."

"Suspect," corrected the ICE officer. "Mr. T is still in custody. I was ordered to release Mr. Gil."

"Are you dense?" Hofstra's cheeks were turning red from streaks crawling up her neck. She leaned in, ready to launch a tirade of insults.

The officer leaned back. "I only follow orders."

Tyler put a calming hand on Hofstra's shoulders. In a measured tone, he asked, "Who gave you the order?"

The officer reached over the desk and held up a clipboard holding a signed release order. Tyler flipped through a few pages. "This was sent via email?"

"My commanding officer sent this from LA but called me personally to carry it out."

"These papers are not properly executed," said Tyler. He held out the clipboard. "The date in the footer doesn't match the date on the order. You do realize that there is a reason why footers are dated separately, right? They teach this day one."

The officer blanched. "I know my commanding officer personally. He called for the release."

"Is his name Terrance Smith?" asked Hofstra after glancing at the clipboard. Terrance's name showed as the requester.

He shook his head. "No, that's his superior."

"Brilliant," said Tyler, "one of the oldest tricks in the book. No one questions your boss' boss. I bet your commanding officer did nothing but rubber stamp this. You've been suckered by a kid with a cellphone and computer."

The circles of sweat in the officer's shirt armpits complimented the bead of sweat running down his temple. He picked up the phone and said curtly, "Get me the US Marshals. Now."

With the phone cradled in his neck, he turned to Tyler and pointed to the exit. "Mr. Gil was released less than thirty minutes ago. He couldn't have gotten far. Get him before I lose my job."

Hofstra blew out a breath. "I wonder who will get him first? ICE, US Marshals or FBI?"

The office turned electric as the officer slammed down the phone and barked orders, sharp and urgent. Agents in the room tossed on their jackets while others got on their phones.

Hofstra's phone buzzed in her jacket pocket. She glanced at the display before she put it up to her ear and turned to Tyler. "The basement dwellers." She silently prayed for more good news.

Tyler nodded and took the opportunity to dive into the holding cell to get Mike T. Mike was their primary hope to find Jay and close out this case. Several hours in the interrogation cell alone usually softens people up. No questions. No good cop - bad cop. Just time alone.

"A hacker in a box? I'm not tracking," questioned Hofstra as she waited for Tyler to return. "I have to get it within WiFi range?"

Tyler brought Mike from the interrogation room still in handcuffs. Shoulders slumped, his eyes never left the floor. His shirt was unbuttoned and tie unfurled over his shoulders. The curly locks on his head hung down, a distraught tangle.

Hofstra grabbed Tyler's arm and motioned for him to stop. She continued her conversation with the basement dwellers with a frown of concentration on her face.

She finished by asking the basement dwellers, "Can you have the hacker-in-a-box ready for me at the parking ramp? Tyler and I are hitting the streets. Karl Gil managed to get released without our permission."

With a practiced motion, Hofstra ended the call with a beep and swiftly dropped the phone back into her jacket pocket. She pulled Mike and Tyler out of earshot of the agents' bustle.

"The basement dwellers are insistent that all of these events are connected to the same person or organization. They have traced multiple activities back to the same source."

Tyler asked, "What about Karl's release? Same hackers did that? No one gets released that quick."

"Coincidences don't happen a third time. Karl is connected to all of this."

Mike jumped in with a shaky voice, eyes still down to the ground. "Karl told me that he wasn't directly involved but wanted to do what he could to de-escalate."

Tyler shook his head. "I don't buy it. He's in deep."

Hofstra studied Mike. He was shaken. She shifted her tone to wrap up. "That's why the basement dwellers want me to bring a hacker-in-a-box along. If we get within WiFi range of where Karl works or lives, they can move on the offense, digging into their technology maze, bypassing the security between their network and the rest of the world."

She turned Mike around to unlock his handcuffs carefully. "Mike," said Hofstra in a whisper, "I'm sorry. I forget what it's like in there. Those holding rooms are hell by themselves. I wish we had gotten here sooner."

Mike nodded. He rubbed his wrists. "I'm not under arrest?"

"Not at all. We're here to help."

Mike tugged at his tie and fumbled with his shirt buttons.

Reading the cue, Tyler said to Hofstra, "I'll meet you at the parking ramp. Get the hacker-in-a-box. Mike and I will attack what donuts are left in the break room and freshen up."

Before she stepped through the door to the elevators, she heard Mike's grateful voice from behind. "Thanks, Kat."

"No," said Hofstra over the cellphone, "we need to split up and cover as many of New York's exits. ICE needs to stake out the airports as they know those areas best. The Marshals need to cover the highways. Let FBI check Mr. Gil's apartment for clues as to where he'd head next. We will handle that."

Tyler waited for Hofstra to hang up. "Nice one. Send them all off on a wild goose chase. We know Mr. Gil is headed home."

"The less traffic we have in the way, the better. Besides, splitting up is always the best approach. They are insurance in case we are wrong."

Mike was in the backseat. "What do you know about this Karl Gil?"

"Well, not just anyone can forge an ICE prisoner release," said Tyler. "Mr. Gil is either directly involved or has an accomplice who is also behind what we think is a forged deportation order for a Mr. Jay Wilson. Someone you know."

"Jay is my best friend." Mike could see Hofstra's eyes dart up to the rear-view mirror in sympathy. She believed him. Mike continued, "He's in a lot of trouble and none of it is his fault."

"I struggle to understand why Jay would be without blemish. There is a reason why someone would go to these lengths," said Tyler.

"He ticked off some kid with undeveloped, pre-teen emotional issues at a coffee shop, for pete's sake. Who knew this guy could erase Jay's life?"

Tyler and Hofstra exchanged glances. Pieces were beginning to fill gaps in the puzzle.

Mike continued in a rush. "The kid got Jay fired from his job. Shut off his power. Evicted him. He even has a fake police record that makes him look like a mass murderer who enjoyed a little sumpin-sumpin on the side."

Hofstra finished for him, "I guess tagging Jay as Paraguayan mob was the final stroke of genius. Deportation."

Mike extended his hand over the seat onto Hofstra's shoulder. From the moment they met, he felt a connection. She listened without judgment. She cared. "Kat, please, help Jay. I don't know if he's alive. Since we last talked, he's gone silent. Disappeared. The same for his girlfriend, who is a dear friend of mine as well. I'll do anything you want. Please."

Without saying anything, she patted his hand.

Tyler looked out the window in silence. He spent much of his life working to be an FBI agent to catch bad guys and bring balance in a world filled with injustice. In a single gesture, Hofstra showed him what his work was really about. The victims and their service to them.

◆ ◆ ◆

The New York traffic had come to a standstill. "Oh no. This can't be happening," grumbled Tyler.

"It's New York," said Hofstra.

Two firetrucks were parked in front of a building draped in scaffolding and plastic. One ladder had already been extended up several floors. A policeman was doing everything he could to coax four lanes of traffic down to one to pass the chaotic scene. All Tyler could hear was honks and curses. One taxi driver had already exited the car and was waving his hands in dramatic bobs, willing the taxi behind him to back up. It was going to get worse before it got better.

"This is going to take forever." Tyler scanned traffic. Cars filled his sight in every direction.

Hofstra bit her lip. "How far to walk?"

"A little less than five miles."

"Our boss is going to hate this." She searched the backseat and found a manila folder and marker. In big letters she wrote, "CAR IS IN NEUTRAL. MOVE SOMEWHERE SAFE. FBI PROTECTED." She tossed the folder onto the dash.

"Does that really work?"

"Last time I did this, the car was found at the bottom of the Hudson. But, no reason why it wouldn't work this time."

"Oh."

She stepped out of the car, pulled off her pumps and walked to the sidewalk with the shoes dangling in her hand.

"Why not leave those in the car? We'll come back."

Mike answered for Kat, "Those are two-thousand dollar Christian Louboutins."

"I bet you wish you were wearing my forty-three dollar Sketchers," retorted Tyler.

Hofstra deadpanned, "I wouldn't be caught dead in 'em."

The three of them cantered into a jog, Hofstra was on point, Tyler in the middle and Mike enjoyed the view from behind.

CHAPTER 18

J ohnny Gjerdes was cheerful. The colors of New York were brighter than usual. Men and women, singularly focused on their destination to eat, work or head home, bobbed and weaved, unaware that Johnny was packing some serious heat. It was his last hit. Simon promised him. He was older than most anyone out working the streets but it was a simple case of being punished for doing a good job. No one else was as efficient, effective or slippery.

But age was tugging at him. One of these days his knees would give out at the wrong time. Or his ears would not pick up a floorboard creak, alerting him to someone behind him. His boss, Simon, knew this better than anyone as he was twenty years his senior. Nothing worked on Simon's body, except his gums for flapping and hands for eating.

Johnny continued reminiscing as he walked to Scott's apartment.

"Son, you're worth more to us teaching the young 'uns your tricks than tearing up the streets.

At some point, these idiots need to grow some brains," said Simon as he searched, wrist-deep, through a large bowl of hard candies on his desk. Nothing annoyed Johnny more than someone rummaging through the very food being offered to others.

Simon's eyes lit up when he unearthed a butterscotch. He popped it in his mouth and continued, "I'm clearing out of this office. I'm setting up at the back of Angioletta's by the kitchen. You guys can find me there for breakfast, lunch or dinner. Other than that, leave me alone."

Johnny wasn't sure where Simon was going with this. He had to be careful. "Who you gonna put up in this nice spot, then? Someone's gotta keep an eye on the pups and run the show."

"Nice spot? I have to walk hallways longer than a football field just to take a dump! My new place is close to the train and walled by concrete, just like it is here. I'm not stepping completely out of the game but need to keep an eye on things until I choke on a meatball."

Johnny nodded.

Simon continued, "I was thinking Frankie should take over."

"Frankie's good."

"No he's not," growled Simon. He pointed a crooked finger at him. "Are you sucking up?"

"Yes."

Simon smiled. "This is your gig, if you'll take it. You'll get your fill of ugly men and one pretty lady."

Johnny raised an eyebrow.

"A little advice. Do what she says and don't let all that pretty blind you. I've seen Kaylee get more done on her phone while drinking a latte than all our pups running the streets." Simon rubbed his face and rolled his eyes. "Why did our mommas have to raise so many idiot boys?"

Johnny nodded in agreement. He wasn't sucking up this time. The boys these days seemed more interested in sneaking away to play video games than learning the trade. They couldn't see beyond their nose or the tent in their pants. This business required a long view and that perspective was rare.

"Finish the job on those three men. If Kaylee says they're dangerous, you better believe it. She's the future and I suggest you listen to every word she says. I don't know how she does it, but more and more of our revenue is coming from her computer magic."

Simon leaned back and waved his hand at his desktop. "Get it done quickly and by the time you get back here, the name plate here will read Johnny the Snake. We've worked hard to build this and you've earned it. Just leave me alone at Angioletta's. Between her meatballs and bosom, I'll already be dead and in heaven."

And, so, the air seemed fresher and the sun brighter on the New York concrete. Johnny felt twenty years younger as he walked in confident, long strides. Word had already gotten out that

Johnny the Snake was taking over. No one had to wonder who had been given that new moniker.

A broad smile broke out on his wrinkled, sun-leathered face as he turned to the apartment lobby doors to Scott's apartment. He whispered over and over to himself, "Johnny the Snake." It sounded perfect. This was going to be one of his better days.

CHAPTER 19

Elmer whispered outside Karl and Scott's apartment door, "I'm not sure about this. An old black man just doesn't fit the stereotype of the mob."

With a dismissive wave, Ted replied, "Just pull your pants down a bit, stand by the door and keep your eyes wide-eyed and threatening."

"I'm sixty-seven years old."

"So?"

"I wear tighty-whities."

Ted paused. "On second thought, just keep your gun visible. All these cockroaches need to see is your steady hand but twitchy trigger finger. Please let me do the talking."

"That didn't sound mob at all."

"I'ma do the talkin'. Stand dere and don't pick yer nose."

"Better."

Ted tucked a brown paper-wrapped box under his arm and confidently rapped the door. His eyes narrowed to thin slits and his chest puffed out. It was swagger, not bluster. Ted had never taken on an adversary of this character, technical wizardry and capability. The world had changed and he was still fighting with his old bag of tricks. It was all he had.

Secretly, he hoped it was going to be enough.

He could hear Scott's voice, "Who is this?" Behind the eyehole, they could hear the quiet scratch of someone lifting a cover to peek through.

Ted thought the voice sounded how a cockroach might sound.

Game on.

"Thank you," said Jay. He sipped the cup of hot water from a can that still had the fading image of the Jolly Green Giant on the side. The flavor, faint cinnamon, was restorative and filled his body with graciousness. "What is this?"

Jer, the most able-bodied of the three homeless men, replied, "I dunno. We don't give things fancy names. Old tea? You'd be surprised how long a tea bag can last." He smiled and continued, "Every once in a while I get a chance to drink a fresh bag and it is way too strong."

The room was warm and quiet. The nervous tension of Jay's arrival was gone. Rising up behind the homeless men, Jay was mesmerized by the neatly arranged stockpile of food resting on planks of wood. They were organized by the color of the package and in the dim light, it was a hint of a rainbow.

"How are your feet?" asked Andy, a voice from inside a large cardboard box. It was the first words Jay had heard him speak since he was taken in.

Jay leaned forward and could only make out Andy's dark outline. "Nothing I can't handle. I'm going to be fine, thanks to you guys."

"You delivered yourself to our doorstep. I hope you understand that we had to wait a while and make sure things were safe," said Jer. "We've got a nice spot here and really don't want to move." Jer rose to add some wood to the fire inside the barrel.

"Hide. Huh. Andy, Jer and Tike. Quiet." Tike's eyes were wide when he spoke but returned to a dead stare at the fire when he finished. His gentle bobs never missed a beat when he talked.

"Right, Tike." said Jer as he poked at the fire. "Quiet is the trick. As our guest, it would be appreciated if you didn't speak of our home."

"I understand. My friend, Jenni from the pantry, told me you might be able to keep me hidden for that exact reason. I'm in trouble."

Jer paused his work of tending the fire. His face darkened. In a rush, he scampered and disappeared into the blackness of the sewer tunnels without a word.

Andy inside the box started crying. It was muffled, but unmistakable.

"No no. Andy. Huh. Huh," said Tike. He quickened the pace of his bobs. His light wispy hair lent the impression of wings flapping in slow motion. "Ok. Huh. Right here."

Tike walked over to the box and tapped it gently between each of his dips. "Right here. Huh. Jay talk. Huh. Talk." Tike connected eyes with Jay. His smile was half-hearted and begging. Jay sensed they needed a distraction.

"My name is Jay Wilson."

Tike's smile broadened. "Huh. Wilson. Huh."

"I was found inside a box, a little smaller than your box, Andy, with the word Wilson written on the side."

Tike continued his tapping on the box and never let his eyes off Jay. Andy's crying turned into soft sniffles. Jay continued, "Uh, I was dropped off an orphanage in that box. No one knows why my first name was Jay. I have no middle name. Apparently, there was a big debate on whether Wilson was my first name, last name or just happened to be on the box that someone used to deliver me and wasn't my name at all."

Tap tap tap tap.

"I was never adopted. Bad timing, I figure. More likely it was bad luck where I was continually in the wrong place, wrong time. As I got older, I got less visits from adoptive parents and more time with foster parents. By the time I was twelve, I grew tired of temporary families. I made it difficult for anyone to live with me. No one wants to adopt a troubled teenager."

"Trouble. Huh."

Jay smiled. "Yes, I was trouble. I ran away when I was sixteen. That was when I met Jenni."

Andy's head slowly peeked out of the box. His long, brown matted hair was all Jay could see. He mumbled, "Thank you, Tike."

Tike stopped tapping and returned to the fire. Andy ran his fingers across his face and hair. He curled up at the end of the box's opening, facing the radiant warmth of the fire and closed his eyes. Streaks of black grime ran down from his forehead to his neck. "Who is Jenni?"

"Everything. Imagine bottling smarts, beauty and an oversized heart into a single person." Jay let out a breath. "She is everything I don't deserve. I am nothing she deserves. Until she finds the right man, I keep her company. She spoke of you. Told me I'd be safe here."

"I remember Jenni," said Jer as he crawled back from the darkness of the sewer without making a sound. Visibly excited by Jer's return, Tike stopped bobbing and pointed urgently at the pile of boxes and bags in the corner.

"Ah, you hungry, Tike?" asked Jer as if he never left. He rifled through the boxes and pulled out a styrofoam box and unclasped it. "Hmm, got some fries in here."

Tike grabbed the box and stared at the fries nestled in the remnants of someone's almost finished club sandwich.

Jay was mesmerized and sympathetic. His

stomach seized into a cramp and brought back his own memories of the creative measures he'd go through to sate his hunger. He was hungry, but not hungry enough to enjoy what Andy, Tike and Jer had to offer.

Jay commented, "Andy was pretty upset when you left."

"He always cries when I leave." Andy's chest rose and fell slowly in the deep breath of sleep. "And I always come back. Like me, he has a little bit of trouble dealing with things up above in the world everyone else lives in. Down here, it's safer because we band together like boys in boot camp."

"Military?"

Jer nodded and tugged at his beard. "Army. I served the same time in Vietnam as Andy."

Jay hesitated. He didn't know what to say. "Thank you for serving."

He leaned his head onto the wall and let his heavy lids fall. He couldn't make sense of this new world. Hungry and disoriented, the blackness of sleep beckoned. And as he always did, he returned to Louisiana.

Jenni's college apartment was a tiny studio at the top floor of a grand home divided into five rentals. The small space provided the convenience of not having much that needed decoration. Jenni, however, knew exactly the right places for the right items to make even the worst of places cozy and welcoming.

"This better be the last degree I frame and

hang up. I'm so done with school." Jenni was standing in the middle of the room while Jay was holding her law degree, elegantly framed, at a potential hanging spot.

"Is this spot okay?"

"A little more to the left."

"There?"

"Yes. I'll go get the hammer."

Jay stood waiting. He laid his head against his arm. The sentiment of Jenni's graduation was washing over him in gentle waves of admiration and fear. This could be it. Jenni was leaving for New York. She had a job offer before she even started her final year of school. As a result, the year was a countdown of dread for Jay.

Click. The sound came from Jenni's camera phone. Jay turned from the wall, still holding up the frame. "What are you doing?"

"You are so cute, just sitting there resting your head on the wall and your butt sticking out. If I had left for lunch, would you still be standing there?"

"Glad to hear you are enjoying the photo op." His dour mood brought snarkiness to his tone.

"What's wrong, Jay?"

"Nothing. Let's get this hung."

Jenni grabbed the picture from his hands and set it on the floor. "You've been quiet these last few days."

"It's been hard to shake thoughts of New York."

"We've talked about this hundreds of times and need to settle on this. Come with me. You can start fresh there."

"It's so expensive. I can't cover tuition and rent. Living in New York is a racket. No matter how I run the numbers, I can't do it unless I decide to be homeless again."

Jenni sat on the couch and motioned to Jay to join her.

"Did you talk to Mike?"

"Why?"

"He wants to go, too. When we start out, we can split things three ways. I know you won't let me help out by paying more of the rent."

"I won't take handouts anymore. I need to carry my fair share."

"I understand but I want you with me." Jenni held his hand.

Jay asked, "So Mike got a job in New York, too?"

"No, but he said he's not going to get a leg up in the fashion industry here in New Orleans. He wants to live in the epicenter of all the trends."

"I think he wants to get out from under his dad's watchful eye."

"That too."

"I suppose we'd be out from under your dad's watchful eye, too."

Jenni shifted. "He'll come around. Don't make that the reason to go with me."

Jay had plenty of reasons to go. However, it

was hard to see around the brick wall in front of him. Call it pride, but it seemed no different than Jenni feeding him outside the food pantry on Tuesday nights. He could not return the favor. Worse, he could not carry his fair share.

"Jay," said Jenni. "This is more than just money, isn't it?"

"Yes." His face did nothing to conceal his agony. The decision was a never-ending roller-coaster. He did everything he could to hit the brakes on his internal debate and settle on a decision.

Jenni watched. She yearned to unravel the demons he imprisoned deep inside. "Can you help me understand?"

"I don't know. It's like I'm packing my bags to go stay with another foster family. Except, as a kid, I had no bags to pack. I had to pack and get ready up here." Jay tapped his temple and continued, "It's hard to explain the mental gymnastics to prepare for a new family. You don't know what to expect. Any bit of normalcy or routine is slipping through your fingers. I'd have nothing to fall back on to feel safe. It's like you're thrown into the ocean. You're just floating and hoping someone is going to scoop you out of the water. You can't run. You can't hide. You just helplessly float on."

Jenni put her head on Jay's shoulder.

Jay continued, "New York is frightening. Terrifying, actually. I feel like we're walking into something that could end really bad. It's like an omen.

Things are good here and New York is like walking straight into the devil's maw. It's not rational, I know."

Jay rubbed his face and took in a deep breath. "I feel like I'm pulling up everything down to the roots to go. It took a long time to grow roots here. Do you know how hard it is to grow roots in quicksand?"

"I don't," said Jenni. "But I hope I'm helping."

Jay nodded and kissed Jenni's forehead.

"Pop-tarts," said Jenni with a smile. "New York is scary for me, too. I can't do this alone, but I've got someone who helped me see the right way to eat pop-tarts. The world is brighter and more meaningful with you in it, Jay. That's all I need."

Hofstra fit right into the New York stereotype. Her cell phone was glued to her ear and she was shouting over the street side din. Her pumps swung side to side in her hands as she power walked barefoot ahead of Tyler in her perfect shirt-suit combo. Tyler had already loosened his tie. His eyes scanned the crowds for Karl's slender profile.

"It doesn't matter," commanded Hofstra to the poor folks on the other end of the phone, "no amount of sirens are going to get your Marshals through these clogged up streets. Take the train and set up a two-block perimeter. As soon as we get there, we're not waiting for a soul. We're going in before Mr. Gil destroys any evidence of the deportation order. His apartment is going to be critical to understanding how they executed all of this technical wizardry. We can't waste a second. I've got Agent Brown with me and we've got this covered."

Warm confidence rose up into Tyler's chest. This was why he joined the FBI. The chance to make a difference. Maybe along the way, blow up a few stereotypes and change a few perceptions. He mouthed to Hofstra, "Three miles."

She nodded and continued, "The basement dwellers tell me that there should only be two men inside. No record of arms purchases. Lots of illicit computer equipment has been delivered over the years, so they think the most dangerous thing inside is an overloaded power strip."

Tyler tapped the small box in his arm emphatically as a reminder. LED lights flashed and blinked all over its silver exterior.

She nodded in response.

"Do not, I repeat, do not enter the apartment until I get our hacker-in-a-box in place. We need to be in WiFi range for at least five minutes for my basement dwellers to work their magic." Hofstra spoke through gritted teeth, "Unless you want a stiletto in your eye, do not enter the apartment until you get my go ahead!"

"Mr. Whedon, we need to chat," grumbled Ted

in a threatening tone through the narrow apartment door opening. He worried his acting was over the top, but Scott's reaction was all the confirmation he needed to continue. Scott was a frozen ghost. His pale-white skin was covered with a sheen of nervous sweat. His oversized frame was covered by a NY Rangers hockey shirt that had seen days-old meals. Crumbs, sauce and grease intermixed to create crusty yellow highlights across his chest.

Withholding any pleasantries, Ted pushed the door open with his shoulder and nodded Elmer on to watch just inside the door. He motioned Scott to the couch and he fell into his seat as if Ted Jedi force-pushed him. After closing the door, Elmer unzipped his jacket halfway, pulled out his snub-nosed Colt Cobra .38 Special and after checking carefully for a full load of ammo, tucked it into his coat pocket. If Elmer had any nervous energy, it was not showing. His steady gaze moved from Scott to the noise behind the bedroom door.

Ted heard it, too. "Who is that, Scott?"

Karl stepped into the room holding a duffel bag, sweatpants and t-shirts hanging out the side pockets.

"Oh," Karl said as he dropped bis bag. "I remember you."

Without a word, Elmer caught Karls' gaze, moved his own eyes from Karl to the couch and back to Karl.

"Yah, I think I'll sit down," said Karl. Instinctively, he raised his hands in the air and weaved through the room to sit next to Scott. When his face was out of Ted's view, he silently mouthed "MOB" to Scott. Ted caught his intent and smiled inside. The two looked as if they were about to be scolded by their teacher. If they blinked, no one would have seen it.

Scott reached for his laptop.

"I don't think so," grumbled Ted. Scott's hands returned to tugging at his jersey.

Ted continued with a nod to Elmer. "My friend and I are here to make a proposition so good that you can't refuse."

Scott opened his mouth to talk, but only could let out a dry gag.

Ted continued, "Which one of you worked all that computer stuff on Jay Wilson?"

Karl was the first to answer coherently. "Who?"

A loud click answered before Ted could. Elmer ceremoniously locked the doors and returned his steady gaze on the duo on the couch. He pulled his gun and turned it on Karl. Ted knew Elmer was enjoying this, despite the dour expression on his face. The days-old grey stubble on his face added to the grizzled, impatient facade.

"I only ask questions once," said Ted as he jerked a thumb at Elmer. "My friend here takes care of people who struggle with answering questions."

"It was me," blurted Scott. "I didn't know who he was, honest!"

"It isn't a concern of mine who he was. My

boss finds your skills desirable and ... difficult to procure." Ted set the brown-wrapped package carefully on the coffee table and removed his leather gloves. The blips, whirrs and flashes of lights from all the computer equipment under the glass coffee tabletop seemed to kick up a frenzied notch.

"W-w-what's in there?" Scott pointed at the box. He correlated the jump in activity with the arrival of the package.

"It's not for you. Someone upset our boss and I need to make a delivery after we're done here. Do not bump the box, please." Ted walked behind the couch and continued talking, "As a gesture of my good will, I'll offer free advice to the two of you about this particular box. Hassan's Camera decided to ignore my boss' business proposition and there will be consequences. Hence my advice. Stay away from Hassan's Camera this afternoon. Things might get a little too hot there, if you get my drift. This box is the kindle for that fire. "

Ted smiled, evil dripping from his teeth. "See how much I care about your well-being?"

Scott and Karl sank deeper into the couch, as far as they could from the box.

"But before I can settle that business, I need to settle this business," continued Ted. "The boss would like to engage your services. You'd be well compensated, I assure you."

"Sure," said Scott.

"Eager to help? I like your attitude already, kid."

Elmer never let off his dead-on gaze. He wished he could burn holes with his stare. Seeing them, cowardly and frozen in fear, only increased his disgust. All the two kids needed were antennas and six legs and Ted would have taken care of business with the heel of his shoe. Cockroaches weren't intelligent, just resilient and resourceful with one goal - to survive. These two were switching their allegiances, without conscience.

That's why Elmer and Ted hit it off so well. Everything they did, they did with purpose. To do right by each other, their families and their country. The cockroaches flaunted the gift they gave. As if the roof over their heads and the safety in their streets were a privilege, not earned by those before them. To Elmer and Ted, it was a sacred honor to propel society to a better place. Early in his career, Elmer felt sympathy to their ignorance. Age, combined with a lifetime of police work, added a heavy patina to that attitude.

Ignorance was not bliss. It was irresponsible. He was going to teach these boys a lesson.

Back in the sewer, Jay reassured Tike. "I'll come back, okay? I'll get you something real good to eat." His filthy clothes were were now dry and warm. Combined with multiple bouts of deep sleep, Jay felt refreshed. He had the energy to find a way back upside and away from the chaos of Central

Park. The claustrophobia mixed with the guilt of sharing the homeless men's food urged him back outside.

Tike quickened his bobs and twirled his hair. "Nuts. Huh. Nut nuts."

Jer snorted. "You are what you eat, Tike." He turned to Jay. "Loves any kind of nuts. I watched him devour a bird feeder full of peanuts."

"No Poop. Huh."

"Yes, it took him three days to poop again. A constipated Tike is not to be messed with."

"Huh, huh, huh."

Jay smiled and patted Tike on the shoulder. "Nuts it'll be. I'll give some to Jer. Andy will have to help manage your portions."

Andy didn't make a sound. He was hidden away in the darkness of his box. "It was nice to meet you, Andy, and thank you for looking out for me."

"I think Andy has had enough excitement over the last couple days," said Jer, "He means well."

The exit between sewers was a rectangular slit, only ten inches high. They laid prone and slid sideways to exit and dropped down to a shelf. Jer pointed. "You took a nap in our woodpile right there."

"That's one way to put it. I had no idea you were right above me. You are my angels."

"More like your hobos from heaven." Jer chuckled. "We've got a bit of a hike ahead of us and it'll be a long, scenic route. It's the only way to stay dry."

They shuffled, in tandem, along the narrow shelf. The shallow waters gurgled in the darkness giving some sense of direction. Jer's steps led Jay forward, purposefully shuffling loud enough for him to follow. Occasionally, indirect ambient light would reveal the rectangular pattern of the blackened brick walls that curved over his head. Where warmer waters would enter, the moist brick would glisten, crystals forming as the mist caught the frigid air of the sewer.

The stench was gone, either frozen or pushed back into the recesses of Jay's olfactory memory. His senses were focused on gleaning anything of his surroundings that would measure his progress or give direction. The New York bustle above his head echoed when they walked by storm water openings.

Jay tried to break the monotony of the trek. "How long have you known Andy and Tike?"

"Years. Lost count," answered Jer.

"Did you find them or did they find you?"

"Andy and I were in a support group together. I, uh, needed some..." Jer's voice trailed off. His shuffling stopped.

"I'm sorry, we don't need to talk about it."

"Just need a moment." Jay could hear his breaths. He sucked air in gulps and forcefully exhaled. It was if he was practicing the breathing techniques used for women in labor.

"Can I help?"

"Are you hands cold?"

"Freezing."

"Put one on the back of my neck."

Jay reached out into the dark. He found Jer's shoulders. Under the layers, he could feel Jer's tense muscles, back hunched and tight. He slipped his hand behind the collar of his hoodie.

Jer let out a long exhale. "That's nice."

"I didn't mean to upset you."

"I, uh, get the urge to hide. Hard to fight it."

"You don't have to fight it. Do you want to hide right now? I'll wait for you."

The tension fell out of Jer's shoulder and neck. "That's the nicest thing anyone has said to me. For once, someone doesn't want to fix me."

"If I didn't like my foster parents, I hid. My favorite place was always somewhere in the basement, if they had one. I was pretty small and could tuck away pretty much anywhere."

Jer's voice broke into a rush. "Yes, somewhere dark. I hated group sessions. Always bright, only one door to exit. Sometimes I'd run forever, down well-lit hallways until I could find a closet or a bathroom where I could switch off the lights.

Andy found me, one time, in a stall. I couldn't fit behind the toilet so it was just my head back there. He didn't care. He helped me. Showed me how to get down here. I don't mind going above ground, to get food or anything and now he can stay in his box and not worry. It's sad, but the children don't let him go anywhere."

"The children?"

"The ones he killed. Napalm. He was clearing hideouts in the jungle; collections of wood huts under bramble. Just a dumb private doing what he was commanded. Those kids hid well, real quiet until they started burning. Children tucked away by their mothers and fathers who were fighting us. He, uh, uh, please switch your hands."

Jay obliged. The warmth was wonderful. He retrieved his warm hand and pushed in the other, ice-cold, against his neck.

"Ahhhh. Thank you." Jer continued, "He said he still hears the children. Except they don't scream anymore, they taunt and question him. Talking in their native language; angry and confused. Of course, he doesn't understand them but thinks they are asking him for their parents. When they aren't begging and calling out to him, he can at least sleep. He says the whispering is the worst.

I can tell when he hears them by the look in his eyes. He's a good man. Just haunted. Let's get going."

Jay removed his hand. He followed behind Jer's hurried shuffle. "There are places that can help Andy. I can figure out something so he doesn't have to live down here."

"Thank you, but it's easier to just survive down here than to try to live to other people's expectations up there. Folks need to let us be. Not everything broken can be fixed. Like a three-legged dog, we can soldier on."

CHAPTER 20

In an alley near Karl's apartment, Johnny the Snake stepped out of view, pulled out his cell phone and called one of the pups, Jeffy. He wasn't the biggest or the brightest, but he was exceptionally diligent in following orders. It fit the bill for what he needed. A distraction was on order. With these days of video-capable smart phones and hyper-sensitive home security systems, he needed everyone's real and virtual eyes somewhere else while he took care of Scott and Karl.

"Hey, Jeffy, need you to pull the eyes of New York away from 2222 East 85th street. Just a block."

The voice was a heavy Brooklyn accent. "Sure boss."

"Snake. Call me snake."

"Sure, S-s-snake?"

Johnny smiled.

"What kind of distraction you lookin' for, Snake?"

"I don't know. Burn something? Drive a car

into a storefront? Make something up, but make sure it isn't too big but loud. I need thirty minutes to get a couple hits in."

"I haven't burned anything in a while. I'd enjoy that. I'll be ready to go in fifteen. Just need to find a save point in this game." Johnny could hear the over-exaggerated boings of a spring cutting through hyper-animated synth music.

"Fifteen is fine," said Johnny through gritted teeth. "Text me when you're ready to go."

Silence.

"Are you listening to me?"

"Sure boss...Snake...Sorry, boss. Got it. I'm on my way."

Snake switched his phone off with a grimace. Two hits, Karl and Scott. Then he'd figure out where Jay Wilson was. All in a days' work and then he can turn his attention to decorating his new office.

"Our boss likes to bring employees onboard without baggage. Less surprises." Ted leaned over Scott and Karl's heads from behind. He imagined himself a gargoyle, watching over his prey, hungry and ready to strike.

Neither Scott, nor Karl, answered.

"Have you done work for any of the other families?"

Scott shook his head emphatically.

"Let me be clear, if the boss finds out later

that you're lying. Your death will be an extended trip, all expenses paid, between feeling miserable and truly dead."

Scott blurted, "I haven't worked for anyone my whole life. Just Karl."

"My contracts have been with legitimate businesses," continued Karl in a rush, "I mean legal ones. No, I mean…"

"Stop," said Ted. "Just answer the question. I don't need your miserable life story."

"No."

Ted stole a glance out the apartment window, raised his eyebrows, and continued talking behind Karl and Scott. "Very good. Do either of you have enemies? Government watching you?"

"No."

"No."

Ted let out a grunt. "I can't imagine you would. Somehow, I don't think you two have done anything productive with your computer skills since you fixed your momma's VCR."

"VCRs aren't computers," said Scott.

"Well, professor, I feel smarter already, but, please, I recommend that you save the lessons for when my friend here isn't looking for something to shoot."

Ted walked around the couch, casually sat in the easy chair by the TV and thumbed Elmer. "Do you have something for my friend here to drink?"

Elmer wasn't thirsty but made no indication otherwise. It was a signal that something was amiss.

Elmer grumbled, "I'll help myself."

Dishes, covered in hardened, dried food, were stacked in impossible angles in the sink and on the countertop. The floor, filthy and yellowing, looked as if it hadn't been mopped in months. Elmer shuddered at the thought of what might be growing in the fridge. Thankfully, a box of Mountain Dew cans sat open on the floor so he could avoid finding out.

He popped open a can loudly to sound busy as he scanned the clutter of paper on the kitchen table. They were Jay's personal files. Taxes, printouts of bank statements and several bills. They all bore Jay's name. Elmer rifled through them quietly to see if any other victims' names would jump out. Everything was Jay. One target.

Movement outside the window over the table caught Elmer's eye. With his free hand, he quietly spread the blinds apart to get a better look at the intersection several floors below. Dark cars with tinted windows blocked traffic at every angle. Men and women in beige uniforms, heavy set with deep green flak jackets with US MARSHAL in white letters on the back, rushed back and forth. A senior officer gesticulated frantically while simultaneously talking on his cell phone. The agents entered Scott's building, flowing like water over a dam.

Blood rushed to Elmer's head as he realized what was happening. The odds that someone else in the building warranted the attention of ICE were too low. Scott and Karl were certain to be the target. Ted and Elmer had only seconds to extricate themselves.

Elmer swallowed air and let out a guttural burp to announce his return to the living room. He said, "The boss isn't going to take lightly that we're spending our afternoon socializing. We've got an errand to run and we must be on schedule."

Ted nodded. "These gentlemen and I were just sorting out some loose ends." Ted returned his gaze to Scott. "So you can't return everything back to normal for this Jay?"

"Not in the next five minutes. I have to hack a lot of different systems. It's not hard, just tedious."

"We don't have five minutes," said Elmer as he thumbed at the door and nodded at Ted, "We need to hike."

"Then the arrangement is off," said Ted as he rose from the easy chair. "There is no way the boss would tolerate this."

Like a mafia ballet, Ted and Elmer simultaneously pulled their guns from their jackets and pointed them at Karl and Scott's foreheads. They shrank further into the couch and shut their eyes.

Scott held up his hands as tears rolled down his face. "I'll fix this. I'll fix it as fast as I can. Before the day is over, this will be fixed."

Karl added, "I'll help."

"Please," begged Scott in a whimper, "please, sir."

With a flourish, Elmer tucked his gun away and turned to the door. "Sir? I like that. A little respect."

"Get started right now," grumbled Ted. "If it's not fixed when we get back, we're mopping up this mess you call your lives. Get to work."

Jay's feet were numb from the monotonous trek through the sewer. It was the same brick. The same babbling sewage. He was still warm, because he stayed dry. Jer was his Sherpa in navigating the sewer's maze. Jer kept kept both of them alert; peppering Jay with questions.

"So you broke into a department store. Kissed the girl. Stole some threads for school. No big deal. That sounds like every teenager's story."

Jay shook his head. "Wow. You'd make a great psychologist."

"I've been probed by more than I can count. I know their tricks."

"They are just trying to help."

"Yes, they think that's what they are doing. I think they have some sick desire to hear my story, my struggles and feed off of it. Better than TV."

"Well, I don't know about that."

Jer stopped. "I'm enjoying this. But not in a sick way."

"You like to hear of my struggles."

"Like I said, not in a sick way. It means I'm not alone."

Jay smiled in the dark. "I've been homeless many times in my life. So, I can appreciate reusing tea bags. My preference was discarded pizza. If I was at the dumpster at the right time, the pizza might still be warm."

"That's a good warm. The bad warm is dumpster-tossed pizza in July."

"I hear you. Most of my days were in Louisiana. It wasn't exclusive to July. But that was why Jenni was a lifesaver."

Jer restarted his slow shuffle. "I'm listening."

"Her dad was a lawyer. He was never home. Her mother was a Louisiana socialite. She was smart, but clueless to the double-life Jenni was leading. Whenever her mom was at a bridge game or a fundraiser, which was an excuse to drink and party, Jenni would bring me inside. We jokingly called it 'playing house'."

"She risked the wrath of her father and her mother's social status. It's bad enough bringing a homeless runaway into the house regularly. It's another thing if he's whiter than snow."

"You don't look white to me."

"That's because I have my sewer face on. Underneath all this poop is your prototypical white male. You couldn't pick me out of the street. Regardless, Jenni's dad did not approve. I met him once and he gave me a look of disgust. For a second, I thought I forgot to put on deodorant. He nosed was turned up and it was involuntary.

He's a smart man. He knew I had little prospect of succeeding in life. He did a very effective job of driving a wedge of doubt between me and

Jenni. I get it and I don't blame him."

Jer asked, "Is he still alive?"

"Yes," answered Jay, "and he hasn't changed. I honestly like the man. He keeps driving one thing into my head, over and over. I don't deserve Jenni."

"Ouch."

"Well, it's true. I don't."

"It isn't your call, Jay."

"Sure, but you can't ignore the facts. Her parents despise me and most of the world will do anything to get between a white man and black woman. That's a lot of hurdles. She needs a successful black man who can give her everything she deserves under her parents' approval. Wouldn't that be perfect? I want her happy."

"Sounds perfect, but is that what Jenni wants? Why isn't she married already?"

"Well, she was in school for seven years. Undergraduate and law school was a grind. I stuck around working on my own degree. I don't think she knew any better than to stick with me. She had plenty of suitors and that was tough. Imagine watching every eligible bachelor eyeing Jenni on campus, circling like vultures with fat bank accounts and trust-fund cars."

"And she stuck with you?"

"Like glue. Afterwards, she got a swanky job offer with a law firm here in New York. She urged me to follow along. I even lived with her for a couple years."

"My friend, I think you've cleared all the hurdles. Hit the jackpot. Won the lottery."

"Indeed I have," said Jay, "but Jenni hasn't. She's single, recently broken up from her under-achieving boyfriend who is now exploring the underbelly of New York. Oh, let's not forget that I don't exist except in police systems and mob hit lists. It's time for her to move on."

"I disagree. It's time for you to stop feeling sorry for yourself."

Jay winced.

"I've been in enough group therapy sessions to say that I've seen this before."

"What do you mean?"

"The constant self-criticism. The regrets."

"Life dealt me a pretty bad hand. I just walk along waiting for the next calamity."

"No, life dealt you a winner. You refuse to see it shining in the rough. Decide what you want and commit to it. What's the worst thing that can happen to you?"

"Not having Jenni in my life."

"Seems like you're headed there by wallowing in this puddle of remorse. Do you want to wait and see things slip away or go all in?"

Jay followed in silence. He replayed his last conversation with Jenni. She did not turn away in disgust when he talked about his time with Jake Flourintale under the bridge. She simply listened and held him. It was his darkest secret. Talking about it was terrifying, like the few slow seconds before a car accident. Afterwards, there was no crash, no impact. Instead, he felt the sense of calm that came from surviving something potentially cataclysmic and the comfort of being somewhere safe.

Jay promised himself there would be no more secrets. No more running and no more hiding. With all his chips, he was going all-in.

Jer broke the silence with a shout up ahead. "We're getting close to our exit. Pull that jacket tight. It's going to get much colder."

The initial explosion was followed by a cacophony of metal raining down on the New York streets. Jeffy had done his job a little too well. The eighteen-wheeler was filled with electronics, but Jeffy didn't know that. All he cared was that the truck's two oversized gas tanks were full when he planted his bombs.

Curiosity killed Jeffy. He wanted to record the spectacular explosion and brag about his handiwork with the other guys. Standing on the street side corner, a block away, he held his cell phone steady. With the camera in one hand focused on the truck, he pressed the detonator in the other.

The flicker of a laptop spinning in the sunlight was a warning. Transformed into an oversized bullet, heavy with compacted electronics, it bludgeoned Jeffy above the shoulders. Even headless, falling to the sidewalk stiff like a domino, Jeffy never dropped his phone.

◆ ◆ ◆

The stairwells were filled with deputy US Marshals moving in a hushed rush, swirling around corners, under the command of silent hand motions. They were well trained in apprehending fugitives but their mission quickly changed to apprehend two suspects behind a major technology breach of government services. It was a matter of national security.

The lead officer paused at the door for the fourteenth floor. Everyone squatted and took a break to catch their breath. No amount of training readied anyone for a fourteen story climb. With his finger on his earpiece, the lead officer whispered, "Ready at stairway, fourteenth floor. Will breach on your command."

After a few seconds, the officer raised his hand, palm open with fingers extended. Five minutes. Deputies at the front and back remained on alert as the other deputies put themselves at ease. They checked their weapons and double-checked the equipment secured to their bodies.

A dull crack, like a distant jet's sonic boom, cut the silence. Eyes darted back and forth to their partners, uncomprehending. Eventually all eyes were on the officer whose finger was back on his earpiece.

"Sir, I believe I heard an explosion," said the

officer in a low voice. "One loud enough to be heard in the stairwell."

After a pause, he pointed at two deputies. "Get to the roof. Five more stories. Take my binoculars. Look east and report back immediately." With a nod, the deputies wordlessly burst into motion up and out of view.

"I've got deputies Alexander and Montgomery heading up," said the officer into his earpiece. "I'll report back immediately. Are our orders to breach still in effect? Yes, sir. Confirmed. We will hold for your command."

In the hallway, outside Scott and Karl's apartment, Elmer closed the door with an authoritative slam. His serious grimace melted into a smile. Without a word, he winked at Ted. A job well done.

An explosion shook the floor under their feet a half second before they heard it. Adrenaline ripped through their already-worn nerves, cold water turning to ice. As life-long New Yorkers, an explosion while several floors high in a building held heavy meaning.

"Forget the elevators," said Ted, who had already tossed his mob personality aside and was back to NYPD, "Stairs. Now."

Fear hastened Elmer's pace. By the time they reached the end of the hallway, they were jogging. Elmer pushed the stairway door open and quickly turned into the well-lit platform. Ted heard Elmer mutter "son of a biscuit" before he tumbled over a deputy at the top of the stairs. He disappeared, head-first, into a gaggle of tan and dark green deputies holding weapons.

Instinct, not rational thought, prompted Ted to reach for his gun. He froze as several muzzles were raised. Tiny red dots of light danced across his face and chest. "Gentlemen, I'm going to pull my hand out. Very slowly. There will be nothing in it."

The lead officer nodded. "Smart."

As he extricated his hand, Ted continued, "How is my buddy, Elmer, doing down there?"

"I haven't been felt up this much since high school," said Elmer, "but they got the hands of Jerry Rice. Never hit the ground."

Ted raised both hands in the air. "I'm retired NYPD. So is Elmer there. Are you folks behind that explosion we just heard?"

On cue, Deputy Montgomery slipped into view from the stairs above. "Sir..."

The lead officer silenced him with a swipe of his hand and returned his attention to Ted. "Keep your hands on your head, sir, until we verify your identity."

Ted acquiesced.

"Deputy Montgomery, continue."

The agent from the stairs above said, "Something exploded in the middle of the street, sir, three blocks away. Initial speculation is that a truck bomb never made it to its intended destination."

Waiting in the apartment next door to Scott and Karl, Johnny heard the explosion and cringed. Too big. It wouldn't be long before the police cordoned off several blocks around the explosion, so Johnny had to move quick. Jeffy was going to be a grand example for the rest of the pups when he got back to the office. The team will certainly do a better job of listening over their inane video games.

Shaking his head, he stepped into the hallway and walked calmly in front of Scott and Karl's door. His singular focus on his objective blinded him from Ted and Elmer disappearing act through the stairway door.

Johnny pulled out his gun and checked that it was fully loaded.

Not that it mattered.

Two bullets were enough.

Out in the street near Scott's apartment, Mike, Tyler and Hofstra were knocked off their feet from the explosion. Glass rained down in tiny shards from the building facade above them. Without thinking, Mike got up and hovered protectively over Hofstra. Tyler pulled at both of them, moving them closer to the building and out of the falling debris. Acrid smoke enveloped them in a blue haze. The unbearable heat dissipated as quickly as it appeared.

"Are you all okay?" shouted Tyler. Hofstra and Mike nodded. Tyler pulled out his phone and dialed with one hand while he shook glass shards from his hair.

"What the hell was that?" he asked. "I need a report on an explosion near Karl Gil's apartment."

After a pause, he turned to Mike and Hofstra and said, "Not an accident. Truck bomb. The marshals spotted it a block away to the east. Had to have been a helluva bomb to knock us off our feet this far away."

The hacker-in-a-box burst to life. Like a droid from a galaxy far, far away, it burbled and buzzed as if it had seen its master for the first time in years. Tyler held it away from his body unsure of what to do.

"We need to help the injured," shouted Hofstra over the clatter of debris still falling. From the sidewalk, she stepped into an office, open and exposed by the now-shattered glass wall. She pulled out the chair from under the desk and pointed to Tyler. "Put it there."

Tyler gently laid the box in the darkness under the desk.

She turned to Mike. "The mystery of your friend will have to wait just a little longer."

Mike nodded with understanding. "Of course. Let's go."

The three of them dodged through cars, hands over their mouths in the thick, black smoke. The shouts of panic slowly evolved into shouts of orders, triage and control.

Under the desk, a Hugo Boss jacket glistened from the glass shards embedded in the fabric. Its sleeves surrounded an elegant pair of Christian Louboutins high heels. Next to the fashionable embrace, the hacker-in-a-box bleeped and blurped, spinning LED lights across its edges spitting out random characters. Letter by letter, the LED spelled out a single word.

CONNECTED.

The computer equipment that enveloped the coffee table in Karl's apartment woke from a lazy chatter of clicks and hums to a frenzied whirr. Tiny blinking lights flashed, the DJ of a discotheque of bits and bytes, dancing across wires and radio waves.

Scotts eyes widened. "Dude, someone's in my stuff." A second wave of adrenaline washed over him, erasing the terror of the mobsters who just left minutes ago.

He worked the keyboard and laptop touchpad with experienced ease. The practiced typing stroke evolved into hard charged pecks and, after a few more seconds, escalated to fist slams like a frustrated toddler at piano practice. "I've been locked out. Thankfully my remote jobs are still running on restoring Jay's backups. Good idea, Karl, to start there."

The blinking lights flashed so quickly that it looked steady. The equipment was working at its peak.

"Something is saturating the network. That's a lot of data," said Scott.

"Someone is either copying your data," said Karl, "or they're putting something in."

"The power. We need to cut the power."

Karl stopped Scott. "You can't stop the restoration process for Jay's files. We're dead if those scripts don't finish."

Scott froze in deep thought. His firewalls were impenetrable. He used special servers to cloak his network traffic. For all intents and purposes, he was invisible to the digital world. For anyone to get into his laptop was impossible, unless someone was on his private network. His eyes turned to the box covered in the brown paper of a grocery bag.

"That's not a bomb."

"I'm not interested in the process of verifying or refuting that theory. Leave it alone," said Karl.

"Why would those guys leave this behind?"

"You said it right after they left. They probably forgot and will be back in a few minutes."

Scott shook his head. "Everything lit up when they came in. I'm sure of it. But things really kicked up after that explosion outside." He leaned over to tear the paper on the package and paused.

"I'm not liking my options here," said Karl. "Die by bomb, die by bullet or die by lifetime incarceration."

"At least this option sounds the least painful. We'll die quick," said Scott as he pulled the box closer. "I love you, man. I was acting like a raging idiot and you stuck with me. I owe you in the next life."

He tore the paper, like removing a band-aid from a toddler's knee, eyes closed in anticipation. It was a shoe box. Scott pulled the lid open and muttered, "This makes no sense."

Karl opened one eye but kept his grimace. "What is it?"

"Peanuts? That's weird. Just some snacks, I think. There is something else underneath. Here hold this."

Karl held a can of peanuts in his hand, uncomprehending.

Scott held up a can of peanut brittle. "Did those guys leave the wrong package behind?"

Karl and Scott shrugged and opened their cans. In a short sequence of quiet pops, the cans shot glitter into a slow falling rain of sparkles with streaks of rainbow-colored paper.

Scott tried to shake the glitter out of the keyboard of his laptop. "Dude. Did those old guys literally glitter-bomb us?"

❖ ❖ ❖

The lead officer conveyed new commands to his deputies huddled in the stairwell of Scott's apartment. "Our orders are to surround the area of the explosion by two blocks, let in emergency vehicles and nothing else. Deputy Montgomery, take Alpha and secure the area. Bravo will stay with me. We apprehend the target first."

Half of the agents slithered away into the darkness of the stairwells below.

With hands on his head, Ted glanced back through the tiny window of the stairwell door into the hallway of floor fourteen. A familiar figure stood, wearing a worn suit and classic fedora. He cocked a handgun with black-gloved hands and scanned the hallway.

Ted ducked out of view. It was Johnny Gjerdes. He motioned to the lead officer to join him as he returned to peek in the hallway. Johnny took in a deep breath, kicked the door in as if he had done it every day and entered with his gun ready, pointed at the ceiling.

Ted couldn't fight the smirk forming on his face. When it all comes down to surviving in desperation, cockroaches eat themselves. That's what separated the human from the roach.

"That man who entered Mr. Gil's apartment wielding a gun is mob," said Ted. "You don't have much time if you want to keep your targets alive."

The officer's eyebrows rose from behind his protective glasses. He pulled the door open and motioned to his team, "Enter and breach."

Ted and Earl followed close behind. Ted could not resist the urge to see Johnny's surprised face. He was certain today was going to end up a good day.

◆ ◆ ◆

"What a loser," said Rage-hat as he watched data scroll down the screen on the wall back in the basement of the FBI building. "What a waste of a good mind."

Bushy-beard nodded. "He would've been a great hacktivist. Look at how he double-encrypted his VPN tunnels through the Dark Net with a tor-clone. Amazing that he was able to maintain any level of network performance."

"Is that why it's taking so long to pull his files?"

"Oh, we're done pulling the important ones. Since we're still connected, I poked around and am pulling residual, disk-level images off his laptop drive. I have a feeling he's just as diligent in encrypting his traffic as he is in deleting his data. I'd like to see if we can grab ghost files before we get disconnected. It'd be a gold mine if we grab his password database."

"So, you're saying this is bonus-level stuff."

"Yep. I'm amazed he hasn't turned off his equipment. It's obvious I'm pulling massive data and if he was online, he couldn't get much done. He must be distracted."

"A swarm of FBI and US Marshals could be very distracting."

"True that."

CHAPTER 21

The sewer was at its brightest. Jer and Jay were walking underneath a busy street. They could feel the low rumble of traffic through the soles of their feet. Every ten steps, a storm drain radiated the light of a day's sun muted by the winter-grey clouds.

Jer was walking in confident strides as their narrow shelf opened to a wide pathway with steel railings between them and the rapid rush of water to their right. Ladders jutted out from the brick and led up to each manhole. Jay wanted to rush up the nearest ladder and sip the fresh air and buy a hot dog from a street vendor. With the police on lookout, he had to trust where Jer said they could safely exit.

As if the heavens opened, an explosion knocked both of them off their feet. The yellow-orange light was first, bursting through the storm drain like fire from the nostrils of a dragon. Afterwards was the sound; a clap and rumble which shook the ground and walls. Jer fell against the railing and hooked his arm in time to avoid falling into the rushing water.

Jay was on his back, legs splayed out, facing the ceiling. The air rushed out of the room and refilled with hot, noxious streams of smoke. It swirled above his head and flowed back out of the downspout in black clouds. Above them, it was eerily quiet for a few seconds. Then people started screaming; pleading for help.

Jer rolled onto his side and called out, "Jay! Are you okay?" Through the billowing smoke, he could make out Jay's figure, unmoving. He clutched the railing with both hands and crawled to him.

"Jay, we need to get out." Jer slapped his cheek gently. Jay's eyes opened and spun in all directions.

"Get up soldier. This is no time for a sissy," shouted Jer as he tugged at his arm.

"Wha...what happened?"

"Shut your trap. Listen to me now. Focus. People need help, Jay. Do you hear them?"

The screams overlapped, rushing in from the openings above their head. Jer pulled Jay to his feet and rushed to the nearest ladder. Catlike in his stance, Jer was on full alert. Halfway up the ladder, Jer paused and commanded, "Stick to me. Fly on flypaper, private. Let's go!"

The sharpness and urgency of Jer's bark cleared Jay's head. His limbs were tender, but the adrenaline quickened his pulse and pace.

Jer tossed aside the manhole cover as if it were made of cardboard and pulled himself into the light of the world above. His hand poked back through the blinding brightness, fingers wiggling to offer Jay help onto the street.

It took a few seconds for Jay's eyes to adjust in the full daylight. Jer's figure, bearing a grey sweatshirt hood that rose from his two layers of winter longcoats, was blackened and stained. He crouched over a man who was missing the bottom of his leg only feet away. Jer frantically unwound the twine that held his boot together and looped it around the man's leg, just below the knee. He pointed at a piece of shrapnel at Jay's feet. "Nap's over, private! Give me that!"

Jay grabbed a long, thin piece of aluminum and rushed to Jer. In sweeping motions, Jer secured the tourniquet by spinning the aluminum around the twine to tighten it. He grabbed the man's hand, placed it on the tourniquet and shouted in the victim's stunned face, "Hold this. Do not let go!" The man nodded, eyes dulled by shock, and laid back.

Jer popped back on his feet. His head was on a swivel, scanning the horrendous scene. His eyes darted from person to person, performing a mental triage. Most of the smoke had cleared in the brisk winter wind. A truck was burning, blown apart from the inside. It's metal body curled outward, like a flower unfurling, with a hot center jutting white-yellow flames. Scorched electronics covered the street in brightly colored boxes, advertising all the big brands. If it weren't for the stunned people walking amongst the debris, it had the look of the electronics junkyards in China, infamous for their child-labor picking out parts to recycle.

Jer focused on a woman moaning quietly on the sidewalk and made his way to her. Her face was covered by her bloodied hands. Long blonde hair rained down in red, matted clumps. Jer, talked in calm tones, encouraging her to move her hands from her face so that he could see the extent of her injuries.

Across the street, a young child pushed aside debris piled up outside the burning truck crying, "Daddy? Daddy?"

Jay stumbled across the detritus to help and slipped; twisting his ankle. A tall man descended on the child and helped the young boy toss electronics and boxes aside. Ignoring the sharp edges of metal and glass cutting into his knees, Jay joined in the panicked excavation. The men cleared the area quickly and found the father trapped underneath, covered in dust, blinking with shock and confusion.

"Daddy!" The father's eyes cleared as the child crawled onto his chest and hugged him. "Daddy, I want to go home."

Jay held the child back. "Easy. We need to make sure you don't hurt your Daddy, okay?" The father smiled and asked, "Terrorists? I was hailing a cab. My son was next to me. I...I... "

The blonde man answered, "Truck bomb. We don't know if there will be others, so we need to clear the area. Are you okay enough to get up? Let's find out what's holding your leg down."

Stunned, Jay turned to the man. "Mike? What are you doing here?"

It took a double-take and a few blinks before comprehension washed across Mike's face. "Oh my god. Jay."

Mike reached out but jerked his hand back. "Where have you been? You look like..."

"Poop? I been swimming in it the last couple days."

"Uh. You aren't kidding, are you?"

Jay laughed. "I ran out of places to hide. It's a long story."

"I've got one even longer," said Mike, "but we'll have to deal with that later. Let's get this guy out."

CHAPTER 22

It was the smell of Scott and Karl's apartment that turned up Johnny's nose. To Scott and Karl, it looked like the snarl of a tiger. Johnny hated slobs. His sensitive nose could pick out someone who skipped a shower. Here, it was the pungent odor of days-old food mixed with piles of clothes that had been worn thrice before thrown aside to be washed. Sweat and rot.

What didn't compute was the fact that the two young men were covered in glitter, as if they had just finished celebrating New Years' Eve in the streets. No matter, work had to be done and done quickly. He could ponder the scene another day.

Johnny held up his gun and asked, "Which one of you cutie-pies is Scott?"

Karl tried again, "Who?"

Johnny smiled, showing a neat row of teeth outdone by two oversized eyeteeth that could have passed as vampiric. "Nice try. But it really doesn't matter. I just prefer to know who's who before I put a bullet in 'em."

"Please, sir," pleaded Scott, "I think you've got the wrong people." He held out his hands in defense. They glittered gold, just like his eyelashes and hair.

"Right, and I'm not Johnny the Snake." He pointed the gun at Scott. He had a laptop on the couch next to him and was most likely the one who broke into the mob systems. "You first. Congratulations, you're the gift for my retiring boss, strawberry shortcake."

Johnny heard the gunshot; a familiar sharp, snap-crack. But he hadn't pulled the trigger. No longer feeling his legs, Johnny fell to the floor and hit the coffee table. Laying on his side and trying to process what had happened, Johnny could feel his blood turning stagnant. It was cold slush and creeping from his extremities to his core.

Like the grim reaper, a familiar figure stood into the doorway with arms crossed, flanked by two crouched deputies holding rifles at their shoulders. The bright lights of the hallway blackened the outline of a large Italian man with hair pulled back into a ponytail. A oversized hand, decorated with rings, flashed in the light and pointed at him.

It was a low growl. "Johnny Gjerdes. You have the right to remain silent."

As his world faded to black, Johnny's thoughts fired a last burst of neuron electrical impulses in a race across dying pathways to comprehend what had happened. The neurons answered in a whimper, a cluster of waning thoughts at a dead end — this was one trap he was not going to escape. Ted Stone. Frozen, dying neurons stuck on a single thought.

Ted Stone.

CHAPTER 23

O ut in the New York street, Tyler helped lift a gurney into an ambulance and shut the doors. The smoke had cleared, along with the mass confusion that arose seconds after the explosion. The most severe medical cases had already been whisked away and what remained were stunned pedestrians, in fine suites and dresses, covered in dirt, blood and tears. Police were slowly cordoning off the area after confirming the site was secure.

Kat was on the phone with Rage-Hat. He asked, "You okay to talk right now?"

"Yup. I'm taking a break." Hofstra's eyes connected with Tyler as she talked. She could almost read Tyler's thoughts. Did they catch the guy?

After a few seconds, Hofstra said, "That's great news. I'll tell everyone." Hofstra put her phone back in her pocket. "Three guys captured. Two alive and one dead. The dead one was identified right away. Pretty famous and slippery New York mobster. The other two apparently need a fresh set of underwear. Scott Whedon and Karl Gil."

"Did the hacker-in-the-box work?"

"Yes, but even better, Scott and Karl have been exceptionally cooperative. Apparently they're confessing in such a hurried babble that the agents gave up taking notes and are just recording video. Best of all. They admitted to everything about Jay. He's clear."

Tyler pumped his fist and then noticed Hofstra's confused smile. "What? What else did he say?"

"There is some chatter on the secured lines about glitter, pom-poms and streamers."

Onlookers politely stood behind the yellow tape police line and talked in low murmurs. As is customary, the rescue teams parked their vehicles to block the view of the aftermath of the explosion. Wisps of smoke rose from piles of molten metal and glass giving the look of an epic comic-book, post-fight scene.

"Kat, I need to introduce you to a couple folks," said Mike with a broad smile on his face. He led Tyler and Kat over to a makeshift water stand next to an emergency vehicle.

Mike called out and Jay turned from the emergency staff holding two bottles of water. Kat was happy the homeless man's hands were full and could not shake hands. He was filthy in every way imaginable. His outfit was decorated with wet patches of black and brown. Clumps of mud hung impossibly in the creases and tears of his clothes. The odor of rotting food washed over Kat in waves. She kept her composure and politely introduced herself. "Katherine Hofstra, FBI. This is Tyler Brown, my partner."

Jay nodded. "I'm honored. Mike said that you two saved my life."

"I'm sorry?"

"My name is Jay Wilson. At least that's what it was before someone deleted me."

Kat stared. She noticed hints of the normal man underneath the homeless facade. His hair, despite the matted clumps, was professionally trimmed. The pants and shirt he wore fit him well. Jay's eyes were clear, icy-blue and alert.

"Thank you for identifying yourself, Mr. Wilson. Will you accompany us to our car, please? It's time we returned you to Paraguay."

"Say what?" asked Mike. He stepped between Kat and Jay, chest puffed out.

Her smile hinted at the joke. "He's Paraguayan mob, Mike. Serious stuff. They smuggle those tiny, yipping dogs into Manhattan. It's a pestilence. We've been working this case for years."

Jay laughed. "By the way, you guys should meet Jer. He saved a lot of lives today." His voice trailed off as he looked around for his friend. He held out one of the bottles of water as if to give it to someone.

"Yes, he was amazing," continued Mike. He scanned the scene. "Where is he?"

"He's fine," answered Jay with a sigh, "I just think he needs a little space right now. I'll introduce you to him when he's ready." He paused and looked at Kat and Tyler. "Is this really over?"

"The pieces of the puzzle are starting to make the picture clear. There might be some loose ends, but I think you can help us tie them up. You're safe. We're on your side again."

Jay sat on the curb and took a long sip from the water bottle. His eyes were distant, processing everything he heard.

He handed his second bottle to Mike.

"Thanks for being the best brother one could ask for."

Mike smiled. "Right back at you."

CHAPTER 24

J enni bobbed gracefully as she refilled everyone's glasses with wine. Despite Ted's protests, Jenni insisted being the hostess despite being at Ted's apartment. She cut off his early protests with a polite wink. "Ya'll need some southern hospitality tonight. It's the least I can do."

The lights in Ted's living room were at their brightest. His worldly trinkets glittered and shone reflecting the mood of everyone in the room.

Ted and Elmer were on opposite ends of the couch, wolfing down finger foods in single bites from the tiny plates they held in their hands. Jay sat cross-legged in an overstuffed chair. His lazy smile was encouraged by the glasses of the excellent wine that Jenni brought to celebrate.

Jay's phone beeped. A text from Mike flashed across the screen.

SHE SAID YES! DATE WITH KAT TOMORROW

DINNER? replied Jay.

SHOE SHOPPING@NOLITA

U DIVA

TAKES TWO DIVAS TO DUET

THAT MAKES NO SENSE

CUZ YOU'RE DRUNK

Jenni returned to her perch on a stool just outside the kitchen. She was ready to swoop in with more hor-deourves. "So, I heard Scott confessed everything."

"Caved like a house of cards," said Elmer. "He couldn't figure out if it was the government or the mob that was after him. He was beyond paranoid."

Ted added, "If you can believe it, Scott hacked the mob's data center. That's what set things in motion with Johnny Gjerdes. He kicked a hornet's nest and started the first ever cyberwar with the mafia."

"Why would he hack the mob?" asked Jenni.

Elmer nearly choked on his deviled egg. Chewing hurriedly, he emphatically pointed at Ted.

Ted leaned back and smiled. "Well, apparently Karl mistook me for being a mob hitman."

"Impossible," said Jay. "You look like a cuddly teddy bear!"

With a smirk, he replied, "For once the stereo-type worked in our favor. I hate to say, my acting job in Scott and Karl's apartment was pretty solid. It's not all just good looks."

It was Jay's turn to ask, "What about the FBI? How did Agents Hofstra and Brown flip from hunting me to saving me?"

Elmer jumped in this time. "Tight lips there. The FBI isn't sharing much. All Hofstra would say was that when they were hunting you, they had people that figured out you were a victim, not a perp. They kept the deportation order open to cap-ture you, but with the mindset that you're safer locked up until they found Scott. These FBI com-puter people are really good. I'm mean mind-blow-ing good."

"Why do you say that?" asked Jay.

"They could find things no one else could pos-sibly find. Ted and I have some interesting news to share. Just found out this afternoon and wanted to wait for the right time. Ted, is this the right time?"

Ted smiled. "It's the best time."

Earl continued, "Jay, these people found your birth certificate. They also found police reports de-tailing the circumstances of your birth."

Jenni let out a quiet gasp. She walked over and held Jay's hand. "Do you have it?"

"Not yet. It'll be here tomorrow. I didn't ask anything more. Wanted you to see it first and do what you want with it."

Jay swallowed hard. "That's going to be the

biggest mystery we solve of this entire mess. How can I thank them?"

"Like I said, FBI won't talk. It's like they have some magic computer hidden away in a basement somewhere. Thank Hofstra and Brown. I suppose they can relay your thanks."

Jenni pressed on. "Did Scott talk about what started all this?"

"Yes. In fact, Scott's confession is recorded on video. I don't think it's worth watching, unless you like hearing cockroaches talk."

Ted leaned forward and connected eyes with Jay. "You did nothing wrong. Scott was having a bad day. Apparently he had eyes for a barista and just as he was working up the courage to ask her out, you blocked his mojo."

Jay was riveted. He wanted nothing more than to know why.

Ted continued, "You touched a nerve, I guess. He mistook you for someone from a privileged life where everything came easy because of family and circumstance. It wasn't personal, Jay. It was revenge against whatever grievances he had of life. Once Scott got started, he couldn't stop. He was not healthy. There is some footage the FBI found by searching social media that would make you shudder. Some of his most nefarious work was signed with the name Deetwuh. What that name represents will likely remain an unsolved mystery."

Jenni chuckled. "How ironic that Jay would become a voodoo doll representing corporate greed and white privilege. Did you enjoy playing the part, Jay?"

"That lifestyle wasn't as great as I imagined it'd be. I'd be happy to go back to being a homeless teen."

Jay lingered on that thought. "So Scott was the one who deleted me from CityTrust?"

"Yup," said Ted.

"Falsified my payments to get me evicted?"

"Yup."

"Cancelled my phone service. Cut my power."

"Yes and yes."

"He's the one who put all those crimes in the police system, too?"

"That was pretty creative. And yes."

"Agent Hofstra told me that I was tagged as an international fugitive. Paraguayan mafia. Immigration control, NYPD, and US Marshals were all after me."

"Yup. All that was Scott. In fact, that's why he's going to be locked up for life. That's felony stacked on felony. I can't imagine he'll see an electronic device ever again."

"The fact that you survived this, Jay," said Jenni, "is not a miracle. You're like my *pepere*. Nothing stopped him and nothing can stop you. When we first met, I thought you were fighting the worst of odds. Then all this...I don't know what to say. You're the strongest person I know."

Jay rubbed his face. Perhaps it was the wine, but every imaginable emotion ran through his head like a burbling, rock-filled stream. The cycle had no pattern but was tied to random flashes of memories and sensations. Relief. Gratitude. Confusion. Anger. Remorse. Serenity. Appreciation.

Love.

A hint of a smile cross Jay's face. "Everything was stacked against me. You, Ted Stone, saved me. I know this is the fiftieth time I've said it, but I'm going to keep saying it."

Ted raised his glass. His brusque demeanor softened not only by wine, but by the satisfaction of justice served, decades old and overdue. "I wanted to choke the life out of you when we first met. It would have been a hug had I known you'd be my connection to Johnny Gjerdes."

Ted continued, "Retirement doesn't suit me. It was hard to ignore what my partners had. They retired to spend more time with grandchildren. They made up for lost time with their spouses from years and years on the beat. Johnny represented, in many ways, the destruction of a life I could have had. You, Jay Wilson, saved me, too."

The room settled to a reverent silence.

Jay had his own news to share. "Tyler from the FBI has been helping me get my digital life back in order. Apparently it's really easy to have your life deleted, but to add it back is another body of work entirely. But I'm totally fine with it. I feel like I have the chance to get this right. There are no dark clouds. It's all green lights up ahead."

"In time," said Ted, "you'll find your normal

again. Walk the streets. Ride the subway. You can go home now."

Jay shook his head. "My old life is gone. And I mean that in a good way." He glanced at Jenni. "Home isn't a place. It's a person."

Jenni, realizing Ted and Earl were going to eat the food faster than she could serve them on their tiny plates, brought the remaining serving platters of hor-deourves to the coffee table between them. She snuggled up next to Jay on the easy chair.

"Jay's moving back in with me."

Ted smiled. "Smart."

"Housewarming party is in a few weeks," said Jenni. "Barbecue in the backyard. I'm bringing my secret Delacroix family recipe to life. A taste of old Louisiana. I have to fend off the wolves when I make them."

Ted smacked his lips. "Will you have room for a new, old friend, then?"

"Absolutely not," said Jenni in a stern voice. "This is strictly a family affair, Uncle Ted and Uncle Elmer. We Delacroix are a choosy lot."

"Uncle Elmer?" said Elmer. "That has a nice ring to it."

Ted's eyes softened.

For so long, Jay sought the familiarity of family. He saw it in the multitudes of foster parents who shared their homes with him. Without words, a simple glance between family spoke volumes over the dinner table; a language developed from years of being together. A gentle nudge when washing

305

dishes. A wink when pulling out of the driveway. Jay saw these things exchanged, a transaction of which he had no currency. For years, he imagined a biological link, born of familial DNA that everyone else had and it was what he was missing. He felt cursed that he'd live his entire life not ever knowing.

No longer. Now he understood. He would do anything to protect what he had gained. He'd give his life for this. For his family.

CHAPTER 25

ONE YEAR LATER

"He's been crying all day," said Jenni in a tired voice. Jay had just pulled into the back-alley driveway of Jenni's house and saw her sitting on the back steps. Right away, he knew something was wrong. Her eyes, tired, begged for respite. "I need a break. I can't do anything to console him."

Jay pulled Jenni into a soft embrace. "I'm sorry. Let me see what I can do. Get some fresh air. Go for a walk. I got this."

The bulkhead doors to the cellar were propped open. Jay descended into the darkness of the unlit cellar. He could hear Tike tapping on cardboard loudly over Andy's crying. It wasn't his usual frantic pace, but familiar and soothing. The refrigerator box was on its side, tucked behind the furnace in the corner of the cellar. Andy liked it enough to spend most of his days there. He occasionally left, but always returned.

A space heater in the center of the room was surrounded by piles of boxes and wood planks that were littered with trinkets and food sorted by color. It was reminiscent of their home in the subway. Jer's sleeping bag, resting on a mattress in the corner, was empty.

"Hey, Tike. How are you?"

"Tired. Huh. You tap? Huh."

"Yes, I can take over for you, buddy. Go on. Take a break." Tike ascended into the backyard in tired strides.

"Andy, do you feel okay to come out?" Jay did not miss a beat, tapping just as Tike did.

The crying continued.

"Can I come in?"

"I'm fine," said Andy. His voice was muffled. "You don't need to tap."

Jay stopped and kneeled. He peered into the darkness inside the box. "Jenni is worried."

"I know."

"It's been really tough these last couple days, Andy. We need to figure something out."

After a loud rustle, Andy poked his head out of the box. Under his wool cap, his face was swollen and red.

"They left."

"I'm sure Jer will be back soon. Tike needs a break. He will be back."

"No. The children."

A chill ran down Jay's spine. Andy didn't talk much about his visions. Doing everything he could to maintain his composure, Jay sat, willing him to continue without interruption.

"I didn't notice it at first. But one by one, they left." He sniffled and reached back in the box for a towel and covered his face.

Andy's voice was muffled. "Then, the last child spoke to me."

Out of the corner of his eye, Jay saw Jer and Tike come down a few steps from outside. In silence, they sat on a step to listen.

"She's just a little girl. The one with the hair and ears burned off. She always stares at me. She sits behind all the ones that shout at me. The angry ones. Her stare. It was the worst. Like she didn't understand."

Andy's cries echoed in the basement. Jay connected eyes with Jer on the stairs. Something was different today and he hoped it was progress. Andy had been stuck in neutral for too long.

"She spoke English. She told me that I am done. She said that I mourned for them enough. Each and every one agreed. And now they are gone."

Jay spoke quietly. "That's good. Right?"

"Yes. Deep down in my own hell and heart, there is a glimmer of joy in that. I think they know I'm sorry. But, I still can't forgive myself. I think they've left me to sort that on my own. I'm not sure if hell is better alone or with them."

Jay rose to his feet. "I'm going to have Jer get you some water. Get some rest."

As he left, Jay paused to put his hands on Tike and Jer's shoulders. They smiled and nodded. Andy will be better.

Jay walked around Jenni's house to the front patio. Jenni and Kat were sitting in cypress rocking chairs they had moved with them from New Orleans. Mike was refilling their glasses. Muddled leaves in the hazy white cocktail was the sign it was Friday night mojitos.

"He's quiet now," said Jenni.

Jay nodded and replied, "It's progress in the right direction. As we know, healing takes time."

Jay took the glass meant for him from the deck rail and took a sip. He paused to watch the clouds float lazily across the sky.

"It feels so good to be able to help. To return the favor. I owe it to all those strangers who've helped me over the years and I can finally give back."

Jay lightened his tone. "It also feels good that it's a Friday."

Mike said, "It takes five long days of corporate enslavement, but yes, we made it to Friday night."

Jenni raised her glass. "To hard work and Friday's reward." Her hand glinted in the sun.

Kat spotted the ring before Mike and gasped. "Is that what I think it is?"

It was as if Jenni was holding her breath. All her words spilled out in a single exhale. "We have a surprise. Well, probably not a surprise for you two.

Jay and I have some news to share."

"Indeed," interrupted Jay, "it took me more than a decade to muster up the courage to ask such a simple question."

Jenni added, "And only a second for me to say yes!"

Mike and Kat jumped from their chairs and enveloped Jay and Jenni. It was a joyful melee of hugs, kisses and playful jabs. Drinks got spilled in the mash-up of shrieks, laughs and hearty congratulations.

This Friday was going to be a Friday never forgotten.

Jay's phone buzzed. "Sorry." He extricated himself, giggling, and pulled out his phone from his pocket.

SCOTT IS DEAD - FIRST OF MANY

Stunned, Jay read the message over and over. His broad smile dropped to a frown.

The phone buzzed again.

ALL INVOLVED IN SNAKE'S DEATH WILL PAY

Jay typed on his phone. WHO IS THIS?

KAYLEE

I THINK U HAVE WRONG NUMBER

THE FAMILY REQUIRES RETRIBUTION

LEAVE ME ALONE

BLUE CAR ON YOUR LEFT

Jay looked up from his phone. An old blue Impala was parked across the street. No one was outside on the quiet residential drive.

The peaceful scene was shattered by an explosion from underneath the car; a ripple of loud pops across its underbelly. The car flipped its rear over front and landed with an exaggerated rocking motion. Yellow and white flames licked out through the smashed windows.

WE WILL BE IN TOUCH

ABOUT THE AUTHOR

M T Clark

MT Clark, the author of DEVIL IN THE WIRE, moved from non-fiction to fiction after being trapped on long international flights with only his imagination and a laptop.

His writing reflects the glorious colors of multi-culturism, the plight and passions of human life and the fascinating discoveries of science and technology.

Being profoundly deaf never got in the way of learning how to speak and lip-read Russian, traveling the Trans-Siberian railroad at age sixteen or discovering the joyous mantras of devotees by walking the temples of Mumbai.

You can find DEVIL IN THE WIRE in bookstores around the world and online. You can read some of cross-genre short stories at https://mtclarkauthor. wordpress.com and can keep up with his latest work on Facebook at https://www.facebook.com/

mtclarkauthor/.